PURSUIT

A Fox Walker Novel

D1227394

Indy Quillen

PURSUIT

Copyright © 2017 by Indy Quillen

Cover design by James T. Egan, Bookfly Design

All Rights Reserved

For information address Treeline Press, 1106 Second Street, Encinitas, CA 92024

Treeline Press, Encinitas, CA

ISBN: 0997777729

ISBN: 9780997777727

Library of Congress Control Number: 2017901317

Treeline Press,Encinitas, CA

Printed in the United States

Treeline Press paperback edition / April 2017

Kindle edition / April 2017

Hey Bro, this one is for you.
To Rocky
And as always, to Michael Q

AUTHOR'S NOTE

The Fox Walker stories are based on real locations in and around the Rocky Mountains and San Juan Mountain Range in Colorado, but please know that many of the names of places are as fictionalized as the characters that inhabit them. Also, although much research went into the understanding of the Ute nation and its culture, as well as their use of the Shoshone language, the Fox Walker character is a creation of my imagination and a work of fiction based on my life-long fascination with the Native American culture. Thus, I did take certain liberties in that creation and use of the language. As for the tracking and wilderness survival skills Walker possesses, these are based on real skills and knowledge many dedicated survivalists use and have shared with others.

A special thanks to the folks at the Denver Criminal Court, who maintained a professional attitude even when asked sensitive prisoner protocol questions, such as are the guards armed during transportation. Also, a special shout out to my Navy SEAL friend, Rick, who made sure I had the needed resources on hand for the creation of my character, Matt Logan. You are the best. I salute you.

CHAPTER ONE

Denver, Colorado

"We, the jury, find the defendant, Matthew W. Logan, guilty as charged of Murder in the First Degree."

The man stood military-straight before the judge. The civilian clothes he wore masked neither his imposing six-foot-two stature nor the years of training and service he had undergone. Cool blue eyes stared straight ahead, and the proud square of his shoulders stayed true as the judge remanded him to custody, pending sentencing.

A rush of reporters scrambled from the courtroom, eager to get their stories in print. During the disruption, the convicted man turned toward the gallery, met the gaze of his younger brother. The slightest hint of a nod from Sean, and Matt Logan turned away.

As the bailiff reached out to take the prisoner's arm, he looked up into Logan's face, and backed off.

Matt Logan walked out of the courtroom on his own, the bailiff trailing behind.

CHAPTER TWO

Pine Valley, Colorado

Fox Walker and Nataya emerged from the dusky shadows of the Colorado wilderness to face the bright lights and bedlam of TV news teams, reporters, and law officers. Walker sighed. They were like flies at a picnic, always finding him, no matter how much he tried to avoid them.

Walker dreaded this part of any search and rescue. The sharp contrast of being immersed in the natural world for hours, or days, then the strain of being thrust back into civilization. Civilization. Now there was a term he had to laugh at. That meant people were supposed to be civil to each other.

He leaned in to help Nataya as she shifted the weight of the bundle she carried. Deputies rushed forward, shielding the two of them from the flash of cameras and shouting reporters. The officers guided them toward a young man and woman, also straining to see over the crowd, their gaunt faces accented by the harsh floodlights of the news crews. Walker studied their eyes, dark-rimmed with

2

stress, but that spark of frantic hope still burning there. He knew that haunted look, parents expecting the worst, but clinging—up to the last moment—to the wild expectation that all would be fine.

Two steps closer and Walker saw the woman break free from her husband's grasp. She pushed her way through the throng of officers and stumbled toward Nataya, sobbing, her arms outstretched.

"Cory!"

The bundle in Nataya's arms stirred. "Mommy."

Nataya presented the squirming two-year-old boy to the woman, the toddler's chubby arms reaching toward his mother. An explosion of camera flashes bombarded them as the young woman pulled Cory to her, mindless of his filthy face and muddy clothes, hugging him and weeping in relief.

Fox Walker turned away, not to avoid the emotional scene, just the cameras. He knew how reporters held a special affinity for photographing him. Nothing like spicing up their story with a shot of a traditional Native American, with long, jet-black hair, buckskin shirt and moccasin boots.

The claustrophobic press of bodies swarmed him, microphones thrust in his face, the clamor of questions. He began to step back. Chief Deputy Harris moved up beside him.

"Sorry about this, Walker."

"It is to be expected. Resort area with a large city nearby, and reporters desperate for a story."

"Look, we've got a Rescue Unit waiting over there to check out the boy before we let the jackals loose for a feeding frenzy with the parents, so in the meantime ..."

Walker sighed. "Yeah, I know. Got it." Over the shoulders of the crowd he watched the deputies shuffle away the parents and little boy. In his mind he heard Grandfather's voice gently reprimand him. *Better you than them.* He inhaled deeply and turned to face the crowd.

He felt Nataya lean her body against him, slip her hand into his and squeeze it reassuringly. He looked down into gray-blue eyes, her sun-tinted face framed by flaxen braids. She gave him a smile of encouragement.

A woman reporter Walker didn't recognize shouted over the others. "Is there a reward?"

"Reward?" Walker felt Nataya's grip tighten. "No. Returning the boy to his parents is reward enough."

Someone else yelled, "What's it feel like to be a hero?"

Walker grimaced. "I'm not a hero. I'm a tracker. It's what I do. Just like what you do is ask stupi—" He felt Nataya squeeze his hand again, harder. "Like I said. That's just what I do."

A TV news reporter pushed forward. "But how did you succeed in a few hours when the sheriff's department and a search party spent all day searching and came up with nothing?"

Walker looked out over the heads of the reporters to the forest behind them, letting his gaze lose focus. "I listened to the trees ... they told me where to look."

He stole a glance at a dozen slack-jawed faces.

A local reporter snickered. "Hey, Walker, better fill in the un-initiated. Tell 'em how Grandfather taught you to track when you were only eight years old."

"Is that true?" shouted the TV reporter.

Walker nodded, slipping into the speech he gave to each new class attending his wilderness survival school. "Starting as a young boy, and until a little over a year ago when Grandfather passed, he taught me how to read signs in nature. Details most people wouldn't notice."

"What kind of details are you talking about?"

"How did they help you find Cory?"

Walker glanced back at the Rescue Unit and the cluster of people still around it. "Once we made it past the jumble of footprints left by the search party, we began searching in wider and wider circles until we found a partial print, the heel of a toddler's shoe. And nearby were broken stems and loose petals where a child had tried to pick wildflowers. From there we watched for disturbances in the soil, over-turned pebbles, broken twigs on the ground. We followed that trail into the trees, finding impressions on moss-covered stones where Cory had stepped, and flattened patches of grass where he sat to play or rest."

Nataya spoke up. "Fortunately for us, Cory did what most boys do, headed straight for mud."

A ripple of laughter ran through the group.

"Having some clear tracks sped up our search," she went on. "Which was important because we needed to find Cory before dark, especially with the smell of rain in the air."

Everyone automatically looked up at the sky, and the mass of purple-black clouds clustering around the mountain peaks.

"Nataya," the local reporter called out. "Six months ago it was you Walker discovered, surviving in the woods, with no memory. Now you're working together. So, what's transpired during these last months?"

Walker slid a protective arm around Nataya's shoulders, but she spoke before he could intervene.

"Now isn't the time to discuss the past. Today is about Cody being reunited with his parents."

The reporter tried again. "But what about Walker rescuing you from that killer? Do you feel indebted to him for saving your life?"

Walker opened his mouth to speak, felt Nataya reach up and touch his arm. He held his words and let her reply.

"Yes, I am thankful. Thankful that it was Walker who found me. And, yes, I'm also grateful to have him as a mentor. For teaching me his tracking skills."

"Is that all he is to—"

Chief Deputy Harris pushed his way through the crowd to Walker and turned to the group of reporters.

"Mr. and Mrs. Taylor are ready to give a brief statement now," he said, nodding toward where the couple waited. "I ask that you have consideration for their young son. Listen to what they have to say, but no questions at the moment, please."

The crowd moved away in a cluster of lights, leaving Walker, Nataya, and Harris standing on the dark fringes.

"Thanks, Harris," Walker said, holding out his hand.

"No, thank you." They shook. "Appreciate it that you could keep them occupied until the parents got composed."

"And Cory?" Nataya asked.

"He's fine. Nothing a bath and hot meal won't cure. Good job finding him so quickly."

"Thanks to you calling us right away," Walker responded. "Which reminds me. We've not had an opportunity to congratulate you on your new position. I know the circumstances were tough, but you'll do a great job."

"Thanks. It's been difficult. There's been a lot of resistance to changing the attitude already fostered in the department when Morgan was here, especially about using outside assistance. I'm just glad the sheriff supports my ideas. He asked me to pass along his personal 'thank you' for accepting our request for help."

"No problem."

"Still, we were lucky in this case that the boy's so young, and we have a storm front moving through. That got everyone to listen to reason about calling you in." As if on cue, a rumble of thunder reverberated through the mountains and a few large drops of water splattered down on them. "And there's our sign. That should break this party up. At least the news teams here in Colorado are smart enough to know you don't mess around with lightning. Are you heading back to your cabin now?"

Walker nodded.

"Enjoy being warm and dry for me, okay?" Harris grinned and waved as he turned toward the lingering officers and the reporters hurrying toward their vehicles.

Walker wrapped an arm around Nataya's waist as they strode along the edge of the dispersing reporters and headed toward their truck. When she looked up at him, he leaned over and gave her a quick kiss, then raised his head—and came to an abrupt halt. A man had stepped out of the crowd and stood in their path. Cory's father.

"I argued with the law about calling you in for this." The man looked at Walker's lynx claw necklace, then the knife sheathed at his side, down to his moccasin boots, then back up again.

"I thought it was a mistake to send the two of you in there, alone. I wanted the sheriff to keep all those officers and volunteers out there until they found Cory. I have to say that I've never been so happy to be wrong about something." The man's smile broke free of the stress etched into his face. "Thank you both. I wish there was something more I could say or do."

"No need." Walker said, shaking the man's offered hand.

CHAPTER THREE

Elk Meadow, Colorado

Nataya rested her head against Walker's shoulder as he drove the rumbling pickup toward home. Through the windshield she watched the gathering gloom of the storm, big splashes of rain occasionally hitting the glass. The clouds hadn't completely let loose of the moisture yet. The warmth of the truck's heater radiated into her tired muscles and relaxed her body.

She let the emotions of the day wash over her, the intensity of tracking the toddler, the high anticipation as they got closer to finding him, rejoicing in the reunion of mother and son. Walker spoke the truth. That finding the boy was reward enough.

Then she remembered the local reporter, and his questions for her and Walker. Recalling the last six months made the memories all too vivid, as if only yesterday Walker had saved her from that ritualistic killer, a man obsessed with ending her life.

And yet, it feels a lifetime ago.

The pickup turned onto the long gravel drive leading to the cabin and she straightened up in her seat. She never tired of watching the scene before her unfold as they passed through the stand of imposing old-growth fir trees, the valley spreading out in front of her. A few drops of rain fell every so often, making little spikes of water sprout from the surface of the lake that lay beyond the cabin. Even with the setting sun hidden by somber clouds, she could make out the mountains in the background, shrouded in mist.

Walker parked next to the cabin, and they each climbed from the cab and stepped up onto the porch. Without a word between them, they stopped for a moment, leaning on the railing and looking out over the valley. Nataya watched the murky clouds roil and tumble over the mountains in slow motion, but steadily advancing closer.

"Won't be long now," Walker said. He turned and unlocked the door.

They entered the cabin and stripped off the heavy buckskin shirts they both wore for tracking. Nataya hung them on wooden pegs by the door, to air, and slipped down the hall to get fresh clothes for them as Walker strode beneath the high-beamed ceiling of the large open room that comprised the living and eating space.

When Nataya returned to the main room she hung back, quiet, observing Walker as he knelt before the wood stove, digging in the ashes with a poker, until he found a few glowing hot coals. She watched him place pieces of tinder on the embers and blow on them until the flames flared back to life, thought about how he had done the same thing to her, in a way. Brought her back to life.

As she had for him.

⌐+ +⌐

Fox Walker sat on the rug in front of the open door of the stove, the warmth of the orange blaze radiating over him. Wearing only blue jeans, his compact, muscled torso bare, he leaned back against the sofa and stretched his legs out before him. He sensed Nataya's presence before he heard her and turned. Her hair, loosened from the braids, tousled about her shoulders as she walked over to where he sat.

He saw the warmth in her eyes before it spread to the smile on her lips. She had pulled on a sweater and handed him a flannel shirt. He shrugged it on, leaving it unbuttoned, and indicated the spot next to him on the rug. She nimbly lowered her body and curled up against him.

They watched the flames in contented silence, listening to the wood crack and pop as the flames consumed it. Their times together were often spent this way. They shared a bond of silent communion with nature and therefore with one another, and were connected in so many ways other than language.

Walker pulled her closer. Such a remarkable woman. A woman brutally tortured and left for dead. But she had survived by retreating to a secret place in her mind, and managed to stay alive in the wilderness long enough for him to find her and save her from that madman. She was a woman with memories of two separate pasts, and yet had managed to weave them into one lifetime. And she had chosen to stay as Nataya, and stay with him.

He leaned over and kissed the top of her head. She looked up at him.

"You still miss him, don't you?"

Walker smiled and nodded. "Yes, as much as you miss your grandfather."

He pulled her closer. "I've been thinking. We have a month before the next group will be here for the spring survival class. Maybe we take the canoe down to the river, spend some time out in the woods?"

"Yes, I would love that."

She smiled at him and they kissed, featherlike touches of lips to lips. He pressed his body against hers, feeling the warmth of her, the kisses becoming harder.

They both jumped when the phone rang. It rarely rang, especially in the late evening.

Walker tried to ignore the intrusive sound of the ancient rotary dial phone, but knew full well no answering machine would kick in to take a message. Nataya eased from his embrace, freeing him to answer. He reluctantly stood, strode over to the phone and picked it up.

"Walker here."

"Fox Walker?"

"Yeah, that's me."

"This is Special Agent Susan Mueller, with the FBI, Denver field office. You don't know me, but I know all about you. Dean McClure, our consultant on that serial murder case last fall—the one you were involved in—sang your praises. He says you were a key player in the apprehension of the murderer."

"Guess you could say that. But I couldn't have done it without McClure's help," Walker answered carefully.

"Well, McClure wasn't the only one impressed with your tracking skills. The Bureau has chosen you as the best candidate for a new search we've got going."

"Sounds like an order."

"Look, I don't have time for niceties here. There's been an escape. A convict being transported yesterday morning to the Denver County Jail got loose and made it into the woods."

"Why is the FBI involved in a county matter?"

"Because the fugitive entered a national forest, which puts him in federal jurisdiction."

"I see." Walker hesitated. Superficially the story could make sense. But since when did the FBI care about someone being in a national forest? There had to be more to it. "So, what was the guy's crime?"

"Crimes, in the plural. First-degree murder, rape, and assault with deadly force."

A flash of memory ripped through Walker's mind. Beloved Haiwi, beaten to death on her bedroom floor. And just when he thought he was over that part of his life.

Then his mind made the connection to what the agent had said. He vaguely remembered a high-profile trial in Denver about a rape and murder. But murders were not FBI matters unless state lines were crossed, or the local law called in advisers. There could only be one answer.

"I take it the victim was associated with the Bureau?" Walker asked.

A pause. "She used to be an agent. Quit to get married and start a family. But, she was a damn good agent when she was here."

Walker nodded. So, when the fugitive entered federal lands, it gave the Bureau the old "jurisdiction excuse" to insert themselves into the case. Which brought up his next question.

"I'm usually the last person to get called in, when everyone else gives up. What made you call me first?"

"Because our convict is in your backyard, Walker. A local rancher found the abandoned vehicle just hours ago, at the edge of the San Juan National Forest. I need someone in there fast, to find his trail. You're the closest, and you know those woods better than any trained agent I can send in there."

Walker heard Grandfather's voice in his thoughts. *Beware of strangers singing praises.*

"So, I'll be working this alone?"

"Yes. I know that's what you prefer. And in this instance, it works for us, too. We need someone tracking the convict in stealth mode. We need an edge."

"An edge? How hard can it be to find an orange jumpsuit in a green forest?" There was a long silence on the other end of the phone. Walker shifted his weight, waiting.

"The fugitive has a history that complicates the situation."

"In what way?"

"He's a former Navy SEAL. Top of the class in weapons, demolition, stealth, hand-to-hand combat. But none of those were his specialty."

"Which was?" Walker asked, already sensing the answer.

"Wilderness survival."

"I see ..."

"Not entirely. He's also armed. And every moment that he's out there alone, the bigger our risk of losing him."

CHAPTER FOUR

San Juan National Forest, Colorado

Fingers of evening sunlight groped through the towering trees, giving Matt Logan just enough light to see by as he sprinted through the woods, leaping over fallen logs and boulders, ducking under low branches.

Freedom!

He had fought for it, in foreign deserts and jungles. Almost died for it. But never before had it meant so much to him.

He vaulted over a shallow creek and scrambled up the slope on the other side. At the top he stopped to catch his breath. Damn good thing he kept in shape after retirement.

Logan had no doubt the Land Rover would eventually be found, but he had taken it as far as he could in the failing light. He figured that even if discovered that day, it wouldn't leave the sheriff enough time to organize a group at that location, far less get the search itself under way. So, he had taken advantage of what light remained of the evening and run through the forest for a solid hour, and probably covered almost six miles.

He glanced around. That nearby grove of saplings would be the perfect spot to change. He slipped amongst tree trunks and removed the backpack he'd found sitting on the floorboard in front of the passenger seat, as planned.

Logan reached into one of the outside pouches on the backpack and extracted the Glock 19 semiautomatic handgun he had liberated from one of the guards. He hadn't needed to fire it during his escape. He guessed the one remaining conscious guard could tell Logan knew how to use it, because issuing a threat had been enough.

With his free hand he reached over and touched another pouch to make sure the extra ammo magazine, the one he'd removed from the remaining guard's gun before tossing the weapon aside, was still there. Check.

Logan hefted the Glock in his hand. A bit top-heavy for his taste, but he knew from experience it was extremely reliable in the field. He released the magazine, then checked the ammo. A full magazine, good. Tilting the gun slightly sideways, he racked the slide to clear the chamber and caught the ejected cartridge in midair, before it could fall into the leaves below.

His hands performed an automatic check of the weapon, taking it apart and inspecting the maintenance, then briskly reassembling it. That guard wouldn't have lasted two minutes in a battle, but at least he knew how to care for a gun.

After thumbing the ejected round back into the magazine, Logan used the heel of his hand to punch it back into position in the gun and racked the slide to load it. Although he figured he could count on having several hours lead on any pursuers, by habit he laid the gun within easy reach. Nothing much more useless than a loaded gun he couldn't get to.

Logan unzipped the main compartment on the backpack and pulled out camo clothes and a shoulder holster. As he slid off the bright-orange jumpsuit and the jail-issued boots, he reflected on his escape. It had gone flawlessly. Victor had certainly come through for him, but then, that's what SEAL team members do. Logan had certainly saved Vic on more than one occasion while in the service. Logan being retired didn't change the equation one bit.

Sean had been a slightly different matter. His younger brother was no soldier, but had begged to help. Logan had agreed only on the condition that Sean not be involved in the actual execution of the escape itself. "That way when you get questioned about it, and you will, you can honestly say you don't know shit." A legit reason. But the truth was that Logan was protecting his younger brother. Just as he had done all their lives.

Logan tugged on the trousers, then the matching woodland camo shirt. Next came the shoulder holster. He slipped in the Glock and adjusted the rig for comfort and ease of access. As he pulled on the hiking boots and began to lace them up, a shadow slid across the ground. He peered up through the trees and frowned. Even the most carefully thought-out plan could be foiled by Mother Nature. A fact he knew well.

The clouds rolling in over the treetops looked full of moisture, and with the wind beginning to whip the trees to and fro, meant he probably would not make it as far as he had hoped before having to take shelter. He rolled up the orange jumpsuit, grabbed the jail-issued boots and shoved them into a nearby rotted-out log. Then he scooped up handfuls of dead leaves from the damp ground and stuffed them into the end of the log to hide the clothes, and scattered more leaves over the top to blend the log into the landscape. He stood and checked out the scene, then kicked around loose leaves and pine needles until the spot appeared undisturbed. Lastly he stepped backward from the site, and, using a branch full of dead leaves, erased his boot prints from the ground.

Logan glanced back at the creek he had crossed earlier and decided it was the perfect place for his trail to completely end. He used the branch of leaves to brush away all his foot prints from this side of the creek until he reached rockier ground. If anyone followed his tracks from the valley floor they would be focused on the smooth-soled imprints of his prison boots. From there on out, any prints they happened upon would be entirely different. His original trail would simply end. He didn't have time to do anything more elaborate, but it would slow down any one following.

Sitting on a boulder, he began checking the other pouches in the backpack. He had let Sean be responsible for the supplies, although he suspected Victor had provided some guidance on the camo outfit because Sean had chosen the correct one for the mountain terrain. Custom tailored, so as not to snag on brush.

Side pockets on the backpack held a stash of energy bars and a couple of stainless steel water bottles. Not that Logan didn't know how to forage for food in the wild, but this would keep him moving, putting distance between himself and civilization. In another pouch he found a small wad of twenty-dollar bills, binoculars, a sheath knife, a multi-tool and one of those little survival tins. He opened the tin to find a flint/striker, fishing line and hooks, water purification tablets, and a compass. He almost laughed out loud. Even though he was a trained special ops guy, it was touching to see that Sean was trying to make the next few days as easy as possible for him. Evidently Sean was more than a little worried about his big brother.

Thunder rolled through the air. Well, he couldn't worry about the weather. Besides, the rain would muddy most of his tracks and delay a search party from even getting started this evening. The locals would be savvy enough to know that being outdoors in the open during a thunderstorm in the mountains, with lightning strikes numbering in the hundreds, could easily be a death sentence. He already had one. Those following him would be more cautious.

He took the change of plan in stride, effortlessly switching to a different strategy. In that sense this little excursion wasn't anything new to him. Just another day on the job.

CHAPTER FIVE

Elk Meadow, Colorado

F ox Walker hung up the phone and stared at it for a moment, only the fire crackling in the silence. When he looked up, Nataya had curled up on the sofa, watching him, alert. But before he could speak, a sudden deluge of rain hit the tin roof of the cabin, causing them both to look heavenward.

"It's here." Walker usually enjoyed hearing the patter of rain on the roof, but the pounding of this downpour threatened to drown out his words. He used the moment to gather his thoughts as they both moved to the windows to look outside. The wind pelted the rain against the panes, caused it to flow in streams down the glass, making it difficult to see anything, except the occasional flash of lightning. But within a few minutes the intensity diminished as the wind slowed, and the rain eased to a steady pour that didn't make such a din on the roof.

Nataya took Walker's hand and led him back to the sofa. "So, tell me about the phone call."

He sat beside her. "A convict escaped his guards while being transported to the Denver County Jail. He fled in a vehicle and made it all the way out here before he ditched it and disappeared in the San Juan National Forest. The FBI is asking for help tracking him down."

Her mouth formed a silent 'o' as she contemplated this information. "I guess they'll want us there at first light. There's nothing we can do this late, and in the rain," she said as she stood. "But, we can get things ready now, to save time in the morning."

"You're correct about the timing. It's just that ... I'll be going alone."

Nataya turned and looked at him. "What do you mean, alone? We're a team. We work together."

"Not on this one, Nataya." The surprise in her eyes made him soften his tone before continuing.

"Look, the escaped prisoner is a former Navy SEAL. A man who specialized in wilderness survival—"

She stood up. "So he's an equal. All the more reason to pit the two of us against him."

Walker shook his head and laid out his trump card. "The Bureau wants me to go in alone on this, stalking the man." He could tell by her expression that she didn't buy it, and her next words said as much.

"I know you could convince them that we work as a team. That we could stalk the fugitive together."

"But this guy was convicted of murder, Nataya. He raped, tortured and killed a woman who used to be an FBI agent."

He saw Nataya's hand involuntarily stray to her abdomen, to where scars lay hidden beneath fabric. A physical reminder left behind by the attacker. The mental scars were more difficult to see. She looked away a moment. Then turned to face him.

"So, we are partners only if the job is a nice safe one?"

Walker cringed internally at the sarcasm sliding into her voice. "I'm sorry. I can't let you get involved in this," he said as he stood, slid his arms around her and pulled her close.

She stiffened in his embrace.

"I'm sorry, Nataya. I truly am," he said, leaning back, his gaze intent. "Look, we've worked together to rescue lost hikers and runaways, and you've done a great job. No doubt about it. We both know your survival skills are top-notch. Your instincts in tune with nature. And over the last few months you've worked hard to hone your tracking skills to near perfection. But this is different. This guy escaped with a guard's gun, so he's not only skilled at survival, he's armed. And a convicted killer."

Nataya pulled away from him. Holding eye contact, she lifted the bottom of her sweater, revealing the scars covering her torso. The angry welts silvery against her tan skin.

"I know what it's like going up against a killer. Don't these prove anything? I'm a survivor. I'm not afraid."

Walker sighed. "This has nothing to do with your courage. You have proven that, more than once. This is about being smart, and knowing what will work best in this situation. I agree with the FBI that my best option will be the element of surprise. I don't see any other way than to go in alone after this guy." His words held an element of truth, but he wondered if she could see through it, could see that his concern for her safety factored into his decision.

"You've made up your mind then."

"Yes, I have."

She stood rigid before him, breathing hard. "Well, I've made up my mind, too. And I think you're wrong."

She held his gaze for a long moment, but when he remained silent he saw her shoulders fall and knew the battle had ended. As she turned and busied herself getting things ready for the morning, Walker watched her tense, jerky movements and knew he had not convinced her.

They both worked in silence, but not the comfortable quiet he had grown used to.

⟛+ +⟛

Walker took one last look at the topo map before getting up from the desk. He had been studying the lay of the land where the FBI had discovered the abandoned Land Rover, refreshing his memory of that part of the forest. Nataya had silently watched over his shoulder as he showed her the path he thought the fugitive would most likely take. Still moody and downcast, she had gone on to bed without him.

The rain had ended while he worked, so when he stepped into the dark bedroom, moonlight poured in through the window. A good sign that it would be clear in the morning.

Nataya lay curled up on her side of the bed when Walker slipped in under the covers. When she rolled over and snuggled against his body, she caught him off guard, but only momentarily. He nuzzled her neck and found no resistance, so he moved up to kiss her. She soon returned his advances with the same warmth, the same intensity. His hands caressed her, finding all the places on her body that he knew she enjoyed, and knew success in her moans of appreciation.

Soon her hands gently pushed against his shoulders until he lay back on the bed and she slid over on top of him. He noticed the moonlight's glint on her scars, and for one brief moment felt the guilt of his decision. She was a survivor and deserved to be going with him, but his heart could not let it happen. He had just found her, found love in his life again after too many years of pain. He wasn't about to risk losing it to this guy.

Then she moved against him, and he lost the thought.

He knew then that this was not going to be one of those panting, sweaty, bang-the-headboard against-the-wall nights. This would be one of those sensuously slow, pleasurably torturing nights. He smiled. Who was he to guess at her change of heart?

⊨⊰ ⊱⊨

Nataya rolled to her back, pale hair fanning across the pillow. She stole a glance at the contentment on Walker's face, acknowledged that same wash of satisfaction. They both turned as one into their favored position, Walker curled up to her back, his arm draped around her. She sensed him relax into a deep, restful sleep, tensions released, as she knew their lovemaking would do.

She lay there awake, thinking about his decision to leave her behind for this manhunt. Tears stung her eyes and she fought them back. She had not forgiven him.

But she loved him, and needed to feel the intimacy of their love before he left. And she wanted him to come back to her, alive.

He would leave her in the morning. But he would leave with a good night's rest, her love in his heart, and a sound reason to want to survive and return.

She would stay behind out of respect. But it wasn't over.

CHAPTER SIX

Elk Meadow, Colorado

Nataya stood on the front porch watching the gray predawn mist linger over the lake, the stillness periodically broken by birds chirping awake from their slumber. Walker emerged from the cabin and came to her side. He rested his arm across her shoulders, and pulled her against him. They watched together as the drab morning sky lightened into soft pink hues. The sun began to peek over the rim of the dark, somber mountains before them when they heard tires crunching over the gravel drive to the cabin.

Walker turned her into his embrace and gazed into her eyes. She saw the intensity there, the love he held for her, and she could not let him see the anger and hurt that dwelled just below the surface. He didn't need that on his mind right now.

The car stopped next to the cabin and she saw the FBI agent at the wheel. She kissed Walker and watched in silence as he strode to the awaiting vehicle. The Ute people, like most Native Americans, don't have a word for 'good-bye' in their vocabulary, and Nataya preferred to follow the tradition.

Although her ancestors were Scottish and English, and not full-blooded Ute as Walker was, she felt Native American in her heart. It didn't matter that her hair shone pale, as did her gray-blue eyes; it was her mind that held to the traditional ways. The ways her grandfather had taught her, and Walker continued.

Long after the car pulled away and followed the gravel drive down to the main road, Nataya remained standing on the porch, staring beyond the lake to the mountains. She couldn't face going into the empty cabin just yet. She stepped off the porch to the grass, still soggy from the previous night's rain, to follow the well-worn path down past the large outbuilding they used for survival classes, to the edge of the lake.

Walker had built a wooden bench at the water's edge when he saw how much delight she took in watching the ducks and geese on the lake. And each day the change of season brought in different varieties of waterfowl as they migrated through the area. She loved the surprise of spotting species she had never seen before.

She sat on the bench, watching the ripples catch and reflect the sun as it rose in the sky, and let the thoughts flow one into the other as they would.

Only six months had passed since she lived alone in the forest. All of nature had been her companion then. Only when Walker came into her life, became a part of her life, did she know what it felt like to be separated from someone. To be lonely.

Nataya leaned over, picked up a tiny pebble and tossed it into the shallow water. She replayed the previous night's argument over and over, trying to be fair about his insistence that he must track the fugitive alone.

She scooped up a handful of stones and began to throw them one by one into the lake, each one farther out than the one before it.

He used the FBI as an excuse to go alone.

Instincts told her his decision had more to do with protecting her, and keeping her out of harm's way, than it did with strategy. He knew they could be more powerful as a team, yet he insisted on keeping her there. Safe.

Nataya sidearmed a stone into the water, causing it to skip over the surface three times before dropping below.

So he wanted to protect her. Why did that make her angry? Nataya sighed. She knew. She just had to admit it to herself. That it hurt her feelings. This was the first time, since they'd been together, that he had left on a search without her by his side, and the sting of that made her feel less worthy.

The next stone into the lake hit the surface hard enough to frighten the nearest ducks. They burst from the water with a flurry of wings, splashes and vocal protests, startling her out of her thoughts.

Nataya stood and dropped the remaining rocks to the ground. Her hands balled into fists, rhythmically hitting her thighs. How was she to learn if not allowed to do anything dangerous?

I need to prove I deserve to be by his side. No matter what the circumstance.

CHAPTER SEVEN

San Juan National Forest, Colorado

Matt Logan pulled his tall frame from the debris hut he put together before the storm hit full force the night before. To lessen the chance of a lightning strike, he chose to build it on a dry rock slope, slightly higher than the ground around him but dominated by a nearby stony peak.

He stretched and breathed in the fresh early dawn air. The rain had stopped after about four hours, around midnight he guessed, by the position of the almost full moon. But that morning every leaf and blade of grass still dripped with moisture.

Logan began the process of taking apart the shelter, removing large slabs of bark that protected a two-foot-thick layer of grasses, brush, leaves, and moss. He scattered the loose debris under the nearby trees. Next he disassembled the wedge-shaped framework of evergreen boughs and tree limbs that leaned against a large branch, used as a center pole. One end of the branch rested on a large boulder, the other on the ground. It all had the appearance of a giant skeletal rib cage. Inside, a thick pad of fir needles and dried leaves kept away the dampness. He had not only stayed warm the entire time, but dry as well.

He realized that some might think him foolish to spend so much time on a shelter for one night. But aside from escape, shelter ranked as his highest priority, far more important than food. During SEAL training, his superiors made sure he learned that lesson, the hard way. So he'd never forget it. As a green recruit, he made the common mistake of most people when lost in the wilderness. He worried first about food, and nearly died of exposure, long before starvation became a consideration. But after years of training, he knew he no longer fell into the category of "most people."

When Logan finished returning all the debris and limbs back to the natural surroundings, leaving little trace of his overnight camp, he took stock of the distance between his current position and the mountains ahead. No doubt about it. The downpour had forced him to stop well before reaching his objective the previous day.

No doubt the Land Rover had been discovered by then, and a search party at least organized, if not already in the woods. At least the rain would make signs of his passage more difficult to discover. He needed to take advantage of that fact and make up for the hours lost.

He wouldn't take time to search for food until he had gone deeper into the wilderness. Thanks to Sean's thoughtfulness he had the energy bars, and, besides, there were plenty of grasses and plants he could pluck while he walked and chew for nutrition, adding fiber to his empty stomach.

He decided to save the few water bottles for when he left the dense forest for the foothills, where water would be more difficult to find. Instead, he drank rainwater from where it pooled in the rock depressions, and as it dripped from the leaves of the surrounding plants.

Logan shouldered the backpack, adjusted the shoulder holster, checked the compass and set off through the trees. The urgency of making up lost time didn't give him the luxury of taking time to hide his trail as he worked his way deeper into the forest, but he used every opportunity to make his trail difficult to follow. To hide his footprints, he stepped on large stones and hard-packed surfaces whenever possible. He took odd angles through the trees, and tried to stay out of the soft dirt that lay just below the leaf clutter. The smaller, shallow creeks allowed him to wade into them for short distances, so that his trail entering the water did not pick up again until farther upstream, on the other side. Anything that he could use to throw someone off and maintain a quick pace, he used.

The local law knew he was armed, so they'd hesitate to bring in dogs. And the sheriff would know a helicopter would be useless. Logan would hear it a mile away. Besides having the dense forest canopy for cover, he could hide beneath a cliff or boulders, and compress his body so that even heat-sensing devices wouldn't be able to distinguish the blob on screen from man or animal.

Besides, by end of the day he'd be through the forest into the rocky mountain-scape, and at that point a search party wouldn't have the expertise to follow his trail. He'd stay within the timberline and use the evergreens to shield his movement. Then he would make better time.

Logan's movement through the woods were so automatic and natural he found his mind free to think and plan. In fact it worked better that way. He could be more creative.

As he toiled through the trees and underbrush, memories of his younger brother, the two of them playing "army" as kids, rolled through his mind. Sean would stay close to home, as Logan had instructed, knowing law officers would show up to question him, maybe even search his place. Sean would be cooperative and helpful, making sure the authorities believed his story of innocence and start looking elsewhere as quickly as possible.

Logan laughed to himself at the thought as he ducked under a low tree branch and clambered over a large outcrop of boulders. Sean had that all-American-apple-pie kind of face that people just automatically trusted. He could have lived in Mayberry, USA. And his actions followed. Even as a youngster, Sean found it difficult to lie or cross their parents. But for some reason Logan would never understand, Sean looked up to him, even idolized him, all their years together. This made Logan fiercely protective of his younger brother, especially after their father had died in the line of duty, saving his partner's life.

Logan became determined back then to let Sean keep that innocence, so rare in today's world, and made more poignant because of his own past escapades and near brushes with the law.

At the edge of a ridge, Logan paused to catch his breath, do a quick check of his direction on the compass and study the lay of the land ahead. Thoughts of his father invariably brought up memories of the funeral. The honor bestowed upon his father by the city and his fellow officers had deeply impressed Logan. In fact, that day an intense longing began to grow within him. To be a part of that kind of loyalty, somehow, some way.

Becoming a Navy SEAL gave him the sense of loyalty that he craved, with his team. They trusted their lives to each other. But enemies were created as well. He hadn't set out to do that, but his aggressive "damn the consequences, this mission will not fail" attitude did not make him popular with the navy officers.

Logan thought back to all the times he had skirted rules and regulations, pissing off his superiors. Like the time he set up a standard practice "attack" with one of the military compounds, then deviated from the plan and covertly took over the entire facility, just to prove his point. That terrorists don't "follow the rules." His ass had been reamed more times than he could count. Yet, he always compensated by accomplishing extraordinary feats when called upon. The more Logan used his instincts as his guide, the better he had performed, and that hadn't been lost on the higher ranks. He garnered a reputation—not all good—but enough good to outweigh the bad. Until now, he admitted, his face grim.

The land had begun to steadily rise, and he could feel the extra effort in the calves of his legs. He figured he must be entering the foothills. The climb into the mountains would slow his progress, but anyone who followed would have the same issues.

And Logan knew those who might follow certainly wouldn't be the caliber of his team, men he trusted with his life. He may be running through the wilderness alone, but he sensed his team's presence with every step, the escape from his guards, the path he took toward the mountains, the hideout they had prepared for him on the far side of the mountain—when they saw that the trial wasn't going well. They were there alright. Sprinting through the trees with him, both running point and watching his flank.

Logan plunged into the evergreen trees and rockier ground. He left behind the deciduous trees of the forest and would travel just below the timberline, staying within the shelter of the firs on the side of the mountain. The air there held the chill of higher altitude, and the nights would demand a warm shelter. But he knew he had hours to make up before he could even consider stopping to build a shelter for the night. He pushed harder.

An open space gave him room to sprint between trees, and in the process he startled a cottontail from its hiding place. It zigzagged across the ground in front of him. A second later Logan felt the rush of air against his head and, out of instinct, dropped to the ground, giving him a ground-level view of a large Cooper's

Hawk as it struck the cottontail, the quick squeal of terror amid the frenzy of flashing feathers and whiffs of fur.

A sudden vision of Nicole flashed through his memory, dark eyes staring into nothing, hair tangled about her. And the blood. So much blood. He was no stranger to the sight of it. But that had been different.

He shook his head, stood and focused on the task at hand. Time enough for those thoughts later. He had a plan. And he meant to complete it.

CHAPTER EIGHT

San Juan National Forest, Colorado

Early morning sun flashed in and out of the car window as Fox Walker and Special Agent Davis sped along beneath th overhanging tree boughs on either side of the road. Walker closed the manila folder on his lap and leaned forward in the passenger seat, straining to look upward out of the windshield to the mountain towering over the trees, a blur beside them. Reading the report during the drive had made the time go fast, and gave him reason not to carry on a conversation. But he had questions that needed answers. "So how in hell did the convict get this far away from Denver without being caught?"

Davis continued to watch the road without a glance toward Walker. "You just read the report. It's all there."

"No, it's not all here. These are just some facts someone wrote out to appease the sheriff's department. There are too many holes in the story."

"I'm not sure I know what you mean."

Walker stared at the man, eyes dark. The agent's grip tightened on the wheel, but he remained silent. Walker tried another angle. "So, given that this Matthew Logan is a Navy SEAL, survival expert—"

"Former Navy SEAL."

"Call him what you want, it doesn't take away any of his skills and experience. My point is, how did he end up in a private prisoner transport?"

"You know what they say, hindsight is always twenty-twenty. First mistake came with Logan being termed by the court as High Profile, instead of High Risk. After that, no one questioned the decision to keep the operation low profile by transporting him alone, using a private service. With city budget restrictions the way they are these days, it frequently happens."

Walker turned to face forward again. "Hard to believe the sheriff's department would allow complete goof-offs to handle this."

"Near as we could find, the service has, or should I say had, a pristine record. You just read their report to the sheriff."

"Yeah, yeah, they followed all the standard procedures." Walker pictured the scene. Logan loaded into the back of the van, handcuffed and shackled. He wore a belly chain, so his hands were in front, a common procedure for a long-distance transport—according to the private transport service. Walker glanced out the passenger-side window. "So did the van have a solid partition separating the prisoner section from the cab?"

"That's what the report says."

Walker's jaw twitched. "What about this whole deal with the van having to stop because cattle wandered onto the road? We both know that's not rare in these parts, but this one doesn't look like an accident, not with the getaway vehicle waiting below the overpass." Walker waited for a response. When he only got silence, he continued. "Seems someone knew the transport van would be coming through that spot, with Logan on board. So, you guys think an accomplice got the back door open for Logan while the cattle distracted everyone?"

Davis stared straight ahead as he drove and concentrated on taking a curve before he spoke. "Maybe you don't know it, but the Bureau didn't have any jurisdiction in this case until the fugitive entered the national forest. We've got the same intel on the escape that you've got there in your report."

"Maybe you don't get it, Agent Davis. I don't care diddlysquat about any official report on what happened. In fact, this isn't even the sheriff's report, only the word of those private transportation guys. Don't try giving me some crap that the Bureau doesn't have any evidence. I know better. I need you to tell me what the Bureau has pieced together. What's the talk around the office about this case?"

"I'm not at liberty to pass along that kind of information. I'm sure you understand."

Walker struggled to contain his frustration in the silence that followed. He spoke, his voice low, the words even and punctuated with silence. "So, let me get this straight. You want me to go walking into this forest, alone. And then you want me to hunt down a known killer—an armed killer. Someone the FBI doesn't even want to mess with. And you want me to do it without knowing what I'm truly up against?"

Walker turned in his seat as far as the seat belt would allow, giving the agent his full attention. "Who the hell do you think you are, anyway? And who do you think I am that I'll do this for you simply because I was hired, without getting the info I need? You can just turn this car around and take me back."

"Okay. Look, this wasn't my idea, you know. The Bureau has their own reason for handling this the way they are, and I'm sure not privy to it."

"Well, they seem to forget that I'm doing you guys the favor."

Davis sighed. "Fair enough. To hell with it. Go ahead. Ask whatever questions you want and I'll do my best to let you know what I've heard."

Walker relaxed back into the seat. "Good. Let's talk about this big hole in the story. The convenient fact the driver doesn't remember anything after the other guard stepped outside to try and move the black Angus cattle out of the way, until he regains consciousness, handcuffed to the back bumper, along with his partner. I'm sure the FBI has managed to get a few more details that are missing from our *official* report here."

Davis nodded. "Yeah, the driver-side door hinges were sprung. Someone ripped open the door with enough force to cause the damage. The driver has bruises on one side of his neck, probably from being yanked from his seat. And there's the lump on his head and mild concussion to explain the rest, the missing gun and keys. His two-way had been stomped on. Ground into pieces."

"Someone? The second guard didn't witness any of this?"

"Nope. Supposedly he had his back to the van, trying to herd the cattle away. And it was noisy."

"I take it the Bureau checked out the site, to see if the second guard's story holds up?"

Agent Davis nodded and took the car into a sharp curve.

Walker placed his hands on the dashboard to steady himself. *Geez, the guy is sure in a hurry.* He heard the agent speaking. Focused back on the conversation.

"Yeah, with all the noise and confusion of the cattle milling around, we believe the guard is telling the truth. That Logan surprised him from behind, held him at gunpoint, then took his weapon, took the magazine and tossed the gun, and then smashed the two-way."

"What about this disappearing act? That Logan backed his way to the edge of the road while he trained his gun at the guard, and then just dropped from sight?"

"Yeah, as unbelievable as it sounds, it could've happened like that. The land on the side of the road at that location drops off steeply to a creek below. Boot prints and tire tracks corroborate that Logan got into a four-wheel-drive vehicle down there, and then drove off across a meadow."

"Interesting. Why didn't this murderer just kill the guards? It would've bought him a lot of time and no eye witnesses."

"Dunno." Agent Davis then chuckled. "Although I bet those guards wish he would've at least wounded them, rather than go back and face their bosses, or the sheriff."

"No doubt." Walker allowed a small smile. At least Davis had finally lightened up from the straight-laced, strictly-by-the-books stereotypical secret agent man. He glanced out the side window as he thought, and watched the dense forest of trees blur by, accentuated by the deep shadows within. "Okay. So at that point the two-ways are useless. But according to the report, when they were stopped by the cattle, the driver called in from the radio in the van."

"Yeah. But it took a while before anyone at the main office noticed that the driver hadn't called in again. After all, it hadn't been a request for assistance, just a report of delay. But once the van didn't respond to later calls, the office sent out another unit to check on them, and notified the sheriff's department."

"So Logan got a sizable head start on everyone. But even at that, couldn't they use choppers to look for him? The guard mentioned a missing license plate. Wouldn't that be obvious, even from the air?"

"Evidently Logan thought of that, too. When we found the vehicle, the plate had been replaced with a stolen one. The vehicle would have blended in with all the other hundreds of Land Rovers here in Colorado. And this guy must have stayed off-road wherever they set up checkpoints."

"Clever. Or well informed."

"Yeah."

Walker watched Davis shut down like a light being switched off. Walker remained quiet until the agent took the next curve in the road, slowed the car and spoke again.

"Right here is where he ditched the Land Rover. You can see it off in the trees at the edge of the forest there." The agent indicated with a nod. "One of the nearby ranchers has a scanner in his house, heard the Be on the Lookout call and went searching. He spotted it just before dark yesterday."

Agent Davis pulled his car behind a flatbed tow truck parked on the side of the road, and the two men got out. He motioned for Walker to follow him toward the Land Rover. A couple of men were hooking up chains to the vehicle while FBI agents roamed within the taped-off section of ground and trees. Walker noticed a couple of sheriff's deputies standing off to the side, observing, and not looking any too happy about the FBI being there calling the shots.

Davis nodded toward the Land Rover. "Of course they'll take the vehicle in and look for forensic evidence. The rain damaged most of the prints during the night, but when we first arrived on scene yesterday we could get a clear bearing on which direction Logan headed. He went straight into the forest here," Davis said, pointing toward a specific spot in the trees.

Walker didn't say anything as he took a moment to survey his surroundings. The road and tree line where they stood sat higher than the valley below because of a steep embankment, the thick mat of treetops sloping downward into hundreds of square miles of dense national forest. But from where he stood, and looking directly west, the woods ran for about ten miles before it angled up the side of the nearest mountain. The deciduous trees, aspen, oaks, Rocky Mountain maple and mountain-ash mingled with evergreens, then thinned and finally ceased as the spruce, junipers, and fir trees took over in the higher altitude, ending at the timberline. Then the craggy mountain reigned over all, magnificent in its immensity, the uppermost section shrouded in clouds.

The agent stood quietly off to the side, waiting. Walker studied the soil and ground cover as he made his way through the heavy brush at the forest edge, then stepped cautiously into the darkness of the forest foliage. He stopped, alert, waiting for his eyes to adjust to the deep shadows. The agent joined him but hung back, out of the way, watching.

The thick tree boughs overhead had kept even the heavy rains of the previous night from hitting the forest floor with enough impact to completely wash away the disturbed soil and leaf litter. Broken twigs, bruised and torn leaves showed Walker where Logan had crashed through the underbrush. Judging by the distance between muddy footprints, Logan had sprinted across the small open space.

The sign made it obvious to Walker that Logan hadn't worried about hiding his entry into the forest. Most likely he knew that it would be a matter of time before someone spotted the abandoned vehicle. The man would make the most of his time by putting the biggest distance between himself and the pursuers as he could. Besides, Logan would know that dogs could be brought in to find his scent and follow.

Which brought up a good question. Why hadn't they done that? The only answer that came to mind was not a pleasant one. Why bring in a search party and dogs to track someone who could sit back in safety and pick them off one by one, as if they were in a shooting gallery.

Okay, so he was back to the Bureau's game. Bring in one man to track the fugitive in stealth mode, and hope the tracker succeeds. Still, there remained one more question to be answered.

Walker turned to the agent. "Are you holding back something from me? Like the fact that Logan's got an accomplice?" He watched Davis look away. "Look, this is my life on the line here, not some bureaucratic game."

The agent faced Walker, giving him his full attention. "The question isn't whether or not he had an accomplice. It's how many."

Walker remained stone-faced for a moment, then countered with a follow-up question. "Any idea who these accomplices might be?"

Davis looked toward the other FBI agents, then down to his shoes, not meeting Walker's eyes. "The man spent half his life leading a Navy SEAL team. What do *you* think?"

"I think I'd like to know where those teammates are."

"Yeah, so do we. The Bureau is trying to track them all down as we speak."

Walker studied the surrounding trees, then turned to Davis. "I need to know everything you can tell me about this man."

The agent nodded. "Understood. But, before I give you the scoop, can we at least walk back to my car? I feel like a sitting duck in here."

Walker glanced sideways at Davis, saw the grim set of his jaw.

Who the hell is this Matt Logan that he can creep out even the guys at the Bureau?

Fox Walker and Agent Davis turned and pushed their way through the underbrush and trees to the open ground. Walker quizzed the agent as they walked toward the car.

"What has the FBI so spooked, anyway?"

"You do understand that's exactly what the Bureau doesn't want me to divulge to you."

"Why, because it might scare me off?"

Davis shrugged.

Both men stopped next to the car. Walker put his hands in his jeans' pockets and looked Davis in the eye. "Look, I always know my prey before I hunt. It's that simple. And we're wasting valuable time."

Davis sighed and pulled out a pack of cigarettes from his shirt pocket. He tapped the pack against the heel of his hand and offered one to Walker, who declined.

"Matt Logan was a legend among his SEAL teammates," Davis said as he pulled out a cigarette, stuck it between his lips and lit up. "On assignments, he pulled out all the stops, did whatever it took to get it done. Whether it was politically correct or not. In his mind, the end justified the means. He earned the respect and loyalty of his men, but gave his superiors ulcers. They spent a lot of time trying to cover for his actions, even though he always completed the assignment. More than a few of the officers were glad to see him retire."

"He's a rogue, then. Not afraid to break the rules. The Bureau doesn't know how he might react."

"Exactly."

"A dangerous man. Any idea why he murdered the female former agent?"

Davis leaned back against the car and took a long drag on the cigarette, then exhaled. "Nope. He never admitted that he did it. Wouldn't talk about it or defend himself. Which didn't help his case."

"How did he end up getting tagged for the crime, anyway? What evidence did they have?"

"They made a DNA match on fingernail scrapings from the victim."

"Had she been raped?"

"Yeah, and beaten, but no semen."

"Still, a Navy SEAL leaving behind any kind of evidence at a crime scene ... didn't that seem strange to anyone?"

"Yeah. Joggers found the body dumped in a public park, near a popular running path. But forensics said she died somewhere else. The house had been tossed. Everything pointed to the fact that he deliberately made it look like a robbery gone bad."

"I'd think a guy with Logan's reputation and training would be more creative than that."

"Agreed. But everything shifted badly for Logan when it came out during the trial that he and the victim, Nicole, met years ago, about the time she became an FBI agent."

"They knew each other?"

"More than "knew" each other, if we can believe the testimony at the trial. Word is that they remained a hot 'n' heavy item during the time she worked at the Bureau, before she left and married." Davis dropped the butt of his cigarette on the dirt by his car, ground it out with the toe of his shoe.

Walker watched the action and cringed at the desecration. "I bet the prosecution had fun with that."

"Yeah, when Logan wouldn't explain why his DNA had been found on the victim, it allowed for speculation that it might have been a crime of passion. Besides, there wasn't any other evidence to lead to anyone else. And everyone, public and law officers, wanted to put someone away for this one. The prosecutor played up Logan's 'bad boy' antics while in the service, his passionate nature, and the jury convicted him."

Walker gazed out over the tops of the trees. "So, since the FBI wasn't involved with his court case, any chance Logan would guess the Bureau is looking for him now?"

"No reason for him to. He knows enough about policies to understand that the Bureau wouldn't be called in by the sheriff, unless he went over state lines, or was a known serial killer or terrorist. Like I said, before his escape everything ran through the sheriff's department."

There it was again. The fact this wasn't normal procedure. Walker knew the Bureau had to have some bigger reason to exploit a loophole and take over the case. "So, he'll be expecting the local sheriff to send in a search party."

"That's what we believe."

Walker checked his pocket for the small pouch containing his flint, made sure the hunting knife at his side was secure in its sheath, then adjusted the ankle strap that held a smaller knife.

"So, you're heading out?"

"Yep."

Agent Davis opened the car door, reached in and held up a small device. "Here's a GPS to take with you. The FBI wants to be able to track you."

"Yeah, I bet they do."

"Look, Walker, they told me you wouldn't carry any communication devices, so this is a deal breaker. No compromise. Besides, it's for your own good. They can keep track of your progress, in case you need help."

"What you mean is, if I stop moving. They'll figure I'm dead and can find the body." Walker smirked at the look on the agent's face. "Hey, it's all good. I know the danger." He took the small, black box from Davis and examined it. "This isn't going to ring or anything, is it?"

"No. Once you spot Logan, you'll flip this switch here, to let the Bureau know you're in visual contact." Davis indicated a small lever. "Once they get this notification, they will move in to your location for the capture."

"So I'm only to find the guy and then give you the target?"

"Exactly."

Walker mumbled as he attached the device to his belt. "And the FBI takes all the credit."

"You say something?"

"Nope." Walker moved to leave, then stopped. "There is something you can do for me."

"What's that?"

"You got something to write on? Yeah. Take down this phone number."

He watched Davis scribble on the paper as he dictated. "I want you to call that number every night and let Nataya know I'm still alive out here."

"You know I can't do that."

"Sure you can. They'll be tracking me."

"Shit. I'll get my ass kicked if I'm caught giving out details regarding a live case."

"This is a deal breaker for me. You figure out a way to make this happen." Walker gave him a piercing look. "Okay?"

Davis studied Walker a long moment, then gave a single nod. "Okay. Consider it done."

"Appreciate it." Walker turned to leave.

"So, that's all you're taking with you?"

"Yep. I like to travel light. Nature will provide everything I need."

Davis watched Walker stride away wearing only jeans, a buckskin shirt, and moccasin boots. He shook his head as he turned and slid into the car seat. He couldn't decide which man was crazier, Matt Logan or Fox Walker.

CHAPTER NINE

Denver, Colorado

Sean Logan collapsed onto the sofa in his Denver suburban house and leaned his head back, trying to exhale all the tension from his body and calm the hammering in his chest. He took deep breaths to dispel the nausea that threatened. Shit. What a day!

He'd known he would be the number-one suspect when his brother made his escape. And Matt had warned him to expect the sheriff within hours, had primed him on what to say. But Sean hadn't been prepared for the FBI to show up later the same day. Just when he thought the worst was over. He could still hear the agent's voice in his head. *We understand you and your brother are very close.*

Why hadn't Matt mentioned that part of the equation? And these guys meant business. Interview? Try interrogation. Sean shook his head in frustration. He wasn't good at lying to begin with, so it took all his concentration to stick to Matt's game plan. But he'd done it.

Exactly where have you been the last forty-eight hours?

Thank goodness he had an airtight alibi for the time his brother had made his escape. *I've just arrived back home from a two-day bike ride in Durango.* Sean had followed Matt's instructions to make sure he was with others who could vouch for his whereabouts during the whole time. *Yes, sir, I can give you the names and numbers of the people I rode with.* He realized that Matt had been right to not let him know anything about the details of the escape plan. Because of that, Sean could answer the questions honestly. And make them believable.

Sean stared at the ceiling of his living room and consciously tried to relax his body. At least he was in his own home, safe from the law, safe from the elements, safe from wild animals.

This was nothing compared to what Matt might be going through. He needed to get over himself. So long as he stayed cool, and followed the plan, everything would be fine. Matt, on the other hand, was running for his life.

Got to do my part, for Matt.

The old TV show *Simon and Simon* came to mind, and he could hear his mom chuckling at how that show was "all about her boys." Matt fit the character of Rick, the hot head, ready-for-action kind of guy. And of course Sean was AJ, the clean-shaven, button-down-shirt brother. They had all laughed together about that.

But he and Matt were living it in real time. In this thing together, as Matt would say. But this wasn't anything like watching the TV show. No one had prepared Sean for how nervous and scared he'd be. And he wasn't sure he wanted to get good at this stuff, either.

But he'd do whatever it took to help his brother.

Anything.

CHAPTER TEN

San Juan National Forest, Colorado

Fox Walker heard Agent Davis drive away from the scene as he stepped into the forest again. Looking around, he quickly registered and dismissed the myriad tracks left by the deputies and FBI agents. Their prints were hesitant, with frequent pauses as they had scrutinized the area. Logan had been moving fast, sprinting through the small open space. Walker recognized this by the way the dirt was torn up and the heavy toe prints dug into the soft dirt and ground clutter.

Walker followed the fugitive's muddied tracks farther into the trees where the officers' tracks disappeared completely, leaving one trail to follow. Good. No accomplices had joined him. So far it was just one lone set of prints.

He knelt and carefully brushed aside the fallen leaves until he found one clean, perfect print. Walker studied it, memorizing the detail of the boot marks, the smooth sole, and how deep the depressions went into the soil. When not sprinting, Logan walked "heel to toe," typical white man.

Walker stepped in a toe-to-heel rolling fashion. It allowed him to set down his foot slowly, carefully, making sure he didn't step on anything that would make a sound, such as a twig snapping under his weight, especially important when stalking someone, or something.

Walker knew he wouldn't always have footprints to follow, so understanding how Logan moved over the ground became critical. The knowledge allowed him to watch for signs of Logan's passing: crushed grasses, pebbles pushed into the dirt, broken twigs in the path, overturned stones and seed pods, even disturbed dirt or moss on the tops of rocks where a boot had stepped. Walker had trained all his life, to not only observe details in nature, but to also see what shouldn't be in the wild, things out of place.

Walker stood and remained still. He took in a deep breath, savoring the smells around him, fallen leaves, the damp earth, evergreens. Leaving behind the civilized world for the wild lands gave him that sensation of coming home again. He could sense Grandfather's presence next to him, encouraging him to immerse his very soul fully into the moment. Walker closed his eyes and listened to sounds of the forest, birdsong, the hum of insects, the creaking of tree boughs in the wind. He could feel the forest beckoning and had to remind himself that this visit held a different purpose. One that included danger. He opened his eyes and thought of his quarry, Matt Logan.

What would cause a skilled, highly decorated military man to become a rapist and murderer? And a man on the run?

Although he had been given a profile of the fugitive, including his height, weight, and body build, Walker knew that by following sign he would soon understand Logan's knowledge of the wilderness, his agility, and how intelligent the man was. The many years of training with Grandfather had taught Walker that he would soon "know" Logan, maybe in ways that the man did not know himself.

As Walker followed the tracks and sign throughout the day, he stayed alert, watching the terrain ahead for anything that offered a hiding place or perfect spot for an ambush. He listened constantly for any reaction from nature around him, a sudden silence of insects and birdsong, or a quick eruption of birds in flight from the trees ahead, warning him that someone else might be in the vicinity. It made for slow progress, but his life depended on not assuming Logan had fled the area and wouldn't be lying in wait for him somewhere up ahead. He thought of Davis's words: *Matt Logan, a legend among his SEAL teammates. While on assignment, he pulled out all the stops. Did whatever it took to get it done.*

Walker crossed over a shallow creek and climbed the incline on the other side, following the tracks to where Logan had stopped for a moment, perhaps surveying which way to go next. But there the tracks abruptly ended. The ground clutter had been disturbed, the prints brushed away. The man had taken the time to destroy the trail. And rain had pockmarked the dirt, meaning the fugitive went through there before the storm of the previous night. He was making damned good time.

Walker knew he would have to do a sweep of the entire area forward for prints if he was to pick up the trail again. He forced away the fleeting moment of frustration when he thought about the precious time he would lose. Instead he remained calm and focused. This would still be quicker than guessing, and possibly heading off in the wrong direction.

Moving in a slow, circular pattern, he began to check for any sign that might have been missed in the cleanup. Just the fact that the ground had been disturbed indicated he still searched in the right location.

When he came close to a group of young saplings, he noticed a substantial amount of scuffling about in the dirt. Logan had spent extra time there, perhaps to make doubly sure he left no tracks behind. Walker noted it, to perhaps further investigate later. He continued forward, still moving in an ever-widening arc, making sure not to miss even a tiny patch of ground.

The tree canopy overhead thinned and the ground became much rockier and sparse before Walker discovered a footprint again. Something about it looked peculiar. He knelt for a closer view and noted a deep-cleated track, like a hiking boot would make. Rain had pitted it, but no way could it be the smooth-soled boots he'd been following, although they were the same size as before. And the depth of the depression remained the same, so this man carried the same weight.

He sat back on his heels in thought. It could be a lone print from a hiker. But what were the chances that the guy would wear the same size boot and be the same weight as Logan? Walker searched for other prints, but found none nearby. And a hiker would have no reason to hide his tracks.

No matter how he looked at the puzzle, there could only be one explanation for it. Logan had changed boots. Once again the notion of Logan having accomplices came to mind.

Walker stood and looked back at the section of woods he had just searched. Time to take a closer look at that spot where Logan had spent so much effort clearing the area of sign. He returned to the clump of saplings and surveyed the land. Nearby lay a rotting old log. Walker knelt and began to rake the dead leaves from around it and from the end of it. Sure enough, bright orange peeked out at him. He pulled the cloth out and shook out the fabric, not surprised to find he held a county-jail jumpsuit. Farther back in the log he found the discarded boots.

So, whoever supplied the getaway vehicle had also left the convict a change of clothes. What else might Logan have acquired? Binoculars and night-vision goggles? A sniper rifle? He could even have land mines. More variables to deal with wasn't what Walker needed at that moment.

Besides knowing even less about what he might be up against, he could no longer watch for a flash of orange jumpsuit. Most likely the fugitive wore clothes that gave him some sort of camouflage amid the terrain. The only good news being that the new, deeply cleated hiking boots would leave prints far easier to track than the smoother soled jail-issued boots Logan had been wearing. Walker had to exploit the positives. There weren't many.

As he continued to follow Logan's trail, it became clear that Logan had begun to make a real effort to leave as few footprints as possible, stepping on rocks and hard-packed dirt whenever possible, yet still he moved through the trees and brush at a fast pace, enough to cause damage. The broken twigs and torn leaves were details many people would miss, but a clear path to Walker. He moved forward as quickly as possible, keeping in mind that at any point the fugitive could double back and set up an ambush for anyone following.

The prints headed toward the foothills. Walker guessed that from there they would be heading up the side of the mountain. It made sense; the terrain would slow them both down, but the ground would become rockier and more difficult to track. On the far side of this mountain a vast wilderness ranged for hundreds of square miles, uncharted territory, a perfect spot to hide, for a long time. Thinking like a fugitive with wilderness survival skills, that's where he'd head.

With the warmth of the noon sun on his back, Walker knelt next to the partial footprint and studied the impression. Studying the amount of rain damage, it revealed this print had been made close to the time of the storm the previous night. If Logan knew his wilderness survival as well as reported, he would have stopped to prepare a shelter before the thunderstorm hit.

Walker stood and thought about the timing of the events. The Land Rover had been discovered at dusk, and if the fugitive did stop to prepare a shelter before the storm let loose, there existed the possibility that Logan may have only had a little over an hour of travel time into the woods before he had to quit for the night. That would mean the fugitive would be struggling to make up valuable lost time.

It would explain why Logan seemed compelled to rush forward through the forest, leaving sign along the way. Although, Walker had to admit, most search parties would have lost the trail long ago. Perhaps Logan counted on that fact. But it seemed a dangerous assumption to make. Maybe the man had no choice. Maybe time played a critical element to his plan.

And Logan had to have a plan. The details of the escape had been well thought out and executed. A man like that would not leave the rest to chance. Which brought up the whole accomplice element again. Did Logan head toward a designated meeting place, to be joined by his team?

Walker began his trek again with a new thought on his mind. Maybe it wasn't so much that Logan was running away, but more that he was running toward something.

Walker hoped he could find the man long before Logan figured out that his dead-end trail hadn't worked, and that Walker followed. And long before Logan met up with any accomplices.

CHAPTER ELEVEN

San Juan National Forest, Colorado

Matt Logan worked his way up the ever-steeper incline as the afternoon sunbeams splashed across a rocky land, highlighting the reds and browns between the contrasting evergreens. Even with the challenge of higher altitude and the ascent, he still managed to flit from tree to tree within the stand of firs. He didn't think about it. He just did it. Years of conditioning made it an automatic response to the situation. And in his mind, he was in battle mode. He had to outwit the enemy and stay hidden. And he would make use of whatever resources were at hand.

Logan glanced behind and down to the valley below. If search parties were already behind him, he felt certain they would be stumped at the dead-end trail he had created the day before, giving him precious hours of time to move beyond their hunt that day. And even if someone did manage to pick up his trail again, it would be nearly impossible for anyone to track him in the rocky terrain ahead. They would lose his trail long before he made it to his destination.

The pressure to gain distance from anyone who might follow lifted somewhat, even though he had far to travel before he would make it to the cabin. The building was just a one-room structure, but it would give shelter and was hidden away in the trees. It would serve his needs just fine. A place where he could hide out and orchestrate his game plan. He found his mind drifting to those plans ... then back in time to the trial ... Nicole.

Logan stopped next to one of the fir trees and leaned his head against it. He had to stay focused. He couldn't think about her at that moment. This escape had more purpose than that. He had a task to perform. And he meant to finish it.

He looked up ahead, above the straggling edges of the timber-line, and spotted a protruding ledge. He estimated that it jutted out from the mountainside at least twenty feet. If he climbed up on top and crawled out to the end, he'd be able to see much of the land below. He could check for activity.

He didn't like it that he'd have a moment of exposure, but the opportunity to see what might be happening down below won out. He stepped out from the security of the surrounding firs and scurried across the open rock face of the mountain.

Logan pulled and climbed his way up the side of the ledge, heaved his body up over the rocky rim, and sat there a moment to catch his breath in the thinning air.

The warmth of the afternoon sun felt good on his face, in contrast to the cooler air of the higher altitude. Logan crawled out toward the edge of the overlook and lay face down to peer over the ledge. Incredible. Even with the thick cover of trees and underbrush, he could see miles of valley floor spreading out as it marched up to the rocky incline directly below him. He spotted the serpentine road where he had driven the Land

Rover. There appeared to be a few vehicles sitting beside the road where he had ditched his ride. The distance didn't allow him to see any details. No problem. At least he knew the Land Rover had been discovered and a search party had either already headed out, or soon would be. But even though the rocky terrain and steady incline slowed his progress, he could see the miles of forest between him and them. And the search party would be forced to travel slower than he, not knowing if he waited in ambush, or not.

Logan brought his attention back to the valley floor. He knew others would find the beauty of the scene emotionally moving, yet he couldn't bring himself to let those feelings surface. He could only see it as a game board where he made moves to outsmart the other players. Successfully completing a mission and the safety of his men in battle, those were the only things he had found a passion for. That was, until he had met Nicole. She had changed everything.

A movement below caught his attention. Something moved among the trees on the valley floor. Too small to be an elk, perhaps a deer. But, instincts told him not to assume anything. The shape moved into view for a brief moment before sliding behind the trees again.

A Man. Damnit!

Logan slid back on the ledge. No way a search team could have followed and gotten this close so fast. He slid off the backpack and pulled out the binoculars, then eased his way to the edge of the ledge for a closer look.

Looking through the binoculars he didn't spot any other people in the area, only the lone man. No search team then. Maybe a hiker. But he knew this remote location had no marked trails, and hunting season was months away. Okay, maybe a lost hiker.

Logan studied the man as he moved between the trees, intent upon every detail. He could only make out black hair and a tan shirt. But as he watched, the man moved in slow motion, stopping often to squat or kneel, as if studying the ground.

He's tracking me!

Logan shook off the sense of stunned awareness and considered the situation. No way anyone could've gotten a search team out there in the dark and rain the previous night. That meant this guy must have set out at first light that morning, and had already traveled far enough to be within a mile of where Logan had taken shelter. Logan had sprinted that distance in an hour, before the storm hit. But still, this guy had covered the same distance, following his trail, in a few hours. The man had to be goddamned good to be able to track him that quickly.

Maybe the sheriff called in a professional tracker. Logan hadn't thought of that possibility. Had been sure the sheriff would bring in a deputized search party. It wasn't like him to miss details like this.

It wouldn't do any good to dwell on his mistake. But no doubt this changed everything. And it sucked in more ways than one. He could no longer head straight to the cabin. He couldn't take the chance of leading this man to his hideout.

Logan did the mental calculations. He had also started at dawn. Had been climbing up into the foothills all day, making his pace slower than the tracker. But he guessed there were still at least three hours of climbing time separating them.

Logan had no doubt that he could redirect the tracker and eventually lose him. But it would take time. He fingered the handle of the Glock tucked into the shoulder holster, studied the distance between them, then removed his hand.

This isn't Afghanistan.

At least he had the advantage of rockier terrain. His boots wouldn't leave a clean print as they did in the dirt of the forest floor, meaning the tracker would have to move forward slower to keep the trail. Logan would be cautious, flitting like a bird between the trees and boulders. What a slow dance of hide-and–go-seek they would be playing. And Logan intended to win. He had more at stake than anyone the authorities could throw at him.

Then it struck him. The man didn't wear a backpack. No supplies. Who was this guy?

⚔ ⚔

Walker felt the hair on the back of his neck rise and a sense of dread. He instinctively lowered his body to the ground. Something watched him ... cougar ... bear ... man? The nature sounds around him gave no warning that anything lurked nearby, still ...

He felt his gaze drawn upward, sliding up the side of the foot-hills above, scrutinizing every shadow.

There! A quick flash of light. Sunlight on metal, or glass?

But it just as suddenly disappeared. Had his eyes played a trick on him? Walker studied the distance between where he knelt and where he thought he saw the reflection of light. Maybe three to four hours of climbing? Hard to tell the true distance looking up at a wall of rock. Experience told him how distorted his perception could be. But it could be the fugitive. Logan's trail appeared to be heading closer into the foothills, where Walker anticipated the fugitive would go. But he could only continue following the sign and see where it took him to know for sure.

He assumed a more crouched position and hid in brush and trees as much as possible as he moved forward. The flash of light had made him think of a rifle scope. He didn't want to become target practice for anyone.

Within thirty minutes, by the sun's path across the sky, Logan's trail did begin to veer off into the craggy landscape, at the base of the foothills towering above him. Walker could see where the fugitive had spent the night sheltered there, using the solid rock slope as a base, away from the trees, and potential lightning conduits. A smart move. But once the storm threat had passed, Logan continued into the mountains.

Walker had guessed right on that one.

⋈ ⋈

Walker's breath grew more ragged in the thin air of the higher altitude. He'd followed Logan's barely discernible trail for hours, up the sharp, gravelly incline. There were no footprints to follow, only slight disturbances in the rocks and pebbles, tiny avalanches of stones from footfalls.

He followed the sign up to the edge of the timberline, which told him he had reached at least 11,000 feet. He stopped when he noticed that the fugitive's trail left the protection of the trees. Why would the man step out into the open and go across the face of the mountain, in full view? Walker scanned the land up above him and spotted a rocky protrusion jutting out from the boulders. That had to have been Logan's destination. The fugitive couldn't pass up the opportunity to get a great vantage point of the valley floor and probably see any activity along the roads as well.

Scrutinizing the rocks around him, he looked for shadows where they didn't belong, listened for any minute noises, then decided to follow Logan's path. He raced across the gritty surface to the ledge, where he discovered a few footprints in the soft, powdery dirt. The fugitive had walked past this spot, but the prints moved on past the overhang. Walker stopped short. Why would Logan travel up to this point, exposed, and not take advantage of the overlook? It didn't make sense.

Walker climbed up, wary that he couldn't see the topside from this position. He had just begun to pull his body over the rocky rim when he noticed the dust on the top of the rock surface had been disturbed. Someone had been there, and recently. He looked closer. The entire surface of the rock protrusion had been brushed clean of prints.

He pulled his body up onto the ledge, worked his way to the end, and peered over the edge. His breath caught. What a view. Mile upon mile of the valley spilled out before him, a creek sensuously winding its way through the green of trees. He remembered the creek on the map he had studied before he left the cabin. He smiled. This gave him confirmation of his location.

His eyes followed the gray stripe of pavement running alongside the forest. He could just make out the vehicles where he took up the chase. Most likely Logan saw them as well and believed a search party headed his way. Walker lowered his view to the trees below, directly at the base of the incline where he had been just hours ago, and tensed.

I could have been seen from here.

He then fully understood his instinctual reaction of feeling watched. Maybe he had been.

Without moving his body, he looked over his shoulder toward nearby boulders and the edge of the timberline, watching for any movement. He couldn't let himself get paranoid. Maybe Logan hadn't spotted him. Still, he slid down off the overhang and crouched in the shadows, studying every sign around him. The boot prints near the ledge took on new meaning. Why leave clear, distinct prints below the overhang, after brushing away the ones on top?

Only one thing made any sense. That Logan had seen him and figured out he was being tracked. Maybe the flash of light came from binoculars. Regardless, the fugitive had obviously tried to make sure he kept following him past this vantage point, hoping Walker wouldn't think to climb up on the ledge and see that he had been spotted.

Shit! Well, this changes everything.

Walker squatted down among the rocks under the overhang, out of view. How close might this fugitive be? Close enough to use his gun? And what about the added supplies Walker worried that Logan might have. Did they truly include a sniper rifle? Logan could be lying in wait for him to come into view, to pick him off. That easy. Walker's jaw tensed.

Had the hunted man become the hunter?

CHAPTER TWELVE

San Juan National Forest, Colorado

Walker crept deeper under the overhang, until completely hidden from view. He leaned back against the cool rock to think. He couldn't worry about the time he might be losing. Maybe the fugitive moved on ahead, maybe not. He had to rethink everything.

He mentally went over all the notes he'd read in the report and what details the FBI agent had given him. Walker believed the fugitive headed directly toward the hundreds of square miles of forests located on the other side of this mountain range. But not just to get there.

He's got a particular place he's heading to. Or at least he did.

If Logan knew that someone followed, he'd probably not continue his quest until he could lead his pursuer off on a false trail, one leading to nowhere, while he doubled back to his original trek. At least that's what Walker hoped the man would do, because the other option meant that Logan would be setting up an ambush for

Walker. But he hadn't shot the guards when he had the opportunity, and that fact still struck Walker as odd.

In Walker's mind, Logan started taking on the shape of a real person. An armed man who had killed before—had been trained in it—but who hadn't lain in wait for Walker to catch up and simply shot him. Why not? Doing so would have simplified Logan's situation. It would have been the smart move for an escaped convict running from the law with only one man tracking him. Only one witness. A dead one. Maybe Logan needed more time to set up an ambush. Maybe he wasn't done yet.

Walker crawled to the edge of the shadows and peered around, both high and low, searching for any kind of movement, any reactions in nature. At first he saw nothing. Then, almost out of view, below and to the south of his position, he saw a disturbance in the trees. An entire flock of crows erupted from the thick evergreen boughs. At that time of the evening, they should be settled in to roost for the night. Of course, a wild animal might have simply gotten too close.

Or perhaps Logan was setting up a false trail, hoping Walker would follow.

Well, Walker would follow, but not until dark.

Evening shadows were already encroaching up the side of the foothill. He wouldn't have to wait long. He crawled under the ledge again, out of sight and safe.

The moon would be full that night, and Walker could track in its low light. He had no choice. Tracking at night would make his job even more difficult and slow, but perhaps keep him from getting shot.

Logan raced between the evergreens, across the rocky terrain, sliding in the loose stones. In fact, the farther he traveled, the more often he let his trail show. After all, he wanted to make sure the tracker followed him. Let the tracker believe he didn't know he was being followed, and grew less cautious the farther away he got from his ditched vehicle. After this many hours, the tracker should buy that.

Angling down into the denser trees again, Logan kept to the same general direction he had been going. But the woods would give him more cover as he hurried forward. He planned to bring the tracker back down into the forest, make sure the man lost the trail, then head back up to the timberline and continue his trek. That way he wouldn't lose precious time having to double back to where he started this game.

At first Logan had been pissed when he discovered the tracker, and stunned that he had been followed so easily. But the more he thought about it, he realized he had a big advantage—being able to rush ahead. And if the tracker had any smarts he would continue to follow cautiously, watching for an ambush. At least he knew he had an adversary, and how many.

The sun would set behind the mountains within an hour. He had better make the most of this opportunity and increase the distance between them as much as possible. He'd rush forward, not stopping until darkness forced it upon him.

CHAPTER THIRTEEN

Elk Meadow, Colorado

Nataya lay on the rug in front of the wood stove. The smell of wood burning, the warmth and light pouring from its open door rolled over her. The popping of sparks in the flames the only sound in the cabin. Her finger traced over the topo map that Walker had studied for hours before he left with the FBI.

She wanted to know every inch of that forest as well as he did, although she had no idea what she would do with the knowledge, yet. But it kept her from going quietly insane sitting there alone, knowing he was out there somewhere, maybe injured, or ...

Stop it. Don't go there.

She halted the thought and stood, stretched tall to loosen muscles, then wandered over to Walker's bow-and-arrow collection. She enjoyed looking at the different types of wood that the bows were hand crafted from, the contrasting colors and grains, each one varying in size. Some only had leather hand guards, while others incorporated woven leather designs. The bow that Walker said had belonged to Grandfather included elaborate beaded decorations.

But the arrows held the most fascination for her, with their various painted and leather designs, the different tip styles and material. She fingered the hand-finished arrows and wished Walker had taken one of the weapons with him. He had his knives, of course, and she knew he was deadly with them, but against a gun?

He had been forced to use a gun once, to save her life, but that didn't change his view of them. He preferred bow hunting or spear fishing, as he had been taught by Grandfather.

She jumped when the phone jangled loudly in the quiet of the evening. She stared at it from across the room, half afraid to answer it. Then ran to pick it up.

"Hello?"

"Is this Nataya?"

"Who is this?"

"My name is Special Agent Davis, with the FBI. I picked Fox Walker up this morning at your cabin. He asked that I call you with some news."

"Okay ..."

"He requested that I call you each evening and let you know that he is safe."

"How can you know that?"

"He's wearing a tracking device. We can see his movements through the forest. He'll locate the fugitive and then send us a signal. We'll take it from there."

"So he won't need to bring in the fugitive, simply let you know where the man is?"

"That's right, ma'am."

"Good. Thanks for letting me know. I appreciate it."

"No problem. Just make sure you don't speak of this to anyone, understand? If my superiors found out I gave you stats about an ongoing case, they'd—well, let's just say it wouldn't be pleasant for me."

"I understand. I won't tell anyone."

Nataya laid the phone in its cradle and stood contemplating the news. Her heart leaped at the knowledge that Walker was well and alive. And how thoughtful that he requested she receive the call. Or was it guilt for not letting her join him? At that moment, it didn't matter, only the fact that he was safe.

Then the realization dawned that she would spend each day waiting and wondering what was happening, in eager anticipation of that call every evening. She turned and looked at the bow-and-arrow display. She had to look at the positive, that at least she didn't have to worry about Walker trying to capture the convict. A relief.

But she had to face another obvious fact. The killer didn't know that Walker was only tracking him, and meant him no bodily harm.

CHAPTER FOURTEEN

Denver, Colorado

Sean ambled into the dimly lit bar, hands jammed into his jeans' pockets, in hopes it appeared he did this all the time, just another local. He didn't meet anyone's glance as he walked past the tables and headed straight back to the darkest corner of the room, where a lone man shot pool. The bear of a man wore a dark, scruffy beard and an attitude that would give anyone pause about approaching him.

Sean stepped up to the pool table, where Victor barely acknowledged him, and picked up a pool cue. He chalked the end as he glanced at the man and waited his turn. Victor, dressed in jeans and a leather vest, continued setting up his shot but spoke, his deep voice low and restrained.

"Did anyone follow you?"

"No. I mean, I don't think so."

"Great. I knew I should never have agreed to this."

"Look, I was careful. Like you told me."

"Sure. Okay, let's make this quick," Victor said as made his shot, moved closer to Sean and lined up for the next one. "I presume you've already had your official visit from the sheriff's department?"

"Yep. And I told them everything exactly the way you and Matt said to do it."

"Good."

"Victor, I want to tell you thank you for helping Matt. I couldn't have done it alone."

"*Jeeesus*. How many times do I have to tell you not to call me by name?"

"Sorry."

"And you're right. You couldn't have done it without me, or at least without being there in person." Then Victor's tone softened the tiniest bit. "And you're welcome. Anything for your brother."

"Yeah, well your plan worked perfectly. But now that the law has looked at me and gone on to other leads, I want to help with the rest of the plan." Sean eyed the table and lined up a shot as if he knew what he was doing.

"That's a negative and you know it. Your brother made that clear. Crystal clear. You already did your part. You're not to be involved any more, in any way, shape, or form in this plan."

"Look at it from my point of view. You know I want to do more to help my brother. I can't just sit on the sidelines and watch."

"That's exactly what you're going to do. This isn't the playground, kid, where you can beg to get picked for the team."

Sean's face flushed, his lips a thin line as he made his shot, the ball bouncing across the table. He hated it that Victor insisted on calling him "kid," even though he was thirty-two years old. "Don't I get any respect for how well I handled that FBI interrogation? 'Cause that's what it felt like. And I stuck to my story like a pro."

Sean looked up to see Victor staring at him. Surprise in his eyes for a second, before the veil dropped again.

"What the hell are you talking about?" Victor said in a low growl. "And be goddamn careful about what you're saying in public."

"Sorry. You got me fired up."

"Yeah? Well, you just made my case."

Sean's jaw clinched in angry defiance. "Just because Matt has always over-protected me, doesn't mean I'm not cut out to learn this stuff."

Victor studied Sean for a long moment. "You've got a point, kid. I'll give you the benefit of the doubt this time. So, tell me about this *interrogation*."

"They came to the house without warning and wanted to ask questions."

"The FBI."

"Yeah. Thought I'd better cooperate or they'd get suspicious. I stuck to the same story I gave to the sheriff. They tried to trick me up, but since I really don't know any details, I could be openly honest about it. I think they believed me by the time they left. But who knows about those guys."

Victor took his time lining up the next couple of shots and made them both before he straightened up and returned to the conversation. "Maybe there is a way you can help out."

"Yeah?"

"Yeah. But I need some time to sort this out and make a couple of calls. I'll be in touch." Victor put the cue stick up in the rack and gave Sean a long look.

Sean knew that look. Matt always looked at him that way. Always played the big brother, out to protect him. The look also said, "I'm ready to lay down my life for Matt."

And Victor wasn't the only one. Others had contacted Sean when Matt had been arrested. Such fierce loyalty. He knew that what he felt for Matt touched on that. But for the first time in his life he wanted to know what it felt like to be a part of a bigger kind of brotherhood.

CHAPTER FIFTEEN

San Juan National Forest, Colorado

Fox Walker stayed in the shelter of the overhanging ledge, out of sight, and tried to keep his mind off the fact that Logan probably moved far ahead of him. It still beat out the option of taking a chance out there and getting shot. By sticking with his decision, he figured that Logan would give up waiting around for an ambush and would seize the opportunity to put a great distance between them.

But it still took every bit of his training to keep his patience during the wait for the sun to set behind the giant shoulders of the mountain. Patience had been his most difficult lesson throughout his years with Grandfather, so the old man had made sure he had plenty of times to practice. The thought made him smile.

It had been a long day, and it would be a longer night of tracking by moonlight, so he took the opportunity to rest while waiting. But it let his mind wander, and thoughts of Nataya intruded. He wondered how she fared back at the cabin. Wondered if she worried about him.

You ass. Of course she does.

That's what was so hard. He had hated leaving her behind. And knowing that she would be waiting and worried about his safety made it that much more unfair to her.

He missed her company, roaming the woods together, sitting by the fire in the evening, holding her close through the night. But aside from missing her company, he had to admit that it would be good to have her with him. They could talk strategy together. And they could discuss the confusing signals he kept reading from Logan. So far, nothing matched with the profile the FBI had given him, except that the man certainly did know how to survive in the wilderness.

But Walker shook his head at the thought. Far better that she wasn't in danger, better that he had made her stay behind.

Still, if something happened to him, would she ever forgive him, or herself? He hadn't thought about that aspect of it until that moment.

A beam of moonlight slid between the rocks and pooled at his feet. Time to get started. Walker crept to the opening between boulders and watched for dark shadows of movement. He concentrated on the night sounds, the slight breeze rustling dried leaves on a nearby shrub, listened for any noise that didn't fit. Finally, satisfied that no one waited close by, he crawled out from the recess and stretched his cramped muscles.

As his eyes adjusted to the dim moonlight, he could see enough light and shadow to pick up the trail at the ledge, starting with the distinct footprints Logan had purposefully left behind for him to follow. He then began tracking Logan's signs of passage through the rock and gravel of the mountainside.

Walker had to admit that he expected Logan to double back and lead him in the opposite direction. So, he was surprised that Logan's trail headed out the same way they had been going before. Maybe Logan hadn't seen him, after all?

That would be a boon, but he couldn't count on it. This guy had been trained in survival, had fought in battles. He most likely had an arsenal of tricks he could use. Walker couldn't assume anything at this point, including the fact that it appeared to be a trail to follow. It might instead be a path leading him into a trap.

⊷⊷ ⊷⊷

Darkness devoured the dim evening light, making it impossible for Matt Logan to keep running through the dense forest. He came to an abrupt halt, bent double, panting, trying to catch his breath. He forced himself to raise his shoulders and straighten his back, taking deep gulps of air to calm his rapid heartbeat until it no longer drowned out the night sounds of the forest.

He had made good use of his one hour of sunlight by running through the woods as fast as the terrain allowed, zigzagging among the trees and boulders. Considering his pace, and allowing for hiking boots and the natural obstacles of the forest, he guessed he had put four to five miles between him and the tracker.

The downside to his quick trek through the woods meant the tracker would have an easy trail to follow. But if this guy had any sense at all he would be worried about Logan setting up an ambush in this deeper cover of the forest and would be advancing carefully, which meant slowly.

Besides, Logan had a plan. With the distance he gained, he could take time the next day to figure out a way to lead this guy off on a false trail and lose him altogether. His mind ran through past missions and decided on his favorite ruse. It would do nicely, and had never failed him. He had been using variations of it all along, as he crossed over the many small creeks and larger streams in his path.

And for extra measure, after he set up the false trail, he'd have the time and opportunity to set a trap, one the tracker would not anticipate. He had plenty of options on that front.

CHAPTER SIXTEEN

San Juan National Forest, Colorado

Fox Walker made his way down the last bit of the incline to the valley floor and stopped at the edge of the dark forest. He listened for any nuances of sound in his surroundings, as well as an absence of natural sounds that might indicate a human nearby. After a moment Walker stepped through the underbrush, careful to make little noise, and into the thick stand of trees, where he waited for his eyes to adjust to the deeper nighttime shadows.

He had tracked Logan through the night down the face of the rocky mountainside and evergreens, at times on his hands and knees in the pebbles and dirt, searching for sign beneath the pale moonlight. After the first hour, he noticed that Logan had lost some of his caution and left behind easy-to-spot tracks. Walker could think of two scenarios that fit the pattern. One: Logan didn't believe anyone followed him and had decided to make better time, and not worry about leaving behind a trail. Two: Logan wanted to make sure Walker *didn't* lose the trail—which could mean a couple of things. Either Logan hoped to lead Walker on a false trail and lose him altogether, or he was leading Walker into a trap.

Whatever might be the truth, Walker had to consider all the options as possibilities, watching for an ambush or a dead end to the trail.

But the darkness of the deep woods made it impossible to track any farther. He knelt at one of the footprints and felt the soil. The moisture level indicated that Logan passed through at least eight hours earlier.

Damn. Those hours of waiting until nightfall had taken their toll on Walker's patience. But exhaustion overran his frustration. There were only a few hours until dawn. He decided to get some sleep, then reassess his situation.

No need to make a shelter at that late hour. He stuffed dry, fallen leaves into his buckskin shirt for insulation and curled up under the low branches of a fir tree, using the soft pad of fallen needles as a bed.

Sleep would come fast, but not before a knot of anxiety formed in his gut. This Logan guy would be miles ahead of him, with plenty of time to plan anything he wanted.

How did I become the hunted as well as the hunter?

CHAPTER SEVENTEEN

Denver, Colorado

Sean Logan checked his rearview mirror after making the turn into the Denver REI parking lot, pulled into an empty spot and turned off the engine. He waited and watched for anyone to pull in behind him.

All clear.

This time he could be certain he hadn't been followed.

He exited the car and headed toward the entrance of the 75,000-square-foot, multilevel brick structure. Victor should be proud of his choice for their meeting. The historical building had once supplied electricity for the Denver streetcar system, but now the vast outdoor-sports supply store, with its many floors and displays, made it a perfect place to "get lost" among the merchandise and other shoppers. In fact, it wouldn't be difficult for two people to spend an hour trying to find each other if they became separated.

Sean pretended to check out various items as he strolled through the store, making his way toward the camping equipment area. Victor stood by a display of camp stoves, looking over the components when Sean arrived. He glanced at Sean then back to the equipment. Sean spoke first.

"This time I *know* I wasn't followed." He saw the hint of a smile from Victor.

"You did good picking out this place to meet."

"Thanks. So, you said that you might have an idea of how I could help my brother?"

"Yeah, I do. This whole FBI issue has me concerned. Why the hell are they involved? The only thing I could come up with is the fact that the murder victim, Nicole, used to be one of their agents. But as far as I could tell the Bureau wasn't part of the investigation, or even visible at the trial. Maybe one of the higher up mucky-mucks has taken this whole thing as a personal matter, I dunno. They do tend to get their panties in a wad pretty easy."

"So what do you want me to do?"

"I know a guy who can get us some insight into this." Victor fished around in his shirt pocket and pulled out a worn business card. "I'm going to lay this card under the camp stove here and move away. You amble over to check out the stove and pick it up. Don't let anybody see that, okay?"

"Sure. But who's this guy? How can he help us?"

"The two of us go way back. His name is Dean McClure and he's a retired FBI profiler."

"FBI?" Sean whispered. "Why would I talk to someone from the FBI? They're the ones out after Matt."

"You didn't listen. I said he's retired. He follows his own rules now. You can trust him. He'll listen to what you have to say. And he has connections that we're gonna need." Victor stepped over to the next stove on display and started fiddling with the parts.

"Okay, if you say so," Sean said as he slid the business card into his hand, then his pocket. "I guess I have to trust you on this."

"Damn right you do, Kid."

"So just what am I supposed to tell this guy?"

"The truth. Tell him every question the Bureau asked you, and your responses. Answer any questions McClure has for you. Give him as much information as you can."

"Wow, you must really trust this guy."

"With my life. Okay, look, go buy one of those disposable cell phones and call McClure. He's expecting you. Make an appointment as soon as possible to see him, okay?"

"Yeah. Got it."

"Good. And when you get back, you let me know and we'll meet again."

Each man took his turn walking away from the display and leaving the store.

When Sean returned to his car and got in, the first thing he did was pull the business card out of his pocket. He read the name, then the address. His mouth gaped.

Seattle?

Would've been nice of Victor to mention that fact. Guess he better take a couple days off from work and purchase some airline tickets. Well, he had asked for it.

He could feel his heartbeat increase with the knowledge he headed for uncharted territory. Then he squared his shoulders, took a deep breath and blew it out.

CHAPTER EIGHTEEN

San Juan National Forest, Colorado

Fox Walker opened his eyes—startled—not sure what had caused him to awaken. He lay perfectly still, kept his breathing shallow while he listened and visually scrutinized every inch of his surroundings. The early morning songs of wrens and chickadees filled the air, and dapples of sunlight peeked through the trees, sparkling on the jewel drops of dew. He stirred then, and recognized the exhaustion caused by his night-long tracking ordeal.

He needed water. The fleshy meat of the prickly pear cacti and succulent purslane plants that managed to survive on the rugged mountainside had given him enough moisture to hold through the day before. But, with the lack of rest, his body demanded more. He knew better than to ignore the signs. Dehydration was serious business and could impair his judgment as well as his skill level. This valley was ripe with many snow-melt streams flowing down out of the mountains, but nothing these days could be considered a safe source for drinking water without first boiling it. And he didn't want to start a fire with telltale smoke, not knowing how close Logan might be.

Walker stretched the stiffness from his body, then pulled a cloth handkerchief from his pocket and began to lay it over the surfaces of rocks and leaves, making sure to avoid poisonous plants. The dew, having been recently condensed, was distilled and would be safe to drink without filtering it or boiling it. He squeezed the water from the cloth directly into his mouth. He performed this routine over and over until he quenched his thirst. The rest of the day he would pluck plants as he walked, and chew them for moisture and nourishment. He then picked up the trail where he had left off.

Walker noticed the tracks took on a different appearance once Logan had entered the safety of dense tree cover. He crouched down to examine a clean footprint. The deep toe indent, and distance between foot falls, showed Logan went from the quick steps on the rocky mountainside to full out sprinting through the woods. He guessed Logan planned to put as much distance between the two of them as possible. It could be good news, maybe indicating the man wouldn't be taking the time to set up an ambush, not yet, anyway. But Walker would still need to move forward through the trees at a pace where he could keep cover as much as possible, and watch ahead for anything that might be a trap.

The sun sat level with the treetops in the morning sky as Walker continued to follow Logan's trail through the forest. The convict's tracks wove in and out of trees and over rocks and boulders, even as he ran through the forest. It made it difficult for Walker to follow him, and forced him to slow his pace often. It gave him evidence that perhaps Logan did know someone followed him. Why else would the man go to so much trouble? Or did Logan do it out of instinct?

When Walker ducked under a low branch of a fir, something about the groundcover underneath caught his eye. He crouched, then crawled underneath the lowest boughs. The pine needles had been moved about, as if to conceal prints. But when he gently brushed away the first layer, he could see the flattened leaves, evergreen needles and moist dirt underneath—an impression large enough for a man's body remained. No doubt about it. Logan had spent the night there.

Walker sat back on his heels to think and tried to reconstruct the previous night's scene, how long he had traveled compared to the distance Logan covered in the same time frame.

He thought about the prints he had found just before he gave in to sleep. They were already eight hours old when he discovered them. That put Logan entering the woods with about one hour of daylight left. Logan most likely didn't stop until dark, since his objective appeared to be to put distance between them.

Walker knew that a normal running pace for a man in good physical condition would be around six miles an hour. That meant he should play it safe and add another three hours, and estimate that Logan could be eleven hours ahead of him.

Damn. He was not only losing hours of time, he was falling behind in terms of miles. He fought the urge to let anger take hold. The larger the distance grew between them, the more comfortable Logan would be. The trail would get colder and colder, with time to cover his tracks better, with time to set up an ambush.

Walker sucked in the damp, woodsy air and blew it out. He had to relax and clear his mind. He thought back to the myriad lessons Grandfather had instilled in his heart and mind over the years. Learning to stay calm and patient in the face of frustration. Never giving up on a trail. Learning to see what didn't belong in nature, as much as what did belong there.

He took up the pace again, thinking as he worked. So what if Logan moved on ahead. It could work to Walker's advantage.

Perhaps after a while Logan would believe Walker lost the trail altogether. Logan might relax his vigilance and get a little sloppy, although Walker didn't have much hope for that, given the man's military background. Still, having such a lead on Walker would play on the fugitive's mind, and, more importantly, on his confidence. Walker knew that when men became too confident, or arrogant, it could eventually result in their downfall.

The sun hung low in its descent toward the mountain peaks when Logan's prints took Walker up to the edge of a wide but shallow creek. He leaned over and let his hand trail into the water. Icy cold. Another stream originating from the melting snowcaps high above, weaving and wandering its way down the mountainside to this valley. Stepping on rocks rising above the water's surface, Walker crossed the creek and checked the bank on the opposite side. There were no prints coming out of the water.

This could only mean that Logan had walked in the water for some distance before emerging from the creek. A trick Walker had watched Logan often use to hide his trail. It meant that Walker had no choice but to walk both sides of the creek, upstream and downstream, looking for sign as to where the trail picked up again. The convict could stay in the water for hundreds of yards to try to throw Walker off the trail. The longer Logan stayed in the water, the longer Walker would have to study the area, looking for sign. And with Walker so far behind, Logan might take the time to do it. A perfect setup to detour Walker and keep him busy for hours. And with it being the end of day, it might even delay him for the night, until he could pick up the trail again in the morning.

Walker took a moment to look back at the prints leading up to the creek. Yes, this was the perfect detour, alright. Too perfect. It didn't take him long to notice that right before approaching the creek, Logan's strides suddenly shortened from a full-out run to a slow, even walk. In fact, each print showed up as a clean, full footprint leading to the creek's bank. Logan hadn't done that in the past. He had barreled into the water at full speed and emerged on the other side, going into a full run immediately.

This could also be an opportunity for the convict to double back the way he came, while Walker wasted hours of time trying to find a trail that didn't exist. A dead end.

Walker smiled. Grandfather had taught him this trick during his preteen years. And he had recently showed Nataya the trick. Well, he couldn't blame Logan for trying.

Walker studied the footprints at the water's edge. He touched the surface, confirming what his eyes told him. These prints held more moisture than the others. He would normally brush that off to the fact that they were near the creek and the soil would hold more water. But there could be another reason.

The footprints were also deeply indented and appeared the tiniest bit "odd," compared to the others he had been following. Walker searched for a particular type of marking.

There.

The print he scrutinized had the faintest hint of a double edge at the heel, as if it had been made twice. A detail not easily spotted unless a person knew to look for it.

It all fell into place. The extra wetness of the prints told Walker that Logan hadn't merely stopped at the water's edge and painstakingly stepped backward into his own footprints, moving away from the water's edge. Logan had taken the time to walk in the creek, perhaps for many yards, and left prints on the other side to lead Walker onto a false trail. Then he had doubled back to this site and meticulously stepped backward into his own prints. But it left water in them from the creek. A tip-off Walker guessed most people would never catch.

An ingenious plan. Too bad for Logan that Walker had used it, and knew how to watch for the indicators.

But Walker needed more than this for proof. He had to find the spot where Logan went off this trail and forged a new one. He followed the prints backward, coming close to the trunk of a large Rocky Mountain maple with dense shrubs and weeds off to the side. There the footprint indentations were lighter. Logan hadn't stepped backward into these prints. Walker carefully dropped to his hands and knees, searching for the tiniest hint of a print off this trail, checking the groundcover and soil under the thick plants and brush.

Long moments later, he found his reward, a small rim-shaped indent in some moss. Exactly the type of mark the edge of a boot would make. A start.

Walker continued to search the ground, sometimes at a crouch, sometimes kneeling. Sign would be difficult to find at the beginning. Logan would have been extremely diligent about hiding his new trail, unlike the one he had purposely left for Walker to follow. Memories of Grandfather in the woods with him floated into his thoughts as he worked. How often had they practiced this type of technique, looking for the most minute sign, the tiniest clue.

The evening light had all but faded, but he searched in an ever-increasing arc around the large tree until he found his next clue, crushed leaves and a disturbance of the fir needles on the forest floor, nothing more. But, to his trained eye, he knew no animal had done this. Only a human stepping onto the ground cover and standing there a few moments could create that specific look. It gave him a direction to take.

Walker looked up through the foliage overhead to the darkening sky beyond. After taking so much trouble to find Logan's real trail, he didn't want to risk losing it. He'd have to wait and head out again at first light.

His emotions were a mix of personal satisfaction at not being duped by Logan's elaborate dead-end scheme and frustration at being forced to stop for the night just as he found the real trail. *Patience*, he heard Grandfather say.

As he prepared to settle in for some much-needed sleep, he considered his circumstances. With the knowledge that Logan had anywhere from eight to eleven hours lead on him, Walker could safely assume the fugitive had out distanced him by at least thirty miles, perhaps more. It would've taken the man an hour or more to set up the dead-end ruse, but Logan had still traveled at a run most of the day. While Walker moved at a snail's pace.

CHAPTER NINETEEN

Elk Meadow, Colorado

Nataya stood alone on the front porch of the log cabin and watched the last stripe of brilliant pink glow disappear, extinguished by the massive indigo pinnacles rearing up against the sky. She remained there, still, as a blanket of darkness covered her and the stars sparkled their way through the void above. When the full moon rose up to greet her, only then did she move to go inside, to the empty cabin.

She felt Walker's presence. Stronger than the other nights. Did he lie wounded out there somewhere, needing her help?

Her fingers brushed the phone receiver as she walked past it, willing it to ring. That night the hours flowed like a lazy summer creek, in no hurry to get to its destination. She sat down at the desk, where the now-familiar topo map lay spread out across the surface.

She studied it every day, guessing where Walker might be. He had mentioned the vast forest that lay on the other side of the nearest mountain. A place where someone could hide out, for a long time. Had Walker guessed correctly? Did he follow the convict in that direction?

When the phone rang, she raced across the room to grab it, heart pounding.

"Hello."

"Nataya, it's Special Agent Davis."

She found her voice, managed to squeak out, "Yes?"

"Walker's fine."

Her breath escaped in relief, and she smiled. "Thank you."

"No problem. Sorry it's so late tonight. I couldn't get to the info at my usual time."

"That's okay. I understand. Listen, Agent Davis, I have a favor to ask." She heard the silence of hesitation before the man replied.

"Yeah. What is it?"

"This is difficult for me, as I'm sure you know, to be here and Walker out there. It would be wonderful if you could let me know approximately what his location is each night." She rushed forward before Davis could protest. "I know you can't give me the actual coordinates, but maybe something ... how many miles he's traveled ... which direction. I could follow along on my map. It would give me such comfort to be able to do that."

Silence.

"Please, Agent Davis ..."

She heard him sigh.

"What the hell. I'm so far up to my eyeballs in shit at this point. Sure. But only the number of miles and a general direction. That's it."

"Fair enough. I do appreciate it so much."

"I hope so. When I get the coordinates tomorrow, I'll figure out the total miles he's gone. I can tell you now that he is headed west. That's all I can give you."

"Thank you, Agent Davis. I'll not forget this."

"Well, actually I'd rather you did. Like it never happened, right?"

"Right."

Nataya hung up the phone with a lightness of spirit she hadn't felt since Walker left. She didn't yet know how she would use this knowledge, but she knew she needed it.

Walker had taught her to listen to her instincts. She had no doubt she would soon understand what to do.

CHAPTER TWENTY

San Juan National Forest, Colorado

Even with exhaustion bearing down on his shoulders, Fox Walker found it impossible to sleep. He tossed about, thoughts flitting around in his mind. Questions about Logan. He gave a sigh and sat up.

With so many miles between him and the fugitive, and the late hour of night, Walker decided a small fire would be safe. He needed to give his hands something to do while his mind worked.

Walker began to gather dry materials to use in building a fire, as well as tiny twigs and slivers of wood for kindling. After selecting items near him, he made his way back to the creek, where he had earlier spotted a few cattails. He pulled his knife and cut the heads from the stalks. The down from the plants would make a light and airy tinder, essential for catching a spark.

On his way back to his camping spot, he gathered larger pieces of wood, making sure they were dry and wouldn't cause much smoke. He stacked them next to where he wanted the fire.

Walker knelt and scraped out a shallow fire pit in the dirt. He put together the tinder bundle and placed it on a large piece of bark, which he laid on the ground in front of him, the kindling close by. He pulled out the smaller ankle knife and the flint he always carried. Using the steel blade to strike the flint at the correct angle, he sent sparks into the tinder. He picked up the bundle, gently blowing into it until flames erupted. He placed the tinder bundle in the fire pit and fed tiny kindling to the flames until the fire grew large enough to consume larger pieces of wood. Soon a small fire crackled, with only a minimum of smoke curling up, concealed by the heavy tree canopy overhead.

One of the short tree branches he gathered had just the right dimension to create a drinking cup. Using his hunting knife, he patiently sawed through the wood, cutting it to the length he wanted. Walker leaned back against the tree trunk and stretched his legs out next to the warmth of the fire, waiting for the fire to produce some glowing coals—for the next step in the process.

Sitting next to the crackling fire, Walker could picture Nataya sitting by the wood stove in the cabin. They might both be alone, but they were connected by that common thread. And it gave him comfort to know that every night she would receive a call, telling her that he was still safe.

Then it struck him. She was alone in the cabin. Alone, for the first time since he had saved her from that madman. Walker felt his insides go cold. Why hadn't he thought of that? What might she be feeling. Was she afraid? What an ass he'd been. Thinking only of his fears and desires.

For the first time since he took this assignment, he began to doubt that he had made the right decision about leaving her behind. He had only thought about the fact that he wanted to keep her safe, protected. He couldn't bear the thought of losing her, like he had lost Haiwi.

He shook his head. He couldn't change anything. He needed to concentrate on what he could control.

Walker rolled up to his knees and, using two sticks like tongs, retrieved a hot coal from the fire, then carefully placed it on top of the wood cylinder. A curl of smoke drifted up as the coal began to scorch the wood.

He returned to his reclining position against the tree trunk and forced thoughts of Nataya from his mind. He needed to concentrate on his present circumstance. And consider what he learned about Logan, so far.

First, Logan hadn't killed his guards when given the perfect opportunity. In fact, the man went to great lengths to not harm them. Well, other than their pride. Okay, he could accept that. Why rack up more murder charges, if the man didn't need to? Yet, it didn't fit with this killer image the FBI had painted. A rogue, former navy SEAL who obviously intimidated them.

Or does he?

Did they send him on this manhunt simply to keep Logan on the run, while they worked another angle? He hadn't considered that before. Anger threatened to bubble up as Walker thought about it. They were knowingly risking his life just to play some game? Unless they knew something about this man that they weren't telling him …

Walker picked up the wood cylinder, turned it on its side and let the cool charcoal drop back into the fire pit. He pulled his smaller knife from its ankle sheath and began to scrape away the burned wood and ashes, creating a deep depression in the top of the wood.

Considering the elaborate scheme Logan hatched for the double back and dead-end trail, Walker believed that the fugitive knew he was being followed. But that couldn't be confirmed yet. The military man had trained as a survivalist. He would naturally try to make it impossible for someone to follow his trail, whether he actually saw anyone or not.

Walker sat the piece of wood on the ground and, using his homemade tongs, placed another glowing red coal on top. He would repeat the action over and over while he rested by the fire each night. The process would eventually hollow out the inside of the cylinder, creating a drinking cup. Later he would treat the inside with pitch gathered from an evergreen, so he could heat water in it. He would merely add hot stones—which had been heated in the fire—to the water in the cup until the water boiled. Because of the high altitude he'd boil it for three minutes to make it safe to drink.

He picked up another log and laid it on the fire, watching sparks momentarily float upward in the heat. The flames danced in a mesmerizing pattern, lulling Walker into relaxation, at last.

But one final thought persisted. If indeed Logan knew a man followed him, he would know Walker could track and survive in the wilderness as well. So why had Logan repeatedly not taken advantage of his own situation? He had multiple opportunities to shoot Walker from a distance, or set an ambush. Why did he spend hours creating a scenario that would throw Walker off his trail, versus just getting rid of his tormentor, with no witnesses? Nothing matched the information he'd been fed. Why?

Matt Logan lay on his back under the shelter of a large evergreen, his hands under his head, staring at the stars that peeked through the branches overhead. The soft mat of fallen needles made his bed, the boughs overhead his ceiling.

But he didn't take the time to enjoy the inspiring view of the Milky Way, or revel in the peacefulness of the quiet night, the chirping crickets and night calls of the Great Horned Owl.

Logan thought about past missions, the tactics he had employed to thwart the enemy. Which ones had been the most successful.

How he could use the resources at hand to modify the needed components. He considered the materials he had in the backpack, fishing line, and hooks. Oh, he knew a good one for those items. The Cong first used the idea, but opium farmers had picked up on it. A nasty way to booby trap a path you didn't want someone following.

Logan thought back to his handiwork the previous day, his elaborate ruse and back-track. But the tracker should have realized that he had lost Logan's trail altogether and would have to spend hours trying to figure out which direction to take. But there wouldn't be anywhere to go.

Logan had spent far more hours than he should have on the task, but for good reason. The clock was running out for him. Time to get back on track. Get to the cabin. He needed the tracker off his trail. Now. From there on out he planned to stay on course and move with the upmost speed possible to meet his timeline.

A niggling thought kept surfacing, though. This tracker seemed superhuman at times in how he managed to keep following Logan's passage through the wilderness. There was always a slim possibility, he supposed. He couldn't take any chances. He'd have to make sure that if the tracker somehow picked up his trail, he wouldn't surprise Logan.

He must make sure the tracker would be the one who was caught unawares, and he'd make sure the man knew who gift-wrapped the present.

CHAPTER TWENTY-ONE

FBI Headquarters, Denver, Colorado

Special Agent Susan Mueller looked up from the phone call when she heard a light tap on her office door and saw her assistant, Agent Rachel Campbell. The assistant peeked in and waved a file folder. Mueller beckoned her in while she finished her conversation.

"Thanks for the update on Walker's progress, Agent Davis. Let me know the moment he activates the location signal for Logan."

Campbell laid the folder on the desk and turned to leave as Mueller hung up the phone.

"Anything here of special interest, Campbell?" Mueller asked as she slid on her reading glasses.

The agent faced Mueller. "Not really. Sean Logan is squeaky clean. Seems like a nice guy, actually."

Mueller peered over the top of her glasses. "I've heard the two brothers are extremely loyal to each other. Doesn't sound like they are much alike, though?"

"I'd say not."

Mueller nodded and opened the folder as Campbell left the room. She skimmed through the report. Her assistant had been correct. In turns of an interesting read, this fit under the heading of "boring." But Mueller still had a difficult time believing that Logan's younger brother had nothing to do with the convict's escape. Then again, Matt Logan was no typical criminal. He knew procedures. He knew what would happen once he escaped. Maybe he planned everything to keep his younger brother free of suspicion.

Mueller closed Sean Logan's folder and picked up Nicole Conrad's file. She'd lost track of how many times she had read the newspaper clippings about Nicole's murder, the sheriff department's reports, the trial transcripts. Yet each time she hoped to see something that had been missed before, a clue, a place to start.

The photo of Nicole clipped to the inside of the folder stared at Mueller. She slipped it free and studied it. Mueller had been a new recruit when she first met Special Agent Nicole Conrad. She had instantly liked Nicole, her independence and self-confidence. She had found her inspirational. It hurt to know that she was gone, especially considering the way she died.

Even when Nicole turned in her resignation from the Bureau, Mueller had admired Nicole's determination to follow the life she wanted. She always followed her dreams.

Mueller flipped through the pages in the folder. Like others in the agency, she'd heard the rumors about Nicole and Matt Logan's relationship, but she had never personally seen any evidence of it. And as far as Mueller was concerned that had been Nicole's private life. It didn't have anything to do with her work. Until now. It became another piece of the puzzle, and who knew where one piece might fit into the other. She had her own set of questions for Logan. She sighed, rested her chin in her hand and stared at her desk.

A dog-eared and stained folder beckoned and she slid it over in front of her. *John Selden.* Mueller opened it, knowing full well its contents, knowing every page and every sentence on the reports. She knew that within the Bureau and behind her back people whispered that it was the "never ending case," and she sometimes felt the same way.

But she had taken the case on with the determination to stop Selden, and she couldn't give up. People like him, who used their wealth and power to abuse the United States' political system, rated up there on the scale of treason in her mind. Greed. Corrupting the very system that served the general population of this country. She found it deplorable. But what made Selden even more danger-ous than most was his secret past. Mueller wasn't the only agent in the Bureau who was convinced he had committed murder while in college, and they had spent years trying to find the proof, a dif-ficult thing to do when there were no bodies.

Nicole's folder still lay open and Mueller pulled out the sheet of paper with the Post-it note attached to the top. Even though she knew the words by heart, she read through the list of cases that Nicole had handled while at the agency, stopping at the one she had highlighted when she first read it. The one telling Mueller that years before she would take over Selden's case, Nicole had worked on this very same assignment, this still unsolved case.

Mueller shook her head and stared across the room.

Whatever did you get yourself involved in, Nicole, that you ended up dead?

CHAPTER TWENTY-TWO

Seattle, Washington

Seattle turned out to be everything Sean had heard about it. His flight landed in the rain, with clouds covering the entire sky. With a few hours to kill before his appointment, he took the rental car out for a drive just beyond the city limits. He hadn't expected the beautiful scenery, or those magnificent trees. The rain did nothing to diminish it. The scenery begged him to keep driving. He wished he had more time to explore, to the mountains beyond.

But instead he stood outside of Dean McClure's office door, suddenly nervous and feeling as if he was about to be interrogated by the law again. He sucked up his trepidation in a deep breath and blew it out, then knocked.

The man who opened the door stood a head taller than Sean. His gray hair did not diminish the effect of the broad shoulders and hard physique of a man who still worked out on a regular basis. But he gave Sean a friendly smile.

"You must be Sean Logan," he said, extending his hand.

"Yes. Thank you for agreeing to meet with me on such short notice."

"No problem. Glad to help any friend of Victor's. Come in and make yourself comfortable. It sounds like we have a few things to discuss."

Sean stepped into the austere surroundings of McClure's office. A desk, dark and immense, and a chair sat at one end of the room. The wall across from the desk held a huge whiteboard. Photographs of all shapes and sizes covered the board, magnets holding them up there, seemingly at random. Sean tried to get a closer look at the photos, but McClure motioned him over toward the leather sofa and chairs sitting by a lone window, casually saying, "You don't want to see those, son." Which made Sean all the more curious, but not enough to contradict the man.

There were a couple of framed pieces of art on the wall beside the window and a table with a coffee pot. The patter of rain created its own melody on the glass panes. Sean found it soothing, and he needed to latch onto anything that could help him regain some calm.

"Coffee?" McClure asked, holding up a mug.

"Yes, that sounds good, thanks."

McClure poured a mug full of the steaming brew and handed Sean the cup. "Yeah, this weather makes a person appreciate a hot cup of coffee."

Sean settled back into the sofa, the rain streaming down the window, the coffee mug warming his hands. He tried to relax. He still didn't have any idea how this retired FBI profiler could help him, but Victor had been adamant about it. And Sean sure didn't have any idea where to turn, so he didn't have much of a choice.

McClure took the chair opposite Sean and leaned back, totally at ease with the situation. Sean sensed the older man appraising him.

"How old are you, son?"

"Thirty-two."

"Victor says that you are just the opposite of your older brother. That you are a law-abiding, up-standing citizen. Matt has lived life hard. You begrudge him for his rough and tough life style?"

"No. And I don't see what any of this has to do with why I am here," Sean said, sitting up straighter, red spots coming to his cheeks. "This isn't about me."

McClure smiled. "Well, yes it is. You've gotten yourself into a pretty serious mess for someone so young and 'up-standing' in society. Now why would a nice young man put himself in this kind of position?"

"Didn't Victor explain it to you?"

"Sure he did. But I want to hear it from you. Why would you go to these lengths to help your brother escape? To make plans well before the conviction came down?"

Sean sat his cup of coffee on the table. His hands were shaking and he didn't want this McClure guy to notice. "Well, to us—"

"Us?"

"Yeah, Matt's SEAL buddies and me."

McClure gave Sean a nod to continue.

"Toward the end it was pretty clear how the jury was going to go. We had to plan ahead for the worse-case scenario."

"But why, Sean? Why did you need to help him escape?"

Sean leaned forward, his face hard, his eyes flashing. "Because Matt is innocent, that's why." Sean stared at McClure in the silence that followed, realizing that his fists were clenched. Relaxed his hands.

"Because Matt told you he's innocent of the crime?"

Sean stood up and glared at McClure. "Yes, that's what he told me. And I know what you're going to say next, that he's my brother and I want to believe him. But do I have any proof?" Sean began pacing the floor. "I know Matt was a badass in the service, did a lot of things I don't even want to think about. But he would never torture and murder a woman. It was all circumstantial evidence. That's all they had."

"What about the fact that they found Matt's DNA under the victim's fingernails?"

Sean stopped pacing and stared at Dean. "I know, it looks bad. But Matt insists that he and Nicole only met to discuss a situation she found herself in, that she wanted his advice."

"So why didn't Matt say this in court?"

Sean stared at his shoes. "I dunno. He would never explain it to me. Just kept saying he had an honor to uphold. That he wouldn't break it."

Both men grew quiet in thought, rain pattering on the window the only sound breaking the silence.

McClure motioned Sean to take a seat again. "Let's hear about this interrogation the FBI put you through. I need you to tell me every word. I know, it's impossible to remember perfectly. Just try your best."

CHAPTER TWENTY-THREE

San Juan National Forest, Colorado

With clear blue skies and sunshine overhead, Walker made his way along the ridgeline. To his left the land dropped off suddenly into a large ravine. At the bottom flowed a stream, a thin thread from his viewpoint. Logan's trail followed a natural pathway along the top edge, where not many trees or shrubs had made a stand in the rockier soil. With the absence of obstacles, such as large streams to cross, or thick stands of trees to maneuver through, Walker had been free to set a steady pace and make up some lost time.

He rounded a curve in the trail and stopped. Up ahead, the path narrowed, with shoulder-high shrubs closing in from each side. The scene put his instincts into hyper-alert. He studied the symmetry of the shrubs and brush in front of him before he moved closer and knelt. He took his time studying the limbs and branches through the foliage, until he spotted a hand-carved wooden peg at ground level. Only then could he see the fishing line attached to it. His eyes followed the line, up through the leaves.

"I'll be damned."

He stood. The almost transparent line stretched tight across the narrow opening—at chest height.

The trap had been set up in a perfect spot, the path of least resistance, and high enough that a small animal wouldn't accidently set it off. But what would happen if someone did trip it?

Walker studied the setup, looking for the trigger that might send a projectile heading his way, or a snare to trap him. After long moments of scrutinizing the shrubs, he found his answer. The line, when bumped, would pull the fish line and release the trigger, which would set off a deadfall trap. This one consisted of a small wood barrier, made of sticks lashed together. When released, it would allow a pile of rocks, stones, and small boulders to fall away at the edge of the cliff, down the side of the ravine to his left.

He stared at it, puzzled. Nothing would come crashing down on his head at the trail level. It made no sense, until he thought about it more. Thought about all those rocks and boulders crashing against the side of the ravine, tumbling for hundreds of feet downward, knocking other rocks loose, adding to the small avalanche, all crashing to the ravine floor far below. It would echo and made a tremendous amount of noise, which would be heard for miles around.

Ingenious.

Instead of some deadly trap that would impale Walker with something hideous, this would simply set off an alarm to alert Logan of Walker's presence, and Logan would know that his dead-end trail hadn't worked.

Walker considered just making his way around the trap, but he didn't want some animal to accidently set it off. He wanted Logan to believe he had lost Walker a long time ago.

He studied the deadfall, put together with what looked like ripcord. So he knew that Logan had fishing line and some type of strong, lightweight rope. What *else* did this guy have access to?

Walker didn't have any rope with him, but a quick search of the land nearby yielded some young fireweed shoots. He sat on the ground and began stripping the stems apart. With practiced speed he began to weave the fibrous inner bark together, creating a continuous piece of strong cordage. Minutes later he held up a two-foot-long cord, the thickness of heavy twine.

Back at the trap, and using delicate care, he tied off the trigger for the deadfall with his handmade string, making sure the pile of rocks would stay behind their barrier. When he felt sure the trap had been rendered safe, Walker used his smaller ankle knife to cut the fish-line tripwire.

One trap down. He could only wonder how many more might await him.

Walker set off on Logan's trail again. As much as he enjoyed the process of tracking, the fact that Logan continued to move farther and farther ahead of him made the work tediously slow and frustrating.

Walker reached the highest point on the ridge, pausing to catch his breath. He had to admit that he had not anticipated being out there so long. His searches commonly lasted just hours to a few days, at most. But then Logan wasn't the average lost hiker.

Walker had gathered edible plants as he moved through the landscape, sometimes eating as he walked. But at this point he would be forced to take time to forage for other foods, like birds' eggs, insects, even small mammals, to maintain his energy. He had no idea if Logan did the same. After all, he had the supplies from when he escaped. Did it include food and water? If so, how much might the fugitive still have left after four days?

Walker sighed and began his tracking again. The ridgeline began to make a descent as the land angled down closer to the stream below. At least he didn't have to go uphill again for a while. He pointedly looked for any positive factor in his situation. But he knew the reality as well. That it wasn't just Logan's ability to survive the wilderness that challenged him. It was more the man's expertise at subterfuge and warfare tactics that made him such a potentially deadly opponent to track.

Walker's thought flashed back to Nataya waiting alone at the cabin all these days. What must it feel like for her, waiting all day, every day, to find out if he still lived?

His mind wandered back to the phone call from the FBI, the argument with Nataya about coming out here alone. He remembered the scene afterward, when he climbed into bed next to her. The vision of her that night came clearly to his mind, and how she surprised him with her warm reception. His mind began to replay the moments of their lovemaking.

Walker took another step and felt his feet go out from under him. One moment solid ground—then nothing. It happened too quickly to react.

He fell backward and downward, his back bumping and scraping against dirt and rock, his arms flailing. He tried to grab at anything to stop his skidding descent, but found nothing. He managed to keep his feet first and cover his head with his arms as rocks and dirt followed him downward. After a few more smacks into unyielding surfaces, he hit bottom with a jolt. He lay back, gasping, as dirt, leaves, and twigs fluttered down on top of him. Once he could suck air into his lungs again, he brushed the debris from his face.

Why was it so dark?

Walker looked upward, seeing only a small patch of sky above. How far had he fallen? He continued to lie still for a moment, making sure no bones were broken. Aside from bruises and being battered about, he didn't feel injured, except his pride. His eyes were adjusting to the dark, and he could make out the forms of tree roots, twisting out from the dirt that surrounded him. Rocks and small boulders protruded from the sides of the eroded tunnel-like sinkhole.

Escape became his next concern. The steep angle of what he guessed to be twenty feet of rock and dirt walls would be a challenge to climb. But the boulders and exposed roots would serve as handholds, and he had his knife to dig out indentions for his feet. He felt confident he could make it out. He looked back up to the blue sky peeking at him from above.

How the hell had he missed seeing this?

Logan!

It had to be. He had camouflaged the opening to the sinkhole, and Walker stumbled right into it. He had let his mind wander the tiniest bit—and now look.

Walker knew he had no one to blame but himself. A harsh reminder that the man he hunted was a more than a worthy adversary. Then it hit him. Logan could have just as easily made the trap a deadly one.

Matt Logan made his way through the last of the evergreens along the timberline he had been skirting. Keeping low, he raced up to the edge of the ridge above. He crouched down and turned to take a quick look back. It had been two days since he led the tracker back down into the woods below and had created the false trail. And he hadn't seen or heard any sign of the man since. None of the traps he created as alerts had been triggered, either. He felt reasonably safe in assuming he had lost the man. But, of course, he continued to check whenever he got to a vantage point where he could see back along the path he had taken.

He lowered his body to the ground and peered over the rocky edge to the other side of the mountain. Only then did he feel safe heading into the forest that lay beyond, and on to the cabin that waited for him on the next ridgeline over.

He sighed. His target was almost in sight. As much as he didn't mind being out in the wild, the stress of increasing his distance from the tracker and working to lose him had taken its toll. He looked forward to having a place to retreat to and regroup ... and a hot meal.

The trek had taken longer than he had anticipated, but he would still hit his timeline.

I just can't afford to have someone follow me any farther.

CHAPTER TWENTY-FOUR

Elk Meadow, Colorado

Nataya gathered an armload of logs from the stacked cord of firewood next to the cabin. As she carried it to the front porch, she glanced out toward the mountains and paused a moment to enjoy the view. The sun hid behind the craggy crowns, but the glassy-smooth water of the lake mirrored their silhouette against the dusky sky. Within the hour, darkness and the moon and stars would prevail, which meant it was almost time for Agent Davis to call her.

She turned and entered the log cabin, crossing the room to lay the logs next to the wood stove. The nights were still chilly in the early spring, and she wondered if Walker stayed warm at night—then laughed at herself. Of course he did. He understood how to be one with nature better than anyone she knew.

She couldn't help but worry about him though, while stuck there alone. Several times she thought about hiking the surrounding woods, had even taken the canoe out on the lake twice, but mostly she stayed near the phone ... just in case.

She walked over to the topo map. Walker had shown her the point on the map where the FBI said the convict's vehicle had been discovered. From there, going east led to the eventual end of the San Juan National Forest, as it ran into the nearest ski resort towns and higher mountains, where only the alpine areas could survive. But the west opened up to hundreds of square miles of untamed wilderness, and plenty of resources for survival. When Davis had let her know that Walker headed in a westerly direction, she realized that so far everything matched to what Walker had guessed would be his route.

Nataya turned, looking at the phone. Davis was late calling, again. It always made her nervous when he didn't call at his usual time.

When it rang seconds later, she hurried to pick it up.

"Hello?"

"Nataya! So good to hear your voice."

She froze for a moment. This wasn't the agent. Who—?

"I know it's been six months, but don't tell me you already don't even recognize my voice." The man laughed.

Nataya smiled then as she realized who was on the other end. "Dean—Dean McClure!"

"Good. You haven't forgotten me so soon."

"Of course not. I wouldn't be alive to say this if it weren't for you."

"Give Walker that credit. I only supplied him some clues. He's the one who figured out how to find and rescue you."

"Yes, he is a remarkable man. But we're both grateful you were helping the FBI look for me, and could give him those clues."

"Thanks, Nataya. But, speaking of Walker, I have a project that needs his expertise. I hate to interrupt your evening, but could I talk to him?"

Nataya hesitated. The agent had made her promise she wouldn't let anyone know about his phone calls, but no one had said she couldn't speak of Walker's mission.

"Anything wrong, Nataya?"

"No. It's just that he isn't here. He's been called away. And I'm not sure how much I can tell you."

It was Dean's turn to hesitate. "Sure. I understand. A confidential job. Do you know when he'll be back?"

"No. He's out in the San Juan National Forest. I have no idea for how long."

Nataya listened to the long pause on the other end. When Dean spoke his voice had an edge of urgency to it that hadn't been there just moments ago.

"He's in the San Juan Forest? Listen, this is extremely important. I need you to tell me if Walker is tracking someone."

Nataya nodded, then realized she needed to speak. "Yes, he is."

"Is the man's name Matthew Logan?"

"Sorry, I don't know the man's name."

"That's okay. Just by chance, do you know, is the man an escaped convict?"

"Yes, but how do you—"

"Damnit. Sorry, Nataya."

"That's okay, Dean. But, how did you hear about the escape in Seattle?"

"No time for that. The fact is I was hoping to hire Walker to track this same guy. I need to find Logan before the sheriff's search team does."

"There's a search team out there, too?"

"What do you mean? Isn't Walker working with the sheriff's department?"

"No, not this time. The FBI people called him. But they sent him out there alone."

Silence. Then Nataya heard Dean muttering, "Well, I'll be damned."

"Dean? Is everything okay?" None of this made any sense to her. She knew Dean sometimes consulted for the FBI. Why would he be hunting for this convict on his own? She felt her body tensing with nervousness.

"Yes. Of course. No need to be alarmed."

"Please, tell me why you wanted to hire Walker to find this man. He's a convicted murderer."

"Maybe. I'm not convinced the man is guilty of the crime. And I'm not alone. I haven't had time to get all the facts yet, but I had hoped to get Walker out there to find the guy before the search parties got to him. Sounds more complicated than that now."

Nataya heard her words before she even thought them. "Send me, Dean. Tell me what message you want to get to Walker and I'll find him. I know I can. I've learned so much about tracking."

"I don't know ..."

"You know I can survive in the wilderness. And I promise that as soon as I find Walker, I'll pass along your message and come right back here. What do you say?" She waited out the silence. Finally, Dean spoke.

"You know, I think this might work out perfectly. You could give Walker my instructions and bring back a report to me. If we need to, we could even keep up some type of communication, verbally, between you and Walker. No one could monitor us that way."

Nataya noticed that the more Dean talked, the more excited he became, mirroring her own excitement.

"How soon can you be ready to head out, Nataya?"

"Dawn."

"Perfect. But how will you know where to start?"

"Don't worry, Walker showed me a map of the area and where they found the fugitive's vehicle. He even pointed out the route that he thought the convict would take. I can do a pretty fair guess at how many miles he's gone each day and enter the forest close to where I think he is." It was only a partial lie. She did make a promise to Agent Davis, after all.

"Sounds like you have it all figured out. Good. There's just one thing, Nataya."

"Yes?"

"Even though I believe there is strong evidence that Logan is innocent of the crime he was convicted of, the man *is* a trained killer. I don't know what he might do if backed into a corner, you know?"

"I understand."

"All I want right now is to have Walker hold off on giving the FBI heads up on Logan's location until I can get some more information, okay?"

Dean relayed the details he wanted passed along to Walker, and Nataya had just hung up the phone, her heart still pounding hard, when it rang again. This time it was Agent Davis. And, as promised, he had the information Nataya had requested. The number of miles Walker had traveled. It was all Nataya could do to contain her elation as she listened to Davis.

I'm going to see Walker.

But, more importantly, she had found a way to help him. It felt right. Which made her remember the nightly calls.

"Agent Davis, I need to let you know that I've been called in on a local search and rescue. I don't know when I'll be back here at the cabin to get your evening phone calls. If I don't answer for a few days, don't worry about me."

"Okay. But I don't feel comfortable leaving a voice mail if you don't answer."

"No problem. We don't have an answering machine anyway."

She hung up the phone and immediately sat down at the desk, studying the topo map to chart Walker's course. She looked at the route Walker said would be the way he thought the convict would take through the mountains, to the vast forests on the other side. Taking into consideration the number of miles the agent said Walker had travelled, she circled the general location where she should find him. Then she looked for the nearest road running alongside the forest, eventually finding a little town that would do perfectly.

She gathered up the few items she would be taking … her hunting knife and flint, some dried meat and fruit. She knew how to forage for food, but her goal would be to get to Walker as quickly as possible. She didn't want anything to take time away from her mission.

She walked past the bow-and-arrow collection hanging on the wall and stopped. She had wished Walker had the weapons with him. Would he care that she borrowed it? Maybe he would be glad she brought it. She picked out the smallest bow, the one he had her use for her lessons. She felt familiar with it and knew she could be accurate with it, if need be. Next she picked out one of the doeskin quivers and filled it with arrows.

Nataya laid out a pair of jeans and a deerskin chamois shirt for the morning, plus the beaded moccasin boots that Walker had given her after he discovered her living in the wilderness. She ran her hand lovingly over the soft hide, then lay down on the bed and stared out the window to the still-waning moon.

Her thoughts went back to her nights alone in the forest, watching the moon rise over the pines at night. The peace and contentment she knew then, before regaining her lost memories, memories of her attack. Walker had saved her life, and helped her find her past again. But she had been the only one who could merge the two memories of her past, and weave them together into one life again. A life she had come to share with Walker. She smiled. Somehow, she knew that Walker watched that same moon and thought of her.

CHAPTER TWENTY-FIVE

San Juan National Forest, Colorado

Logan trudged up the steep grade of the canyon, his boots heavy and cumbersome in his state of exertion. He concentrated on the warmth of the morning sun on his back, visualized it spreading energy into his weary body. The strenuous physical work these past few days had been one thing. But adding in the mental strain of shaking his pursuer had exhausted him.

Logan stopped to catch his breath. Anyone following behind him would be faced with a steep cliff rearing up from the valley floor. But as an exploring teenager, Logan had discovered this small, hidden canyon running alongside the cliff, giving him a much easier route to the hilltop. It was still a good workout, but not near as challenging and dangerous as the cliff wall.

He glanced down to the valley floor, to the solid rock wall below. To anyone looking up from that viewpoint, the cabin would be completely hidden from view. It sat back, away from the cliff edge, on a level plateau, surrounded by the woods. It couldn't be much more perfect for a hideout. Logan forced his legs up the last few feet and pushed his way through a stand of shrubs and brush.

And there it was.

He stared through the trees at the hunter's cabin. It appeared so much smaller than he remembered. The wood had weathered over the years, and weeds and brush had overtaken the ground around it. On the opposite side of the cabin, the land stayed level for several yards before angling down to a creek, then back up toward the mountains. Snapshots of scenes flashed through his mind ... he and Sean running and shouting in the trees, their father commanding them to "settle down," but the next moment chuckling at their antics.

His father had chosen this location and built the cabin over the course of one summer, commandeering the boys' help. He swore them to secrecy, telling them it was for hunting expeditions. But Logan knew he had used the place more for the solitude than anything. A place he could retreat to for peace and quiet. Years later Logan would realize that his father knew the structure was illegal, having been built on national park land. That knowledge endeared his father to him even more. Maybe because of the rebellious attitude he didn't know his father possessed, until then.

But Logan admired the cabin's location for another reason. No one knew it existed except he and Sean, and Victor. But even so, out of habit Logan made his way through the brush and skirted the perimeter of the building, going from tree to tree.

He checked for specific markers that Victor said he had put in place after he got the cabin ready for Logan, thin threads stretched between trees at a man's chest height. If someone had been around the cabin recently, the threads would be broken, without the trespasser even noticing. Logan watched for footprints, both human and animal. He didn't want to startle either species unexpectedly.

Once he had secured the perimeter, he made his way over to the ramshackle outhouse that sat off to the side, located the key Victor had hidden under a rock by the foundation, then walked to the front of the cabin. He opened the door and slipped inside, closing the door behind him.

Standing with his back against the wood of the door, he looked around the single room. It hadn't changed from what he remembered. No one had used the cabin since his father's death ten years earlier. But he had no time to be sentimental.

He breathed in the old-wood smell, mingled with a slight hint of lemon oil, most likely from Victor cleaning away years of dust. At the back of the room, and in the center of the wall, stood a small, freestanding wood stove. A memory surfaced. The first time his father had put him in charge of keeping the fire going all night, and his pride at being successful.

Maybe coming here wasn't such a good idea. It brought back too many memories. He shook his head. He didn't have a choice. There hadn't been time to come up with an alternative.

Logan glanced around at the rest of the cabin, at a simple cot bed with blankets and a pillow. A small table next to the cot held a kerosene lamp, the only source of light for the room, except the tiny window on the opposite wall.

At the foot of the bed stood his old footlocker. Sean must have given it to Victor to bring up. Matt opened it. In it he found a change of clothes and a warm jacket. There was also a camping towel and washcloth, made of fabric that would wick away water and dry out quickly.

Logan remembered taking baths as a kid in the large, galvanized-steel tub that sat next to the wood stove, his father heating the water on its top. There was also an old chamber pot in the corner for the nighttime when he didn't want to head outside to the outhouse. Logan grinned.

All the luxuries of home.

On the wall to his left, next to the small window, stood a compact kitchen cabinet with sink and counter space. There was no faucet at the sink, though. He would use the hand pump, standing at attention just outside, to bring water up from the well below.

No need for bottled water here.

Logan checked the cabinet underneath the sink, noted a cast-iron skillet, a metal saucepan, and enamel coffee pot for use on the wood stove top, where he would be doing his cooking.

He opened one cabinet above the sink to find a few plates, bowls, and cups, cooking and eating utensils, can opener, and extra kerosene for the lamp. He opened the second cabinet and smiled. Sitting among the cans of soup and stew, and packages of dried meat, dried fruit, and crackers, was a large green-glass bottle with a note attached. A bottle of Ardbeg Scotch. His favorite. Logan picked it up reverently, read the message "Home Sweet Home" and laughed out loud. No doubt Victor's donation to the cause.

For one brief moment he smiled.

Like coming off a field mission. Just need my teammates to help me kick back and celebrate.

Except this mission was just getting started.

He slid off the backpack and laid it on the cot, then adjusted the shoulder holster to a more comfortable position.

Time for some hot food. He had no qualms about having a fire in the wood stove. The cabin sat on the backside of the mountain range from where he had ditched the Land Rover, along with the tracker, who was most likely still trying to find Logan's trail.

Logan grabbed the matches and a fire-starter stick from his backpack, and knelt on the floor in front of the stove, a stack of firewood close by. He opened the door on the stove and made sure the damper was open. At the sight of the old ashes from years ago came a stab of melancholy and the rush of memories. Again, he forced the thoughts aside and laid some small logs in crisscross fashion on the cold ashes. Then he added the starter stick and lit it. The crackle of flames and smell of wood burning soon relaxed his taut nerves.

What is it about a fire that is so soothing? It's like it's wired into our DNA.

Once the fire took off, Logan stood, grabbed the enamel coffee pot and headed outside. He walked over to the iron water pump, primed it, then pushed the lever down and pulled up a couple of times, until a steady stream of water flowed easily. He filled the coffee pot, took a long drink from it to quench his immediate thirst, then carried it inside and set it on top of the wood stove to heat.

Logan sat on the cot and opened the backpack, pulling out the survival items Sean had thoughtfully included. When he came upon the remaining fishing line and hooks, he paused. He and Sean used to fish in the stream down the hill from there. He might try his luck. The mere thought of fresh-caught, pan-fried trout made his mouth water. He would check it out the next day.

Then he opened the side pocket containing the extra ammo magazines and the pleasant thoughts dissolved. This was no vacation. There were other people out there who would be hunting for him. probably already were, and it wasn't just the law. In fact, law enforcement was the least of his worries.

CHAPTER TWENTY-SIX

Elk Meadow, Colorado

Nataya sat up in bed with a start, awake but sensing the edges of a dream as it faded. She tried to recapture it … something about falling … and darkness. But the fleeting images slid away. Gone.

She swung her legs over the edge of the bed in the still-dark bedroom and looked out the window. The sky had begun to lighten. It was the hour of day she called "the in between time." Not quite dawn, but past the night hours.

She wouldn't be able to get back to sleep, so why not get an early start? She pulled on the jeans she had laid out the night before, slipped the deerskin chamois shirt over her head and laced up the front, moving quickly in the chilled morning air. Next came the moccasin boots, the soft hide conforming to her feet from the many miles of use.

Nataya padded through the main room to the kitchen space. She had wrapped up some beef jerky and dried fruit to take with her. The packages were tucked into a pocket as she made her way to the wood stove. There should only be a few remaining hot coals at that hour, but she opened the stove door to confirm it, then shut it and damped down the stove. The smoldering coals would soon burn themselves out.

She could feel her heart quickening as the time to leave arrived. Over six months had passed since she had been out in the wilderness alone. But instead of being wary, she looked forward to the solitude. Her grandfather had taught her to love being in the wilderness, gave her books on how to survive, taught her how to identify plants. That knowledge had kept her alive when the killer had left her in the forest to die. But it was the Native American teachings her grandfather had passed on to her that had given her mind a refuge to shelter in, a place to hide from the terror she did not want to remember. She had no fear of being alone in the wilderness. It had been her home, her sanctuary.

Nataya walked over to the counter by the door and picked up the rest of the items she had laid out the night before. The flint went into the front pocket of her jeans. She strapped the sheathed hunting knife to her belt, picked up the quiver of arrows and slipped the strap over her shoulder, letting the leather pouch rest against her back, then grabbed the bow.

Nataya slid the key ring from its hook by the door and gave the room one last look, trying to think of anything else she might need, then noticed the topo map on the desk. She hurried to the desk, folded the map and tucked it into a back pocket.

A rosy hue glowed behind the silhouetted trees, dark against the eastern sky, as she exited the cabin and locked the door. She stood a moment in the morning quiet before she crossed the wooden porch and stepped off. She slid the cabin door key off the ring and placed it up under the porch step, in its hiding place. The gravel in the driveway crunched under her feet as she walked to the pickup truck.

She trembled with excitement, or nervousness, it didn't matter which. The fact that she could be on her way, that's what mattered. No more waiting alone in the cabin.

⚞⚟

The morning sun peeked above the trees as Nataya downshifted the truck and slowed for the curve ahead. She should be close to the turnoff she wanted. When the road straightened, she could see the Pine Ridge Motel and parking lot on her right. She pulled in, found a spot next to the main building and parked the truck. The bow and quiver stayed behind on the front seat as she walked to the door marked "office." An elderly woman stood behind the counter when Nataya entered.

"Hello. I'd like to get a room for the week. Do you have any openings?"

"We do. You can have your pick of any of these," the woman said as she indicated the rooms on a layout at the desk.

"I'd like that one, on the end."

"It's yours."

Nataya handed the woman money for the room, took the key and exited. She pulled the truck over to the end of the building and parked in front of her room. It could stay parked there, and no one would think anything about it sitting for a few days.

She got out and walked over to the passenger side to retrieve the bow and arrows, making sure no one could see what she carried to the room, unlocked the door and entered. The small room smelled of old wood and cleaning products. Although the furnishings were out-dated, the owner had tried to make it comfy.

Nataya closed the curtains in the main room. She laid the bow and quiver on the bed, pulled the map from her pocket and spread it out on the small lamp table by the bed. Sitting on the edge of the mattress, she studied the map under the dim light.

She had chosen this motel because it sat at the edge of the San Juan National Forest, directly north and perpendicular to the route Walker had pointed out on the map, the route he thought the fugitive would take. For anyone trying to traverse the mountainside and reach the wilderness on the opposite side, it would be the quickest way, and would allow the person to stay camouflaged in the evergreens of the timberline. If Nataya took a direct path south for several miles, she should cross Walker's, or the fugitive's, trail.

Knowing that she wouldn't be close to finding any prints for several miles meant she could move quickly through the woods for around two hours before having to slow down and start watching for footprints or signs of passage in the ground cover. She hoped to pick up a trail before noon, while she still had hours of light to track.

She folded up the map and returned it to her jeans' pocket, filled one of the glasses in the room with water and drank it all, then prepared to leave. Shouldering the quiver and bow, she pulled a corner of the curtains back and peeked outside. No one was around. Yet another reason she had picked this little out-of-the-way place.

She slipped out the door, and with her back against the wooden building, slid around the corner. She bent down and tilted up the edge of a large rock lying next to the building foundation and placed the room key and truck key under it for her return. Then she walked straight into the woods behind the motel.

Thick bushes and shrubs at the forest edge thinned as the tall trees took over and dominated the sun. Nataya loved the feel of Mother Earth under her moccasins, the connection of energy and strength. She breathed in the woodsy damp smell of the forest, noticed the tree branches full of spring buds ready to burst open, and the tender green shoots of newborn plants bravely pushing their way through the dense cover of the forest floor. Overhead a crow cawed his early morning greeting.

"Good morning, *haih*," she called to the bird, its black feathers glinting in the sunlight.

It's good to be back home in nature.

Walker favored his right leg as he trudged up the steep grade of the incline. During the process of climbing up and out of the deep sinkhole trap Logan had set, he realized more than just his pride had been bruised. Aside from the various sore places on his back and elbows, he had managed to twist his knee in the fall. So far the injury hadn't kept him from continuing his pursuit of Logan, but the pain of putting his weight on the knee had certainly slowed him down more than he wanted, something that plagued him more than he'd ever experienced in his many years of tracking.

He had spent the morning watching for more traps as he traveled through the last of the deep woodland, finding and dismantling two more. All non-lethal. All merely signal alarms. Walker caught himself breathing a sigh of relief when he left behind the dense trees and once again began his trek up the more open, rocky timberline of the mountainside.

Any tracks he found were many hours old. The fugitive had used his time wisely, and put at least twenty-plus miles between them, while making sure to impede the progress of his pursuer at every opportunity.

If Grandfather were still there with him, he would tell Walker there was a lesson to be learned. Walker tried to think of what it might be, but so far he only knew a slow burn of frustration at the situation.

Still, Logan had not made full use of his advantage. Walker knew he could very well be lying at the bottom of that sinkhole, impaled on various pointed stakes, dead or dying a slow, painful death. This contradiction between the portrait of Logan that the FBI had painted, and what Walker had witnessed out there in nature intrigued him.

There could only be one reason why Walker remained alive.

The man has morals, that's why.

Everything pointed to the conclusion that this convicted killer had chosen not to kill. At least for the time being.

The question on Walker's mind was whether or not he was willing to stake his life on that conclusion.

CHAPTER TWENTY-SEVEN

North of Boulder, Colorado

S ean Logan pulled his car off the side of road at the sign for
Boulder Falls, and joined other vehicles parked in the gravel
turnout. After opening the door, he swiveled in his seat to get his
legs out of the car and slipped off his loafers. He pulled on a new
pair of hiking boots, laced them up and got out of the car.

His destination was easy to see from the road, a stunning waterfall cascading down the mountainside, over boulders and cliffs.
Mostly only the locals from the town of Boulder knew of the little
path leading to it from the road. Sean walked along the gravel
turnout until he found the worn, narrow path, then followed it
downhill through the grasses and boulders.

A few people with cameras on tripods stood at the base of the
waterfall, snapping photos. The crashing rush of water muffled
nearby noises as it spilled into the pool at its base. No one paid
Sean any attention as he passed them by and continued, until the

trail made a bend back away from the falls, into the trees where Victor waited for him.

Victor fell in step with Sean without breaking stride. They hiked a few minutes farther along the path before either spoke. Victor broke the silence.

"How did your meeting go with Dean McClure?"

"Fine, I guess. I told him everything the FBI asked me, plus my answers to their questions."

"And ...?"

"He seems as perplexed as we are about why the FBI would be involved, and finds it odd that the FBI jumped at the chance to claim jurisdiction when Matt escaped into the San Juan National Forest."

"So he agrees that it looks like an excuse to get involved?"

"Yes, he does." Sean lengthened his strides, trying to keep pace with Victor. "He knows a tracker, named Fox Walker. Someone we can trust to find Matt and let him know the Bureau is involved. But this is where everything gets even stranger. McClure gave me a call this morning. Don't worry, I gave him the number for the disposable phone," he quickly added when he saw the look on Victor's face. "When McClure tried to contact Walker, he found out the FBI had already hired him to track Matt. He's out there now."

Victor stopped and looked at Sean. "Shit, Logan has no idea. He's expecting a search party, not an expert tracker."

Sean nodded. "Fortunately for our team, McClure knows the tracker's companion—just as capable in the wilderness as this guy. Her name is Nataya, and she's already headed out there to find Walker and tell him not to let the FBI know of Matt's location."

"That's good." Victor nodded and resumed walking along the dirt path. "But why would these two strangers agree to do McClure's bidding? By all rights your brother's a convicted felon."

Sean smiled. "Because, it seems that he helped Walker save Nataya's life about six months ago."

"Really. Okay, I'd guess that gives us a good enough reason to trust them." Victor sprinted up a slight incline and waited for Sean to catch up. "But that still leaves us with the question of why the FBI is so intent on getting involved in this case."

"Yeah, McClure thought about that one for a while," Sean agreed, stalling a moment to regain his breath. "He speculates it has something to do with the fact Matt knew the victim, when she was one of their agents. Beyond that he's stumped. Said he is going to do a little snooping. Quietly, of course. Once Nataya gets word to Walker not to give out Matt's location, she will report back to McClure. In the meantime, we wait for him to contact us again."

Victor shook his head. "No can do. The plan is for me to meet Logan at the cabin the day after tomorrow. He should already be there by now."

Sean took the lead, trying to set a slower pace. "McClure made it clear to me that now that the FBI is involved, if you or I try anything like that we'll be endangering Matt's safety. It's one thing for you to stay low profile so the sheriff's department can't question you, but he's confident that the Bureau is also trying to locate you, and they have more resources at their disposal."

"Okay, I can accept that. But what about Logan? He's waiting for me. Says he has a mission to carry out."

"McClure said Walker can contact Matt when the time is right and let him know the score."

Victor stopped walking, staring out to the trees beyond and back to Sean. "I hope this tracker knows how to do that without getting himself shot."

Sean swallowed hard and looked at Victor, who motioned to turn around on the path and head back toward where they'd parked their cars.

Sean walked in silence for a few steps, then spoke up. "There's something else that came up during my conversation with McClure. Something I'd like to ask you about."

"Sure, kid. What is it?"

"It's about the victim, Nicole."

"Yeah, what about her?"

"All that stuff they said during the trial, about Matt and Nicole being … lovers. Was it all true?"

Victor walked another couple of paces before he answered. "Yeah, it was. They were quite the hot item during those years, before she left the agency and married someone else."

"What about what they said about him killing her because she rejected him? About it being a crime of passion?"

"Do you believe that?"

Sean shook his head. "No way."

"Good. The only person who could convince me it's true would be Matt telling me to my face. Matt loved Nicole. But she left the Bureau because she wanted 'a husband, kids, and a home with a white picket fence.' The whole deal, she told him. Matt knew he couldn't give her that. He loved her enough to let her go."

"What about the fact Matt wouldn't talk about any of this at the trial? He refused to even defend himself. What was he hiding?"

"That I can't tell you. He hasn't shared it with me. But just between you and me, kid, I don't think he ever stopped loving her."

"So why didn't Matt ever tell me about her?"

"You were barely a teenager at the time. It's not like you had much experience with the subject. Besides, his goal was always to shield you from the realities of the world."

"Protect me."

"Yeah. Protect you. And it wasn't such a bad ideal to have, especially after you lost your dad at such a young age."

"Yeah, I know. But can you understand why I want to help him now?"

Victor put his hand on Sean's shoulder as they continued walking the path. "Maybe, kid … we'll see."

CHAPTER TWENTY-EIGHT

San Juan National Forest, Colorado

Nataya stopped to catch her breath and glanced up at the sun overhead. She had been sprinting through the woods wherever the terrain allowed it and knew she should be happy with the progress she'd made. But she had hoped to find Walker's tracks by this time.

Still, she had to be close. She had just passed over a small creek that, according to the topo map, meant she had traveled six miles into the forest.

She would slow her pace and watch for anything that showed passage by a human through this part of the forest. To outsiders it might look like an impossible task. But she had an advantage. The topo map let her see the elevation of the hills and depth of the valleys, as well as the creeks and larger streams. And Walker had taught her that tracking people held many of the same principles as tracking animals, in that most of the time they would naturally follow the easiest course while traversing the wilderness. She would keep that in mind and watch for prints along the streams and creeks. People always gravitated to water, since they needed it for survival, but they could also use the waterway as an easy path to follow to their destination.

She pulled a package from her pocket, selected a couple of slices of dried apple and ate them while she surveyed the land before her. Below this ridge lay a valley with a large stream running through it. The map showed that it originated in the foothills above. It would be an excellent way to move forward without losing direction, and an almost direct path to the forests that lay on the other side of this mountain. Walker had been sure this would be part of the route for the fugitive. She would check for sign as she got close to the waterway.

She tucked the package back into her pocket and began her decent. Turning her body sideways, she placed her footfalls carefully on the steep slope, while holding unto tree trucks and shrubs to keep from sliding downhill. When she reached the valley floor, she approached the stream slowly, watching for any tracks or markings that indicated someone had been through the area. She found raccoon and deer tracks leading to the shoreline, where the animals had come down to drink, but nothing that looked like human prints.

Nataya studied the surrounding land and thought about where the fugitive and Walker would have been coming from. If they did venture into this valley, they would have approached it from the other side. She walked downstream until she found a fallen tree spanning the width of the water. She leapt up onto the log, crossed over the stream and jumped down on the opposite bank.

Then she moved in slow motion, studying the ground for anything that would tip her off that one of the men had been there … impressions in the softer ground near the bank of the stream, pebbles or twigs pressed into the mud.

Nothing.

But she wasn't ready to give up. She'd try moving to higher ground and take her time searching for evidence of their passage.

Thirty minutes later, she found her reward. A footprint. But it wasn't Walker's. A deeply cleated hiking boot made this impression. She knelt by the print, studying it. She hadn't thought the fugitive would be wearing hiking boots. Wouldn't he have prison-issued work boots on? Maybe she had accidently stumbled onto the prints of a lone hiker. She tried not to be too disappointed. If one man found this spot, others may have found it also, perhaps Walker. She looked closer at the footprint. The cleat marks in the dirt were sharp and perfect. Too perfect. These boots were brand new. Any hiker with enough experience to hike this wilderness would have well-worn boots. That gave her some other options to consider. Maybe the fugitive had an accomplice, and been given some supplies, a change of clothes?

She decided to follow the prints for a while, see where they headed. Before long the trail led down toward the water. The prints were clear and easy to follow in the moist soil. Nataya stopped, then knelt and examined a soft impression made in the smooth mud at the edge of the bank.

There. Walker's moccasin print. The two of them had hiked together enough that she would recognize it anywhere. Her heart raced with excitement and anticipation.

I found him.

She allowed a moment for celebration, then forced herself to grow calm. Keep her mind keen.

She continued to follow Walker's trail to the edge of the stream, where he had knelt, and up the bank to higher ground. Walker definitely followed the hiking-boot prints.

Could it be just coincidence? She had to trust that Walker knew something she didn't.

She studied Walker's footprints in comparison to the hiking boots. The two sets of prints were made hours apart, perhaps a full day between them. That gave her hope that whether the hiking boots belonged to the fugitive or not, she still had a chance of locating Walker before he caught up with the man and let the FBI know the convict's location.

She had the rest of the day to track Walker, and even though she could tell that he moved forward with caution, he clearly didn't worry about hiding his trail. She would be able to move quickly and make up hours of time. She felt sure the two men would continue to follow the stream up the mountainside. She would hike until almost dark, and hopefully be able to locate Walker the next day.

She couldn't stop the smile that spread across her face at the thought of seeing him again. Then the smile faded. What made her think Walker would be happy seeing her?

It's more likely he will angry about what I've done.

Fox Walker had tracked Logan all day through the deep valley, following a large stream fed by snowmelt, until the tracks veered straight up and across the face of the mountainside, staying just at the edge of the timberline, the snowcapped peak rising far above them.

He followed Logan's tracks up out of the timberline, surprised that the man left the cover of trees for open ground. He studied the landscape ahead. Didn't spot any way for someone to hide for an ambush, so he continued, limping to favor his injured knee.

The trail then rounded over to the backside of the mountain, where the vast wilderness waited. Walker figured Logan must have wanted to get above the tree line so he could get a clear perspective of his location and see his destination.

Walker crouched, then dropped to his belly and inched his way up to the edge of the summit. He peeked over, watching for any movement in the open space leading to the sparse tree cover below. Nothing moved except the tops of the trees in the wind. This was good news, considering his limp didn't make him the most agile person right then. He would have to cross quite a bit of open ground with few evergreens to use for cover before he could reach the timberline below. And he'd like to know Logan wouldn't use it as a shooting range opportunity.

He bet Logan's tracks entered the trees again just ahead. So far the fugitive had taken a close route to what Walker had guessed he would follow.

Walker started to push his body upright when something caught his eye and he lay back down. Across the valley and up on a high plateau directly in front of him, a thin line of smoke rose through the trees. He watched the telltale smoke trail as it became stronger … studied it … this wasn't from a campfire. Only smoke rising from a chimney would look like that. Which meant someone used a fireplace or woodstove. Which meant there was a building of some sort over there.

This was national park property. No residential houses allowed. Maybe an illegal hunter's cabin. Maybe Logan's? Could the man be holed up in a hideaway over there? That would make sense. Walker believed the man had a destination in mind as he traveled.

It gave Walker a target to keep in mind as he followed Logan's trail, and an idea of how many miles and hours away his destination might be.

All I need to do now is get close enough to confirm it is Logan out there and activate the GPS before Logan changes his mind about not killing me.

CHAPTER TWENTY-NINE

San Juan National Forest, Colorado

 ox Walker stirred awake from a dream … the wisps of memory floating away … a few vivid scenes remaining. Nataya had been there in the dream. There had been flames from a fire and she materialized from deep within the trees. Walked to him through the fire.

He sat up, for a moment expecting to see her. But only bird song greeted him. The bright orange of morning sun glowed up from behind the trees. *Damn.* He had slept far later than he wanted, but remembered that he had tracked until darkness took over. His body merely tried to recuperate its strength. He stretched and surveyed his position in the light of day.

He had camped at the base of a steep cliff and, although he couldn't visually see it, he knew the smoke he had spotted the day before had come from atop the ridge above. Even though he had followed Logan's trail for most of the way, Walker had picked out landmarks to use as guideposts and markers, to know when he neared his target. Toward dark, he had veered off from Logan's trail. He had to be getting near the area where he had seen the smoke. The last thing he wanted to do was follow Logan's trail up the incline, only to walk right into the man's line of sight, and the sight of a gun, for that matter. He had no choice but to make his way up the cliffside. It would keep him from being spotted from above.

The climb would be difficult and time consuming for anyone, but with his knee still injured, the challenge would be a tough one. Walker dreaded the hours ahead of him.

All the better reason to get started.

〰〰 〰〰

As relieved as Matt Logan had been to finally complete the first part of his quest, making it to the cabin, he realized that this waiting around for his meeting with Victor wasn't going to be easy. He and Victor had made plans that they would meet that day, but he wished they had set a specific time. He looked at the fishing line and thought of the nearby creek. But he didn't dare leave the area for fear of missing Victor.

So he busied himself with cleaning the gun, pumping water from the well and eating some of the dried food, ones that didn't need to be heated or cooked. As he worked, his thoughts turned to all that had transpired, and how he ended up there, hiding out from the law. He allowed the thoughts to flow through his mind, finally letting down his guard, letting the memories come forward. He relived the shock of his arrest, the nightmare trial, his desperation for escape. And Nicole. He hadn't allowed himself one moment of emotional release. Not one iota of grief to escape.

Flashes of the crime scene photos streaked through his mind. He felt the agony again of being made to look at photos of Nicole's tortured body, all the while being interrogated by the sheriff's department.

Logan jumped to his feet and kicked the cot frame in frustration. *How in blazes did I end up here?*

Hiding out from the law. Making plans for revenge. And no hope for a future?

He couldn't do this. Sitting and waiting meant he had too much time to think. He grabbed the shoulder holster and slipped it on, then picked up the Glock from the bedside table and slid it into the holster.

⊷⊷ ⊶⊶

Fox Walker felt the perspiration running down his face. He couldn't blame the weather. The sun felt good on his back, and a cool breeze wafted up the cliff's face. But the stress of the two-hour climb up the sheer rock wall, not to mention the pain in his knee, had taken its toll. His hands trembled with the tension of holding onto whatever shallow indentions or stony projections he could find. He stole a glance upward. Worked to keep his balance.

Almost there.

Walker focused every fiber of concentration left in his body for the last few feet of painful climbing. When at last he reached the ridge, he gratefully pulled his body up over the edge and crawled forward onto the level surface of the plateau. He let his body collapse and lay prone in the grass a moment to recoup his strength and let the throbbing of his knee subside a bit.

Once he could breathe easier, Walker pushed himself up to a low crouch, slowly putting weight on the injured leg, testing his knee. The pain was bearable, so he made his way through the jumble of weeds, shrubs, and trees in front of him, keeping hidden. It didn't take long to catch sight of a small cabin nestled in the woods.

Walker realized his advantage. That he had spotted the smoke earlier and knew someone was up there. And he had made the correct decision to scale the cliff wall to get up to this position. Otherwise he could've been spotted long ago.

He dropped to his belly and snaked his way closer to the cabin, hiding behind bushes and trees. As he angled in toward the back of the building, he had to wonder how he could get a look at the occupant without being caught, or shot. He heard a door open and close. He immediately rolled behind a shrub, stopped and waited.

Soon a tall man came into view as Walker peered between the branches of the bush. He calculated the guy to be over six feet, broad shoulders, fit and athletic. A weight that matched the footprints Walker had been tracking. Walker could see that he sported a military haircut as well. Everything fit the description he had been given of Matthew Logan. If only he could get a clear look at the man's face so he could compare it to the photo in the file the FBI shown him.

The man strode toward a pile of logs and Walker could see that he carried an axe.

As the man came closer, Walker could clearly identify him as Logan. His instincts had been right. He had his confirmation.

All he had to do was get back to his camp, notify the FBI and wait for them to show up. Of course, first he had to get out of there. For the moment, Walker had no choice but to wait and watch.

Logan picked up a log, sat it on a tree stump, then proceeded to wield the axe and split the log neatly in half with one swing. Walker studied the man as he worked. After few more swings of the axe it became clear to Walker that Logan was working out some type of frustration. His movements became jerky—harder— as if anger had seeped in, until they took on a frenzied action that bordered on dangerous.

Just when Walker feared that at any moment Logan's actions would result in serious injury, the man stopped, stood completely still for a few moments, breathing hard. Then Logan did something that took Walker by total surprise. Still standing in the same spot, the man lowered his head and Walker swore the big man's shoulders shook, as if he wept.

━━┼ ┼━━

Nataya stood still, listening to the sounds of nature around her. She had followed Walker and the hiker all the previous day along the stream in the valley. There weren't many clear footprints to study, only signs of passage in the ground cover. But she believed Walker to be injured. Even the few prints she found showed that he favored his right leg. It could be his ankle or knee, or worse, an open wound of some sort. She had been anxious to get to Walker before he could contact the FBI, but a new anxiety seeped in.

When the hiker's tracks suddenly veered up out of the tree line, Walker had followed as well, across the mountainside and up to a ridge. Nataya did the same. When she reached the summit, she could see where someone had lain on the ground, most likely to survey the land on the backside of this mountain.

She followed the sign, skittering across the open space until, with relief, she entered the safety of the trees again.

She had entered the vast wilderness that Walker felt the fugitive would flee to. A place to hide for as long as need be. It all made perfect sense to her—until Walker suddenly stopped following the hiker's tracks.

Nataya stopped, confused. Did this confirm that the hiker wasn't the fugitive?

She studied the footprints of both men again. The footprints were made many hours apart. The men had not met face to face. So what made Walker change his mind? Was it simply coincidence that Walker and the hiker had been taking the same path?

But it didn't matter. She had no option but to continue following Walker, and trust him yet again that he knew something she did not. Besides, he still limped. And Walker knew the healing plants better than she did. Why didn't he take the time to care for his injury? Why did he feel pressured to keep up this pursuit in his condition?

Nataya took up Walker's trail again and followed it as quickly as she could without missing sign. Within an hour his tracks led her to where he had made a campfire. It had been doused with dirt and sand, but by digging into the ashes, she found still-warm coals. The fire had been burned recently, most likely from the previous night, up until morning.

Walker's injury had definitely slowed his progress, which was probably why he kept pushing himself forward. Meanwhile, she closed in rapidly.

Nataya left the campsite behind and excitedly followed his path through the trees, noticing that Walker headed steadily toward the wall of the ravine. She soon found herself smack up against the base of a formidably steep cliff. Tracks proved Walker had taken this route.

She leaned back and stared upward. It would take hours to make it to the top. She checked the sun's position and shook her head. She'd risk getting caught up on the cliff face with the sun setting on the opposite side. Not a place she'd want to be in the dark.

Nataya had no choice but to wait out the night. She brushed away the disappointment of being so close to catching up with Walker, then having to set it aside for the night. But she wouldn't do him any good at the bottom of a cliff, splattered on the rocks.

She looked back at the woods behind her, remembering Walker's deserted campsite. Perfect. She'd make use of it that night and tackle the cliff after a good night's rest. Besides, she needed to hunt and replenish her food.

She made a quick note of the landmarks around her. She figured she could cover a two- to three-mile range, maybe less, depending on how quickly she found game. Then she'd head back toward Walker's old campsite and be there by dark.

CHAPTER THIRTY

San Juan National Forest, Colorado

Fox Walker slid his right hand down to the next protruding ledge, then placed his right foot cautiously, before fully committing his weight. Then started the entire process over again, only this time moving his left hand and foot. He had spent two hours working his way down the cliff's face. His right knee throbbed with the strain, and he tried not to stress it any more than possible. One misstep and he had a long fall before the ground would find him. He wouldn't be as lucky as the sink-hole tumble.

At least he wouldn't have to make that climb again. He had his visual of Logan that the FBI wanted. And it looked conclusive to Walker that Logan had made his destination and wouldn't be moving soon.

Walker decided to return to his camp of the previous night. The location sat far below the ridge from the cabin, and around a bend. Ideal for keeping his presence a secret from Logan. Even a small campfire wouldn't be spotted. It also would encourage the

FBI to enter the forest from the north to connect with Walker. That would keep them out of the valley below the cabin, where Logan could possibly spot them.

Walker gave a sigh of relief as he finished the last of his decent, planted his feet on solid ground again and entered the shelter of trees. He had just enough daylight left to get a shelter put together. And he could finally take the time to tend to his injury. He might as well be comfortable while he waited for the agents to show up.

As Walker made his way through the woods toward his camp, he began, out of habit, to gather the leaves of edible plants … purslane, lamb's-quarter, and dandelion … plucked and saved to eat later. And he picked the tender, just-poking-through-the-soil nettle tops. He would brew them into a tea to help ease the pain in his knee.

When Walker reached the camping spot, he laid the gathered leaves and plants on the ground next to the fire pit. As he straightened up, something about the charred remains of the fire made him look again. He squatted next to the blackened pieces of wood. Something, or someone, had dug around in the ashes and cold coals. He checked the ground for prints—human or animal—but found none. But the surrounding grasses had been disturbed. A curious bear could've made his way through. It would be consistent with the sign he found. He would make sure to keep a fire going all night to keep away larger animals, just in case. At least he knew it wasn't Logan.

Walker slipped the GPS from his belt. But as he stared at it, he had to admit he didn't feel quite right about this whole setup with the FBI. Maybe it came down to the way the FBI had drawn up the picture of Logan as a hardened, convicted killer.

Walker checked the sky. The sun would soon sink behind the mountains. No reason to go ahead and trigger it at the moment. His time would be better spent assembling a debris hut and gathering a supply of firewood to last the night. He'd have plenty of time to trigger the device after he lost the light.

Within minutes Walker had a small fire going, making sure the wispy smoke wouldn't be visible above the foliage overhead.

The sun sank behind the mountain and still Walker found chores to keep him busy, finding excuse after excuse to keep busy setting up his camp, instead of facing the decision that awaited him.

He placed a few small stones near the flames to get hot. He would soon transfer them to his homemade cup, where they would cause the water to heat and boil, and at the same time steep the tender nettle tops into a tea.

And still Walker found himself stalling the inevitable and wondering why. He picked up a long straight tree limb, thinking he could use it to craft a fishing spear.

Without warning, the memory of watching Nataya fishing this way came to mind.

She lifted her legs slowly, gracefully, stepping through the waters of the cold Colorado stream like the herons and egrets that fished the waters, her spear raised and poised like the beak of the birds, ready to strike.

Walker smiled at the memory. An ache of longing ran through his body. He missed her in more than just the physical sense, but still, there was that, too.

He had been alone most of his life, except for the mentoring he received from Grandfather, since he was eight years old. He still missed the old man.

But this was different.

To be honest with himself, he had to acknowledge that many times during this pursuit of the fugitive, he had wished he could talk to Nataya, show her what he saw, share how he read the sign and ask for her opinion. He loved teaching her. And she appeared to love learning. He didn't know anyone else, besides Grandfather, who could commune with nature on the same level he did. It bound them together as a couple, and as partners in work.

Thinking of going home to her made him remember the GPS device. He pulled it from his belt.

Why do I keep putting it off?

There wasn't anything else he could do, other than what he'd been hired to do. Trigger the lever and sit back and wait for the FBI to show up at his camp, so he could point them to Logan.

Then he could go home, to Nataya.

He fingered the lever, without triggering it. After all, who was he to question the FBI? They hired him to track and find this man. He'd done his job. It was time for him to get back to his own life. Leave this Logan guy to his own fate.

His thumb slid to the lever again, then stopped. Walker looked up and listened. The woods around him had become completely silent. Too silent, no crickets, nothing. Something, or someone, was nearby.

He slid his free hand to his knife, fingers encircling the handle, and slowly pulled it from the sheath. He looked away from the fire, tried to let his eyes adjust to the dark shadows of the surrounding trees. His body tensed for action.

"You won't need that."

The voice breaking the silence startled him—but not as much as whom it belonged to. He froze, watching the woods beyond the flames of the fire. Then she stepped through the trees and stopped, just as she had in his dream, except this time she appeared as a warrior princess, complete with a bow and quiver of arrows.

"Nataya."

She smiled, slid the bow and quiver to the ground and held out her arms to him.

Walker dropped the GPS and his knife, and limped to her. He didn't care why she was there, just happy to see her. He held her in a tight embrace, not saying a word. She clung to him for a long moment, then pulled away and looked down at his leg.

"You're injured."

"Don't worry, it will be fine. How did you find me?"

"Before I explain that, first I need to ask if you have let the FBI know of the fugitive's location?"

Walker glanced back at the device lying on the ground. "No, I was just getting ready to do that when I felt someone's presence and—"

Nataya released a huge sigh. "Good." She leaned down to pick up the bow and quiver, then turned to Walker. "Please, let's sit by the fire while I prepare this squirrel I've brought." She indicated the small animal hanging from her belt. "We have so much to talk about."

Walker stared in confusion, but followed her directions, picking up the GPS from the ground and returning it, for the moment, to his belt.

Nataya began cleaning the squirrel while Walker built a simple spit by setting up two Y-shaped sticks on either side of the hot coals of the fire. While they both worked, she relayed everything she had learned from McClure's phone call. Walker began to whittle a skewer from a straight stick as she told him how she had gotten updates from the FBI agent, so she could figure out Walker's location. He laughed out loud.

"You've been very clever."

Nataya smiled and handed him the dressed squirrel. "And hungry."

Walker skewered the carcass, turned it over the flames to sear the flesh, then propped it up over the fire to finish cooking. He turned his attention to Nataya. They sat together and stared into the flames for a long moment before he spoke.

"I'm glad you're here."

She leaned into his shoulder. "I was afraid you'd be angry."

"I should be. You put yourself in danger, still are. But, I'm grateful you could give me McClure's message. I've been having my own doubts about this entire situation." Walker explained about all the times that Logan had an opportunity to ambush him, or cause his death, but instead had spent the time misleading and delaying him. "If this man is the killer he's been portrayed, he wouldn't have left the guards alive, or me. Logan has deliberately chosen not to kill. I get the feeling he's indeed a man on a mission, but he's not willing to take collateral damage on this one."

Nataya stared into the dancing flames before quietly speaking. "McClure still has concerns. That's why even though he doesn't want you to turn Logan over to the FBI, he definitely didn't feel comfortable with you confronting the man. Even the timid possum will turn and viciously attack when cornered."

Walker turned the skewer to let the squirrel roast evenly then leaned back from the fire, thoughtful. "McClure hasn't been out here in the wilderness with Logan, like I have. I believe I know this man, now. He's no doubt a trained killer. But he's no murderer."

Nataya took a long look at Walker before she replied. "If that's the case, I've got a plan."

CHAPTER THIRTY-ONE

Seattle, Washington

Dean McClure poured another cup of coffee and stood looking out his office window to the Seattle city lights below. Rain again. But he didn't mind. Where else would he go?

He'd made his choice many years ago. His career over his marriage. It hadn't been a conscious decision, but once he understood himself better he doubted he could have ever changed the course of his life. McClure recalled, at the young age of nine, telling his Mom, "I think the most perfect job in the world would be to sit in a room, undisturbed for hours … just to think." He smiled at the memory. Being a profiler was who he was. It wouldn't have mattered who he worked for. And that's why, even after retirement from the FBI, he still worked as a consultant.

McClure turned. The only light in the room flowed from his desk lamp. It beckoned to him and he allowed it to pull him there. He sat down at the desk and stared at his notes, the many scribbled pieces of paper, and the faxed photos of Logan and Nicole. In a sense, that's what he needed to do. Profile the very agency he had worked for, for years.

None of the bits of data made any sense just yet. He needed to arrange them in some type of order. McClure picked up the photos of Logan and Nicole.

They knew each other. That had to be the key to this somehow, and not the way the jury thought. Someone had made it far too easy for the court to find a solution.

Dean stood up and carried the photos to The Wall. He used magnets to stick up the two photos on the whiteboard, Logan's on the left and Nicole's on the right. At the bottom and center he used a marker and drew a circle. In the middle he wrote *FBI*.

McClure took up a different colored marker and wrote between the two photos, *Logan and Nicole knew each other. Past lovers.*

Under Nicole's photo he wrote, *Left Bureau, married.*

Then he added under Logan's photo, *Escaped into National Forest.* From there he drew a line down and connected it to the FBI circle, adding, *Excuse for FBI to become involved. Why?*

Lastly, he penned *Logan's DNA on Nicole's body* under Logan's photo and stepped back from the board.

He leaned against his desk, crossed his arms over his chest and stared. Every puzzle made sense once he could put all the pieces together correctly, to make one cohesive picture. He just had to figure out all the parts before he could put them together.

McClure understood far too much about how the Bureau worked to dismiss the fact the FBI had suddenly taken an interest in this, stating to the media that it was "concern for public safety." There had to be a bigger motivator than that.

Logan knew Nicole.

They would think the same thing Dean did. That there had to be a tie-in somehow.

Logan's DNA was found on Nicole's body.
Only one explanation for that.
Logan and Nicole had seen each other that day.

He wrote it on the board between the two photos. Then thought about the implications. Past lovers. Maybe not so "past"? He drew a question mark under the word "past." But he couldn't fathom the FBI getting involved over an infidelity. Something else. Maybe something from Logan and Nicole's past? Dean ran his hand through his hair, staring at the board. One fact became apparent to McClure, and he wrote it between the two photos.

Logan may have been the last person to talk to Nicole before she was murdered.

Now that could very well be what got the FBI's interest. Why they wanted to track him down. He connected the FBI circle with this latest note.

The big question still remained, though. Why? Nicole had given up being an agent years ago, married and settled down, was raising a family. What might she know that the Bureau would be interested in?

In his mind, McClure ran through what he had read about her, a success story from what he remembered. Nicole had been living her dream, married to a well-to-do, fast-tracked, career-politician husband, raising a family, living in a beautiful home, a nice neighborhood.

Politician. That caught McClure's attention. Remembered seeing her husband's name on her information. He wrote *Jeff Conrad, politician* under Nicole's photo on the board, then shuffled through the papers on his desk, unable to find any additional notes on the man. McClure hated politics, tried to avoid it as much as possible. He certainly didn't keep track of politics in Colorado. He sat down at his desk and turned on his computer.

A quick search made McClure sit up straight in his chair. He had been expecting some small-time council member, but Jeff Conrad served in the Colorado State House of Representatives. Not such a small fish after all. Looked like he was being fast-tracked for bigger things, too. From what McClure read, Conrad had a remarkably pristine record for a politician. But what could anyone truly believe?

McClure pushed himself away from the desk, walked closer to the board. That could very well be it, though. Nicole had, after all, at one time been an agent. Her husband, deeply entrenched in politics. It would be all too easy for a former agent to fall back into old habits. What if she discovered some bit of intelligence, maybe something she wasn't supposed to know? He had to consider the flip side of that equation as well. That she could be helping her husband hide something. An illegal operation?

Something didn't feel right about that prospect. He read back through his notes on Nicole.

Nicole had deliberately made huge changes to her life. Left the Bureau, created the future she wanted. What might she be willing to do to preserve it?

McClure picked up the marker again and made a note under Nicole's photo.

What did she know? Is that the real reason she ended up dead?

He studied his markings on the board, the arrow starting at the FBI circle, asking *why they had involved themselves in finding Logan,* followed it to the fact that *Logan may have been the last person to talk to Nicole,* connected that arrow to his last note, asking *what did Nicole know?*

McClure had to believe that was key to why the Bureau would be involved. They needed to talk to Logan. They wanted to know if Nicole spoke to him before she was killed.

Maybe the Bureau suspected the same thing. That she ended up dead, not from a robbery-gone-bad, but because she knew something that got her killed.

Dean looked at Logan's photo. How did he get pulled into this? Did Nicole become frightened and turn to Logan for help? Why not her husband?

Dean walked across the room to pour himself a cup of coffee, thinking about the possibilities. He made his way back to The Wall, considered their past relationship. Perhaps Logan had helped her when she was in the Bureau … or … she had been hiding something from her husband. Perhaps she was frightened, confided in Logan, maybe asked for help. For whatever reason, the two of them met on that day. And it was a distinct possibility Logan was the last person she spoke to before she was murdered. What if Logan knew something about her murder. Something too dangerous to use for his own defense?

Which brought Dean back to *why did the FBI get involved?* Dean sat his coffee cup on the desk.

They want Logan. They believe Logan has knowledge they need.

But why didn't they attempt to talk to him earlier?

Or maybe he can point the finger to someone in the Bureau.

Dean's heart rate increased. What if someone in the Bureau let Logan take the fall, but once he had escaped, feared Logan would get to the right people and tell all? They needed to contain him. A new thought came to mind. One he liked even less.

Hell, maybe they didn't need him alive after all.

They could be using Walker to track Logan down, keeping him busy while they focused their energy and resources on a different game plan. Once they got the location from Walker and moved in, all kinds of accidents could happen.

CHAPTER THIRTY-TWO

San Juan National Forest, Colorado

*M*att Logan looked both ways down the hallway, making sure no one followed, then used the hotel key and entered the room quietly. He slipped off pieces of clothing as he walked toward the bed, a shoe here, a shoe there ... then the socks ... trousers. He unbuttoned his shirt as he stood beside the bed. She smiled up at him, raising her arms to welcome him.

He slid under the covers, pulling her into an embrace, his lips hungry for hers. She hugged him tighter, her lips pressing his with passion, her body moving against his. She pulled back to look into his eyes—and Logan screamed.

Nicole's tortured face and body lay bloody against his, her eyes open, staring into nothingness.

Logan sat up straight, breathing hard, sweat covering his body. *Where am I?*

The cabin's dark interior slowly came into focus as he forced himself to calm down. But had he actually screamed out loud?

He stood up, trying to shake the memory away. He glanced at the thin blind covering the window. Enough light behind it for morning, but no sun yet.

To dispel the dream from his mind, Logan dressed, thinking about the fact Victor hadn't shown the day before. He had no idea what it meant. Had the sheriff found Victor? Held him for questioning? He and Victor had made sure Sean had a solid alibi, but Victor didn't have one. The two of them had planned for Victor to keep a low profile. Stay out of sight, free to help Logan without others knowing.

Logan tried not to let the worrisome thoughts grow into panic. There could be a logical explanation.

He functioned best when he could lead the way, take charge and make things happen. This waiting around didn't work well for him. Never had.

He slipped the shoulder holster on and automatically ran a check on the Glock, then picked up the enamel coffee pot and sloshed it around. Almost empty. He would have to get some water before he could fix his morning coffee. And boy did he need coffee.

Logan walked to the window, pulled back the corner of the blind and peeked outside. An early morning fog still lay close to the ground, shrouding the trees in gray. But the stillness that prevailed soothed his taut nerves.

Logan opened the cabin door, started to step out—but came to an abrupt halt. His right hand dropped the coffee pot and automatically slid up to the gun, but then hesitated. The clang of the metal against the cement step reverberated in the quiet. He felt his jaw drop in stunned amazement, but grappled back his composure as he stared ahead at the apparition.

Under the branches of a large evergreen, and veiled in the swirling mist, sat a man and woman, cross-legged on the ground.

Another dream?

Logan blinked. They remained.

Where did they come from? The man was Native American and wore a buckskin shirt, his black hair hanging over his shoulders. The tracker? No, he had traveled alone.

The woman's skin was deeply tanned, but her hair was a sun-bleached blonde and lay in long braids. She wore moccasins, like the man, as well as a buckskin shirt. Although she didn't look Native American, her dress and attitude said otherwise.

Logan's brain scrambled to understand what he saw. Had he been transported back in time while he slept, waking in a different world? A place where people could just appear and sit there like that, waiting? *Eerie.* Neither of the people spoke, nor moved. Only watched him intently.

Logan stared as well, realized he had frozen in position, his left hand still on the doorknob, ready to slip back inside to safety, his right hand resting on the Glock. He should have caught these two long before they reached the cabin.

Seconds ticked away as Logan studied the man and woman, taking in the details of their clothes, their calm but intent expressions. Then he spotted something else. The man had a large hunting knife lying on the ground in front of him. In front of the woman lay a bow and quiver of arrows.

What the hell?

Okay, so they brought weapons with them, and were making a show of being unarmed. But Logan wasn't stupid enough to think they couldn't grab the weapons in a flash and attack him.

As he continued to stand there, considering his options, the man gave a simple hand gesture for him to come join them.

Logan surprised himself by letting go of the door and stepping forward. All his fighting instincts screamed against the move, and yet he sensed no fear. But he walked cautiously toward the couple, watching for any movement of betrayal. They watched him just as alertly.

When he reached the place where they waited, he sank to the ground and sat facing them. Logan glanced down at the weapons on the ground and moved his hand to the Glock, sensed the two tense, so he paused. He showed them that he was removing the gun with just his fingers, then laid it on the ground, as they had done with their weapons.

Logan's thoughts raced, trying to figure out why these people were there, why they had approached him, what did they want? He kept reminding himself that this act was real and dangerous and not just a dream he would wake up from. Yet it didn't feel real at all. He finally found his voice and spoke.

"What do you want?"

The man replied. "Only the truth. We come to you as friends, Matthew Logan."

"It seems you have the advantage. You already know my name."

The man gave a simple nod. "My name is Fox Walker." He then indicated the woman next to him, "And this is Nataya." The woman smiled, but remained silent.

Walker continued. "We don't mean to take advantage of you. This seemed the best way to reveal ourselves to you, without you feeling threatened."

Logan struggled to make sense of the situation, notions and theories bouncing out of control in his mind.

Reveal themselves. How long have they been watching me?

He finally managed to stutter out his question. "Why—why have you been watching me? And why do you think I would feel threatened?"

Walker spoke. "I was hired to track you, after you made your escape."

"You!" Logan grabbed for his gun as he rushed to get up. Found the point of Walker's knife already touching his throat. He held his kneeling position, staring into Walker's eyes, holding his breath.

Nataya leaned forward, putting her hand on Logan's shoulder. "We're not the enemy. But have no doubt. We will protect ourselves, if need be."

Logan sat down, still wary. Who were these people, and why would they think he would trust them? As if she read his mind, the woman called Nataya spoke.

"I know, we are asking you to trust complete strangers. But we are here because of your brother, Sean."

Logan's heart thumped hard against his ribs upon hearing his brother's name. "Is he okay? Nothing's happened to him, has it?"

"He's safe," Walker said as he also sat back, but still held his knife. "A man named Victor asked your brother to contact Dean McClure. And McClure is a friend of ours."

Relieved to hear that Sean was okay, Logan struggled to not look as confused as he felt. The more he heard, the more nothing made sense.

"So Victor knows someone named McClure, and that same man is your friend? Who is this guy?"

Walker gave him a look, as if he weighed what to say, then spoke. "McClure helped me save Nataya from a serial killer six months ago. We both consider him a friend."

Logan's initial surprise had worn off, his mind cleared, and he wanted some answers. "Let's start at the beginning, Walker. You were called in to track me. It's you I saw following my trail."

Walker nodded.

"I set traps for you, created false trails, but here you are."

Walker nodded again. "Only because you chose not to kill me."

Walker's answer took Logan by surprise.

He knows I am a trained killer. But not a murderer.

This man had vexed him for days and, yet, Logan had to respect him. And not just for the man's tracking skills, but for his insight. Maybe he could trust him.

Logan then looked at Nataya. "And then Sean contacted this Dean McClure guy, and McClure called you. Why?"

"McClure called trying to reach Walker, to hire him to find you. I told him about Walker already being in the forest, tracking you. McClure had an important message for Walker. I volunteered to find Walker and pass along the information."

"Information?"

"Yes. McClure wanted me to tell Walker not to turn you over to the authorities when he located you. To just watch you, for now. McClure wants to believe your brother, Sean, that you didn't murder that woman."

Logan looked at them both. "And what about you two? Do you believe I am innocent?"

Walker spoke first. "That's why we're here."

Could this all be a trick? Why would two total strangers put themselves in danger, supposedly to help him? He sat silent for a moment, processing all this new data. The man and woman shared in the silence. He had to find a way to test what they were telling him and bump it up against facts he knew. "One thing I still don't understand. Why Victor asked my brother to contact Dean McClure. What prompted that?"

Nataya answered. "Victor became concerned about the FBI questioning Sean, and McClure is—"

"What? The FBI talked to Sean?"

Nataya nodded. "Yes. Sean told Victor about the incident. Victor knows McClure, a retired FBI profiler. Victor had Sean relay his experience to McClure, in hopes the man could figure out why the FBI is involved."

The FBI involved? Logan tried to wrap his mind around it. He looked at Walker. "It wasn't the sheriff's department that hired you, was it?"

"No, the FBI called me in."

"Damnit." Logan picked up a smooth stone from the ground to throw in frustration, looked at the two people calmly staring at him, and instead began to roll it around in his hand as he thought. Okay. So if he did believe these people, where did that leave him?

The FBI?

It had to be because of Nicole's past with the Bureau. But that was years ago. He replayed their last conversation in his mind. She had been frightened, almost in panic. He had never seen her act that way. Logan looked up to see Walker and Nataya watching him, waiting. "I need some time to think. Maybe you both can come back here later this evening?"

Walker shook his head. "It would not be a good idea. I cannot come near this location again after today." He indicated the small device on his belt.

Logan stared at it in disbelief. "GPS?" Watched Walker affirm it with a nod. "Shit. They're tracking you?" He worked to suppress the beginning stages of panic, heard Walker reply.

"As long as I keep moving and don't trigger this switch they will think I'm still tracking you. Nataya and I will spend today setting up a new camp. We'll be down over the hill," he said, pointing toward his intended location. "Come see us when you are ready. But Logan—"

"Yeah?"

"Don't wait too long."

CHAPTER THIRTY-THREE

Seattle, Washington

Dean McClure ran his hand through his hair in frustration as he bent over his copy of the trial transcripts scattered across his desk. Everything looked hunky-dory on the surface, but something smelled rotten in between the lines.

He stacked the papers together, set them aside and stared out the office window. It was one of those rare, sunny, spring days that tugged at him to go outside. Earlier he had gone out for a short walk, to clear his mind, but this case intrigued him, and soon he found himself back inside reading through the transcripts again.

He opened his Contacts on his phone to Special Agent Wilson's number, one of his buddies at the Denver regional FBI office. Buddies or not, McClure had had to tread ever so carefully during his previous call, asking Wilson questions about a case he had no part in. McClure used the excuse that Sean Logan's family had contacted him, strictly as a friend, concerned about the FBI's interview with Sean and the question, "Did they need to hire an attorney?" Agent Wilson had promised to check it out for McClure.

McClure dialed the man's number, surprised when the agent answered.

"Morning, Wilson. I expected to get your voice mail."

"What can I say? I'm in a rare mood of feeling *sociable*." Wilson laughed. "What's up?"

"I know I haven't given you much time, but have you had a chance to check into that situation you and I discussed?"

"Oh, yeah. I did get you some intel, although it's not much. Interesting, though. When I checked with the satellite office in Durango, which covers the region where Logan escaped, they referred me back here, in Denver. Guess it makes sense, considering the Joint Terrorism Tactical Force is here, if they should need a chopper. Anyway, there is an open case on Logan's escape, but it's all hush-hush. I was able to find out that your boy, Sean Logan, isn't a suspect, although I believe they are keeping an eye on him. Hope that helps the cause."

"Sure does. Thanks, Wilson. I appreciate it. I can't blame the family for having concerns. It will be nice to give them some good news. They certainly haven't had any lately."

"Yeah. You're right. I also heard the Bureau hired that tracker guy you worked with, what was his name—"

"Walker."

"Yeah. That's the guy. There's some questioning among some of the agents as to why an outsider is involved, so I'm not sure what's up with that. But I know you two are friends. Just thought you might like to know."

"Yeah, thanks. Which brings up a question. You didn't happen to hear any tidbit about *why* the Bureau has decided to go after this Matthew Logan guy in the first place, have you?"

"Nope. Like I said, no one wants to be nice and share their toys in the sand box on this one. Sorry, man."

"No problem. This helps me take care of what the family wanted. Just curious, you know. Hard to not be involved in these cases anymore."

After a moment of silence Wilson answered. "Yeah. We miss your expertise in the Bureau, McClure. No one measures up to what you did. We hate it that you were forced to retire. Didn't make sense, if you ask me, but they never do."

McClure gave a bitter laugh. "Yep. They never do."

"You know, I was just thinking. Not sure if you would find this interesting or not, but when I did my nosing around on this case, I heard some rumors. And remember, that's all they are. Heard rumblings that the Bureau has been snooping around about Nicole Conrad's murder. Probably just because of Logan's trial and such, but you never know."

"Thanks, Wilson. I appreciate the tip. You take care and try to stay out of trouble."

"Yeah, just like you do."

McClure smiled and hung up the phone. He stared at the scribbled notes. The fact the Bureau was keeping this whole case so quiet told McClure more than Wilson might think.

It could only mean one thing. The FBI had a hidden agenda in the works. But why?

And what does Logan have to do with any of this?

CHAPTER THIRTY-FOUR

San Juan National Forest, Colorado

Nataya pulled the bowstring taut while she kept an eye on the quail. The woodland sounds and pungent scent of evergreens surrounding her faded into the background as she concentrated. She released her breath, relaxed and let loose the arrow. Watched it find its mark.

As she walked to the downed bird, she thanked the spirits for the catch, and she thanked the quail for giving up its life that she might have food. She added it to the other quail hanging from her belt. Then Nataya began searching through the tall grasses at the base of shrubs until she found the quail's nest, gathered a few of the eggs and put the rest in another nest for that hen to incubate.

The late afternoon sun peeked in and out of the clouds above, one moment lighting the trees with vibrancy, the next, deep shadow as she made her way back to where she knew Walker prepared their new camp.

She wove her way through the trees and stepped into a small clearing, just large enough for a shelter and fire. Walker looked up and smiled when he saw the birds she brought back.

"I believe you've grown more attached to that bow than I am. And maybe a better shot."

Nataya laughed. "I do enjoy hunting with it."

"When this is over, I'll make a bow that fits your size better, if you want. But for now, consider that one yours."

"Thank you. I'll take good care of it, I promise," Nataya said as her fingers caressed the wooden bow.

She sat down next to Walker and helped him feed twigs to the fire he had just started. They then added larger sticks and soon the campfire blazed brightly, sending off waves of warmth against the growing chill of late afternoon.

While Walker collected firewood for the night, Nataya located a large rock and moved it to gain access to the moist soil underneath. Using the wooden cup Walker had made, she added water from a nearby creek. She began to mix the water and soil, creating a large pit of mud. Then she began to clean the birds by removing the entrails, but left the feathers intact.

Walker returned, stacked logs next to the fire and sat down to help Nataya cover the quails with a thick layer of the sticky mud. They worked in silence, the sounds of nature the only backdrop. Once the birds were prepared, Walker scraped away dirt to form a pit next to the main fire and shoved in hot coals to create a place to cook the fowl. Nataya broke the quiet.

"Do you think Logan will trust us, or take this opportunity to run?"

"Not sure, but his options are pretty slim. He knows the FBI is tracking me, which means they can guess his general location." Walker leaned over, picked up the mud-covered birds and placed them on the hot coals, then added more coals on top. "He could take off and try to get a large distance between us, like he did before, but he knows now that I'm capable of finding him again."

"He took a big risk, trying to escape."

"Yeah, and I can't believe he escaped only to be out here being constantly hunted. Logan always has a game plan. That much I've learned about him."

"So you think he escaped in order to carry out some sort of strategy?"

"It's the only thing that makes sense to me."

"We need him to trust us, to tell us his plan, if we are to help him."

"Yeah, well that's going to be the challenge." Walker helped Nataya cover the quail eggs in the leftover mud. "Logan didn't become a SEAL team leader by just trusting anyone."

Nataya took the mud-covered eggs from Walker and gently laid them on the coals to cook, along with the birds. Once the mud cracked and she knew they were done, she would save them for breakfast.

The two of them cleaned up and relaxed by the fire, enjoying the solitude while they waited for the meat to fully cook.

The sun had almost set when Nataya decided the birds were close to being done. She used her knife to clean some roots she had saved for cooking.

Nataya looked up from her work to see Walker tense and hold his position while staring into the surrounding trees. She held still as well. Walker motioned for her to continue. Then he relaxed into his cross-legged position next to the fire. He pulled out his knife and began to whittle at a piece of wood. Nataya continued her task, but cast curious sidelong glances at Walker.

Then she sensed what had caused Walker's behavior. The birds nearby had ceased their chatter, insects silent. Something was close by, in the trees. She concentrated on the unnatural quiet, wishing she was as quick as Walker to pick it up.

It startled her when Walker called out, loud enough to be heard a good distance into the woods.

"Logan, come join us at our fire and share our food."

For several seconds, nothing happened. Then a quiet rustling in the brush, and Logan stepped out from the shadow of the forest into their camp. He wore the shoulder holster and gun, but carried a metal container by the handle. Nataya could tell by the way he held it that it contained something heavy. He said nothing, but stood there as if waiting for someone to speak.

Walker simply motioned for Logan to come join them and returned to his task, keeping his knife in his hand, working at the wood.

Logan's long-legged strides brought him to the campfire where he presented the metal container to Nataya. "Water. It's safe, from the underground well by the cabin."

Nataya smiled up at Logan, delighted. "Thank you." She took the pot and sat it on a hot, flat stone to heat. She knew exactly how to use the unexpected gift. They could have pine-needle tea with the meal.

Logan joined the two at the fire, sitting opposite Walker, keeping his eye on them both, yet trying to make his movements look casual and relaxed. It gave Nataya hope. He hadn't run. And at least he willingly exposed himself this way, to meet with them.

Now if we can gain his trust.

In the meantime, she noticed Walker never let the knife leave his hand, even though he made it appear that he merely whittled at the piece of wood. She knew how quickly he could turn it into a weapon.

The smell of the roasting birds made Nataya's mouth water, and she was sure both men felt the same way. She checked the large, cracked mounds of mud and nodded to Walker. Using two sticks as tongs, he slid the odd-looking objects onto the ground, Logan watching from his seated position.

Walker grabbed handfuls of leaves to protect his hands while he pulled open the mud balls. The birds' skin and feathers peeled away, stuck within the mud, and exposed the moist meat inside. While they waited a moment for the meat to cool, Nataya gathered some pine needles, crushed them a bit with a rock, then added them to steep in the boiling water.

The three of them positioned themselves around the cooked quail and joined in the feast together, pulling apart the pieces of meat, juices dripping off their fingers.

They ate in silence at first, enjoying the food and the crackling warmth of the fire. But when they had eaten enough to quell their initial hunger pangs, Logan thanked them for sharing their food with him. He complimented Nataya on how well it tasted, commenting that he had never tried cooking birds that way and wanted to know more about it.

When they finished eating, and all the bones were picked clean, Nataya heard Logan give a long sigh. She waited patiently, along with Walker, for Logan to speak. They wanted him to take the lead. They were there to listen to his story. But when he finally spoke, his question surprised Nataya.

"I need to know. What do you want from me?"

Walker gave Logan his full attention, his gaze never wavering. "The truth."

"The truth about what?"

"Why you are here in the wilderness. We need to understand your story, if we are to help you."

"And just why would the two of you decide to help me? Who's really calling the shots? The FBI did hire you, right?"

Walker nodded. "Yes, the FBI hired me to track you. Which I did. But what I do from here is determined by what you tell me, here, now."

Logan looked frustrated. "You talk in circles. I'll ask you again. Why would the two of you want to help me?"

Nataya spoke up. "It's partly because of McClure's phone call to me. He wants to believe Sean is correct. That you are innocent of the crime you were convicted of."

"*Wants* to believe. See, he's not even sure."

Walker spoke up. "True, but McClure has good instincts. If he has doubts about you being guilty, there must a valid reason behind it. The other part is because the man I tracked, and came to know in the wilderness, is not a murderer."

Logan looked long at Walker. "Thanks for that. You're right. I've killed a lot of men in my career, but I'm not a murderer. And I didn't kill Nicole."

In the moment of silence that followed, Nataya picked up the wooden cup. She quietly stood and walked over to the metal pot and scooped hot pine-needle tea from the container. She went to Logan first, knelt and offered it to him. When he looked at her, not sure, she drank from the cup, then handed it to him. "We are here to help you, Logan. No one has authority over our thoughts. We decide what we believe."

He took a sip, then took a longer drink before handing it back to Nataya. When she turned her back to Logan to hand it to Walker, she smiled. Logan had no idea that he participated in an important ceremony.

Walker took the cup, took a long drink, spoke. "This is our pact to you, Logan. That we will help you hide from the law until you can prove your innocence. We will help you, in any way we can, to complete your plan."

"Is that what you think this is all about? Just me trying to prove my innocence?"

When Walker didn't react, but only continued to watch Logan, the man jumped to his feet.

"This isn't about me. It's about honoring Nicole. It's about getting justice for her." Logan clenched his fists, arms tight with tensed muscles. "It's about tracking down Nicole's killer and giving that bastard my own form of justice."

"You're talking about killing someone for revenge," Walker said quietly.

"Damn straight that's what I'm talking about."

Walker waited a long moment, then spoke again, calmly. "But Logan. You are not a murderer."

Nataya watched Logan's demeanor gradually shift. He unclenched his fists, the muscles of his arms relaxed, and his shoulders slumped. He looked at the two of them, pain in his eyes.

"But you don't understand. I know who killed her. That bastard Selden threatened her. I must do something to avenge her death."

"Killing Selden for revenge will never bring you what you seek. But there are other ways," Walker said.

Nataya continued watching Logan, but had sunk deep into her own musings. What kind of man would go to these lengths to avenge a dead woman? Risk his own life. Be willing to kill for her? Only one answer came to mind.

He was still in love with Nicole, and there's a whole lot more to the story than Logan is telling.

CHAPTER THIRTY-FIVE

San Juan National Forest, Colorado

Nataya moved through the trees in stalking mode, mostly for practice, but partly so she wouldn't alert Logan she was near his cabin. No reason to startle him that early in the morning. After his visit to their camp, he appeared to trust them, but better to use caution for the time being.

She placed each step carefully, starting on the outside edge of the ball of her foot and rolling it inward, feeling for any obstruction that would make a noise and reveal her before she put all her weight into the step. She leaned forward as she moved, her knee raised high as she lifted her leg and braced her hands on her thighs. Walker had taught her how to use this technique to get close to game.

Nataya made her way to the large tree where she and Walker had previously sat, waiting to meet Logan. She lowered her body to the ground and made herself comfortable. She listened to the chickadee's morning song and relaxed into the moment, using the time for quiet contemplation, found her mind drifting to comforting memories.

She looked up at her grandfather and pointed to the plant. "This is milkweed." He nodded, his kind eyes watching her, and she grinned. "I know. That was too easy. How 'bout this one?" she said, indicating another plant, "it's lamb's-quarter." He smiled, waiting for her to continue. "Also known as wild spinach." She could tell he was proud of her. It made her want to do even better. She skipped to the next grouping of plants and studied the leaves. "Ooohh—jewelweed. I can use this to rub on my skin if I accidently touch poison ivy."

Nataya came out of her reverie reluctantly. Some of her favorite memories from childhood centered around her time with her grandfather, always teaching her about nature, prompting her to learn about the Native American cultures and encouraging her to do her artwork.

But he became her best friend when her parents were killed in an airplane crash, just as she entered junior high school. He made sure that she had the means to later attend college and earn a living. She missed him terribly, which helped her understand how much Walker missed *his* friend and mentor.

The door to the cabin opened and Logan stopped in the doorway, stared toward her and shook his head with a look of wonder. She stood up and walked toward him. "Walker asked that I come here in place of him, because of the GPS. He has an idea about how to deal with it."

"Yeah? How so?"

"He didn't tell me, just asked me to see if you have anything waterproof in the cabin, like a plastic bag or something similar."

Logan looked at her curiously. "Sure. Let's go in and look."

They emerged a few minutes later. Logan emptied a plastic bag of dried fruit into Nataya's hands and stuffed the bag into his pocket. She handed Logan some of the pieces, and they both ate as they walked away from the cabin.

"Nataya. That's a name I've never heard before. Is it Native American?" Logan asked.

"It's Shoshone. It means 'dance the woman's dance.' "

"Nice."

The two of them continued to walk through the trees, in silence, while Nataya desperately tried to figure out a way to bring up the topic she wanted to discuss. In her mind she replayed the conversation she'd practiced, lying awake most of the night. She wanted to get it right. Get Logan to open up to her. She summoned her courage and dove in.

"I think it's very brave of you to want to avenge Nicole's death."

"It's not about bravery. It's about honor."

"I don't understand."

Logan glanced sideways at her. Nataya sensed him gauge her trustworthiness before he continued.

"Nicole came to me, frightened, afraid for her life. She asked for my help and I failed her. I owe it to her to find her killer."

"I see. So what made her so afraid?"

Logan remained quiet for a few steps, then spoke again. "Nicole heard something about a man named John Selden. An important man, in the fact that he is extremely wealthy. And he has used his wealth and political donations to become powerful. Something about what she heard reminded her of an old case she had worked on while at the Bureau."

"So she started investigating it again?"

"Yes, but only because Selden had recently befriended her husband. If this guy had a questionable past, she didn't want it to reflect badly on her husband, or his political career."

"But Selden found out she was digging into his past?"

"He must have, because he threatened her. She came to me, frightened. Then later that same evening they found her dead."

"So, you're convinced Selden killed her, to make sure she didn't talk."

"Exactly. I think she might have had evidence that could ruin him."

"Didn't Nicole have notes or something you could use against him?"

"He made it look like a home robbery had taken place, but I'm sure it was only a cover so he could look for whatever evidence she might have had. They must have found what they wanted on the laptops they took, because when the house was searched by the sheriff's department, nothing was found."

Nataya leapt over a small fallen tree and turned to wait for Logan. "So that's why you couldn't bring all this up during the trial. You had nothing to support it."

Logan nodded.

"But it seems there had to be a way to defend yourself against the murder accusation."

"You forget. I was with her that day. I'm sure Selden has figured out she talked to me. He can make sure I don't live long, inside or outside prison. I could only hope that when I didn't reveal anything in court he'd assume I didn't have any evidence. Besides, like I said before, this is about Nicole. It's not about me. It was better it went down the way it did."

Nataya remained quiet, thinking about this as they walked the last few yards to the campsite. Something didn't feel quite right.

There's more to this than what he's willing to reveal to me.

Walker looked up as Nataya and Logan stepped through the trees into the campsite. Nataya looked thoughtful, making him wonder what they might have discussed on the way to the campsite.

"Good morning," Walker said.

Logan gave him a smile and nod, while Nataya walked over to where she had stored the mud-cooked eggs. She gathered one for each of them.

Then Walker noticed Logan had pulled a plastic bag from his pocket, which brought his focus back to the reason for the meeting.

Logan handed Walker the plastic bag. "Is this what you need?"

"Yes. It's perfect. This saves us time."

"What's this all about anyway?"

Walker held up the GPS device. "It's about this. I've been trying to figure out what to do about it, and I think I've got a plan."

"Care to share it?"

"That's why I asked you here. Yesterday, and today, I've left camp during the day and gone out into the forest, then back to the camp at night. I'm attempting to make it look as if I've lost your trail. That I'm going out in a different direction each day, hoping to find your tracks again. I've been stalling for time until I could find a solution to this GPS situation."

"And you have?"

"Yeah. During my ranging through the woods today, I found a deep and fast moving snowmelt stream that heads down this mountainside, into the valley far below."

Logan looked at the plastic bag in Walker's hand and got a slow smile. "I think I know what you're thinking. We can keep the GPS moving for the FBI to track. But it'll be going the opposite direction from here."

"Exactly."

"Excellent plan, Walker. You'd make a great SEAL."

Walker grinned.

The three of them sat down as Nataya handed them the eggs, showing Logan how to peel back the mud with the shell adhered to it, leaving only cooked egg inside.

Walker spoke as they ate. "I believe we should deploy the GPS device today, and figure out a plan of action from there."

"Sounds like it's out of the question for Victor to meet with me now." He looked to Walker. "And I gather we won't be staying near here?"

"I was hoping you would agree on that point," said Walker.

Logan nodded. "I do. Once we deploy the GPS, I think we need to move as far away from this location as possible."

"Good. In the meantime, Nataya is going to return, contact Dean and give him an update."

Logan looked to Nataya. "What about being our liaison for future updates?"

Walker tensed, saw Nataya glance at him. They had argued about this the night before. He wasn't excited about her becoming a part of the scheme, but she had already made it clear to him she wanted to do it. And, in the end, he had to agree that it made the most sense. He let her answer Logan.

"Walker and I agree."

Walker nodded to Nataya, and she pulled out the topo map and laid it out the ground.

The three of them gathered around so they could study the map. Walker pointed out their current location. "Here's the stream I'm talking about. See how far it flows down into the valley floor? That should keep the GPS moving long enough for us to travel farther into the forest." Walker jabbed his finger at the map. "Here, on the opposite side of the mountain."

"Looks good, Walker. So where and when do we set up our next contact point with Nataya?"

Nataya spoke up. "I'll need two days to hike out of the forest, get back to the truck and drive to the cabin. Give me another day to call Dean and get any updates from him."

"I think we'll need you to stay close to the phone for a few days," Logan said. "Give McClure a chance to contact Victor or

Sean before you come back out here. You'll be our eyes and ears, and it's vital we know what is going on out there."

Walker acknowledged his relief to hear Logan's suggestion. The more time Nataya spent at the cabin, safe, the better he felt about the whole deal. He nodded in agreement. "Besides, we'll need that much time to get as far from here as possible."

Logan added, "Yes, I'd like to insert ourselves deep into the wilderness, until we can learn more about why the FBI is involved, and figure how to proceed from there."

Nataya studied the map, then looked at Walker. "Where do you think you'll be in about five days?"

Walker indicated a spot on the map. "We will follow that stream for navigation and to be near fresh water."

Nataya looked hard at it. "Do you think you could move into this nearby section of the forest at about the seven-day mark, just long enough for us to meet?"

Walker examined the terrain on the topo map. "Yeah, we should be able to do that. Puts us a little closer to civilization than I would like, but there are a lot of ravines there. Should make for good hiding places and shelter."

"Good," Nataya said, pointing again to the map. "Because right here the road runs along the edge of the forest for a mile or so, and there's a small community where I should be able to find a place to safely leave the truck. From there I can hike into your lo-cation. Should take no more than two days." She looked at Walker and Logan. "That's it then. We'll meet up again in a week." Nataya folded up the map, stood and returned it to her pocket.

Both men stood as she did, Walker suddenly realizing how much he would miss having Nataya with him in the woods. He had grown used to her company again, still thought about their love-making beneath the stars.

He opened his arms to her, kissed and hugged her, hoping she could sense the enormity of his love through his embrace. When she pulled away, she reached up and touched his cheek with her fingertips, then turned and walked away, looking every bit the warrior princess … with her deerskin shirt and high moccasin boots, the bow and quiver over her shoulder.

Walker turned to Logan and saw that the man had lowered his gaze, giving them a moment of privacy. Walker took a deep breath, then spoke, determination in his voice. "Okay, Logan, now we get to see how much you know about evading the enemy, and how much I know about surviving in the wilderness."

Logan gave him a nod.

The sun sat just at noon when Logan and Walker reached the stream, its waters running deep and robust. Walker stood at the shoreline and watched the current for a moment, waiting until a large piece of wood floated by before picking up the pace and following it for a couple of yards downstream. Then he returned to where Logan waited. "Perfect. We can weight the package so the pace will look as if I'm walking alongside the stream."

"What about rapids and small waterfalls? It's going to collide with large boulders and logs along the way."

"Yeah, we'll have to put padding around it to protect it. Let's gather some of this moss."

Both men pulled up sheets of the moist, cushiony plants. Then Walker picked up a handful of mountain maple leaves, wrapped them around the GPS device to protect it from the moistness of the moss, then added the thick layer of protection. Logan held open the plastic bag while Walker slid the mass inside. Then he sealed the top-locking strips together until only about two inches remained open. He blew air into the small opening, causing the bag to puff up like a balloon, then quickly sealed it. He handed the package to Walker to inspect.

"Looks good," Walker said as he hefted it in his hand. "Let's test it in the water. Go downstream and I'll release it. We can see if the weight allows it to float at the speed I want."

Logan sprinted downstream a couple yards and crouched down at the shoreline, waiting. Walker placed the package in the water, released it and watched as it bobbed toward Logan. Walker followed alongside on shore until it reached where Logan waited, who grabbed it as it passed by.

Logan stood up holding the wet package. "That pace work for you?"

"Yeah. Perfect. Let's do this."

Logan walked over to where some large rocks protruded above the waterline. He stepped from stone to stone until he reached the middle of the stream, then squatted and released the package. Both men watched it float downstream. "So, Walker, how long before they figure out they've been duped? What'd you think?"

"I've been trying to calculate that. When night falls and it's still moving I hope they believe I've found your trail again, and I'm anxious to catch up. I tracked at night one other time, so it shouldn't alert them to anything suspicious at first. If we're lucky, about evening time tomorrow, it will have made it down the steepest grades and dumped into a pool at the base of the mountain. There we can hope it floats slowly around a bit before it finds its way to a narrow creek that flows across the valley floor. That's two full days."

"Only two days?"

"Well, I figure that once it makes it into that shallow creek, it's going to probably get hung up on something, just a matter of time. Once it stops moving, they'll still be waiting for me to trigger the switch, to lock in your location. Might give us a third day before they become alarmed and take action."

"What kind of action?"

"I have no idea. Maybe they come looking. I have to say this is a first for me."

Logan surprised Walker with a chuckle. "Yeah, this isn't like any of my typical missions, either. Maybe that's good. It doesn't fit any previous scenarios for them to draw from, even if the Bureau calls in a SEAL to help them plan strategies."

Walker hadn't thought about that possibility.

Just what we need. As if FBI agents won't be enough to deal with.

CHAPTER THIRTY-SIX

Suburb of Denver, Colorado

Victor tried to shift his body into a more comfortable position in the driver's seat and gave a heavy sigh. Damnit. He hated stakeouts. They sounded glamorous to everyone except the people who were actually forced to endure the grueling, mind-numbing hours of painful boredom.

But he didn't have much choice. He couldn't go near the cabin for fear of leading law enforcement to Logan. And that's where Logan had planned to show him the rest of his strategy, and what Victor's role would be, moving forward.

So, he did the only thing he knew to do. Continue with his surveillance on John Selden, as Logan had originally requested. Logan wanted to know Selden's daily routine, where he frequented, who he saw, were there any set schedules for certain activities. Victor was to look for reoccurring habits and patterns of behavior.

He hadn't been told why, or how they were going to use the intel once he had it. But he had to face the fact that Logan's request contained all the earmarks of the type of gathering someone would use to set up a hit. Not that it mattered. He trusted Logan, with his life.

Victor slid down in his seat, peering through the steering wheel as he saw Selden walk out of his office. A distinguished-looking man, impeccably dressed, and as always, sporting two bodyguards. They went with him whenever he made a public appearance, which had made Victor curious. Selden dealt primarily in commercial real estate, so just why did he feel the need for protection? Obviously Logan knew something about this guy that Victor didn't and had good reason for wanting the observation.

Victor watched and waited until the car carrying Selden pulled away from the curb before he started his own vehicle and entered traffic, following at a distance. He varied the length between the two cars and changed lanes often, flowing with the traffic.

If Selden followed his weekly routine, they would be heading for the golf course, which, he admitted, wouldn't be so bad. The day had turned balmy with pleasantly warm spring breezes, and Victor didn't mind taking advantage of it by hanging out near the grounds of the country club. It would certainly beat sitting in his car outside Selden's office. Selden spent most of his time there, hence, so did Victor. But at least during all those long hours, Victor had been quick to notice Selden's group of tight-lipped, unquestioning lackeys scurrying in and out of the building on a regular basis, obviously carrying out orders from Selden. Absent were the smiles and cordial handshakes Victor had witnessed in social settings. It appeared that Selden's private life carried a vastly different tone than his public one.

The driver for Selden's car pulled into the country club entrance while Victor drove past, made a U-turn and pulled off the side of the road, under some trees, to wait. He turned off the engine and rolled down the windows to let the fresh air flow in.

The quiet and peacefulness of the surrounding grounds made him wish all the more he could be out there in the forest with Logan, and he wondered how his buddy might be faring at that moment.

Waiting around to hear back from McClure and Sean made him itchy to take matters into his own hands. But he knew they spoke the truth. He couldn't go anywhere near Logan.

Instead, he thought about what he could report to Logan when the time came. Without ever meeting Selden face to face, Victor still felt he had a pretty good handle on the guy.

Selden's demeanor to the outside world displayed a solid wall of self-confidence, bordering on arrogance. The public image he fostered centered on attending various social and political circles, moving with ease among the people. He appeared to know a wide variety of "movers and shakers," and they seemed to know him as well.

So why the bodyguards and close-knit group of ass-wiping worker bees who constantly buzzed around him?

It told Victor the man had secrets, had surrounded himself with a tight circle of *associates* whom he trusted, people who would follow his orders without hesitation.

Victor knew Logan expected him to form an impression of Selden based not only on facts, but also perception and reading between the lines. And Vic wouldn't be afraid to give Logan exactly what he thought about John Selden. That the man was a full-on, grade-A, piece-of-shit, sleaze bag. A man up to his elbows in no good, and probably had a valid reason to fear for his life.

Beyond that, Victor had no proof for the gut reaction he couldn't get rid of.

That the man is far more dangerous than he appears to the outside world.

CHAPTER THIRTY-SEVEN

San Juan National Forest, Colorado

Fox Walker and Matt Logan hiked through the forest, neither speaking, the only sounds their footfalls in the ground cover, and birdcalls high above them in the wind rustled treetops. Walker struggled to keep up with Logan's long strides. He never traveled through the terrain at such a fast pace, occasionally crashing through the underbrush, making a noisy passage. It felt unnatural. But Walker understood the need to make as much progress as possible in the next few days, so he said nothing. It would only be a matter of days before something caused the GPS to stop its movement. Then, who knew what would happen? What might the FBI do?

The Bureau could very well decide to drop in agents to search for Walker. Agents would find the device and know instantly it had been deployed as a decoy. Following the stream back to its source would put them close enough to the cabin to make its discovery a possibility. Logan and Walker knew they had to plan for the worst-case scenario.

Once they released the GPS into the stream, they had returned one last time to the cabin. Logan gathered all the packages of dried food and non-perishables that he could fit into his pack. They would need energy to move forward rapidly and wouldn't want to take the time to forage for food.

Then they had made the cabin appear untouched, as if it still waited for the owner to appear.

They hid Walker's campsite as well, and brushed away footprints from both locations. They wouldn't have time to hide their prints once they got moving, but they could certainly make it near impossible for anyone to find the beginning of their trail.

Ahead, Walker saw Logan break into a sudden sprint to gain enough momentum to make the leap over a small stream, then he stood on the other side of the bank waiting for Walker to catch up. Walker made the jump and joined him. Logan pulled out a compass from the backpack and studied it.

"Looks like we could head up over this ridge to save some time."

Walker looked back at where they had come from, then the lands before them.

"If we stay in this valley and follow the creek here, we'll soon find the main stream that feeds it. Like I told Nataya, that stream will eventually lead us to the section of forest she indicated as our next meeting place. It's a longer way, but it is easier and keeps us near fresh water."

"Sounds good to me," Logan said, slipping the compass into the backpack. He started to move when Walker grabbed his arm, making Logan freeze in his position.

"It's okay, just a deer," Walker said as the young doe came into view, making her way to the edge of the creek to drink. Walker saw Logan's hand ease toward his gun. "No."

"Why not?" Logan whispered.

"We don't have time to clean a deer and properly prepare all the meat so it doesn't spoil."

"So what? We need some fresh meat."

"We'll have meat, without the waste. Just enjoy the beauty of her." Walker still held Logan's arm and could feel the man's tension, but Logan stayed still and watched the scene play out in front of them. Walker took in every detail, the sound of the creek water tumbling over the rocks, the speckles of sunlight filtering through the trees. After a few minutes he could tell Logan's breathing had slowed, relaxing into the moment.

The doe drank her fill, then made her way across the water, bounded onto the shore and into the bordering trees, breaking the spell.

Walker began to follow the creek, peering into the water for fish or frogs. Logan slowed his pace to walk next to him.

"You're really into this 'being one with nature' shit, aren't you?"

Walker took a few more steps before answering. "If you mean that I respect all life, then yes."

"But you hunt and kill animals, I'm sure."

"Yes, I do. But only for true survival, and never for sport. I am grateful for what nature provides, and I thank the animal or plant for giving up its spirit so that I may live. That's why I won't kill an animal if I can't use every part of it. Nothing must go to waste." Walker expected to hear Logan laugh at him, but instead the man grew silent.

When Logan spoke again, his words were thoughtful. "When I learned how to survive in the wilderness, it was just another 'test' that I had to complete. Another skill that made me stronger and better than my enemies. I never learned to appreciate nature. In fact, I thought I was badass enough to fight against it. Beat it. But then on one training mission I got caught in a blizzard, in the mountains. I almost died. Even with all my skills and big, bad attitude, Mother Nature laughed in my face and showed me how puny I was against her."

Walker chuckled. "You didn't respect her. She was teaching you a lesson."

"Yeah, well, unfortunately as soon as I was safe again, I forgot about it."

"It is not too late to learn."

Logan glanced sideways at Walker. "So how were you able to track me? It seemed almost superhuman how you could follow my trail."

Walker smiled. "No special powers. Grandfather taught me from the age of eight years old how to track. First the mice and voles in the grasses, even birds in the snow, then larger animals. It's more than just following prints. It's about 'knowing' the creature you're tracking. That's how a tracker can know that an animal or bird will be in a certain place at a certain time."

"Are you saying you 'know' me? That's how you tracked me?"

"Partly. When you had the opportunity to ambush me, you chose not to. That told me something about you. When you had the opportunity to set a lethal trap for me, you chose a nonlethal trap. That told me more about you."

"It showed you my weakness."

"No. Just the opposite. You showed great character, strength, and courage."

Logan stopped walking and turned to Walker. "How so?"

"A weak man, without character, would have taken the easiest path. He would have waited in an ambush, killed me and went on his way—without thought as to what he had done—except save his own hide."

"I never thought about it that way." Logan turned and began walking again. "All I know is I killed as my job, and was damn good at it. Ruthless even. That's what I was trained to do. But, this ... this was different."

Walker nodded in understanding, then both men picked up their pace again, hiking through the valley as quickly as the terrain allowed.

The sun sat close to the mountaintops and spread its colors across the sky like a child's finger painting when, up ahead of Walker, Logan startled a dusky grouse from its hiding place under a conifer. It ran across the ground, but before it could lift off into the air, fell suddenly. A small knife protruded from its side.

Logan spun around to look at Walker, surprise on his face.

Walker calmly went to the bird, paused a moment over it, then removed the knife. He wiped it clean, replaced it in his ankle sheath and picked up his catch. "Now is the time for meat, with no waste."

The two of them set up a quick camp before darkness settled, picking a spot under the dense foliage so that smoke from a small fire wouldn't be noticed from a distance.

Walker pulled out the large sheath knife at his waist and began cleaning the grouse. "I'll show you first-hand how Nataya prepared the quail with the mud. I can use the same method for this larger bird."

Logan started putting together wood for a fire. He glanced sideways at Walker. "That knife is unique. Looks handmade."

"Yes, Grandfather created the handle from a deer antler, from my first kill. It was an initiation of sorts."

"Your Grandfather has taught you many things, it seems. Does he still?"

Walker shook his head. "No, he passed on a year ago. But the lessons he gave me will stay with me my entire life."

"Is he the one who taught you how to throw that knife?"

Walker nodded.

"Well, you're damn handy with it. I have to ask, have you ever had to kill a man?'

Walker hesitated, then continued with his task as he spoke. "Once, but not with my knife. I was forced to shoot a man, to save Nataya from certain death. But that didn't make it any easier."

Walker removed the entrails from the carcass, began to coat the bird in mud for cooking. "The hardest one was the time I didn't kill the man."

"What do you mean?"

"I was a young buck. I fell in love with a beautiful woman on our reservation, long hair, black like the raven, a smile that took my heart." Walker smiled a bittersweet smile at the memory, then it faded. "Alcoholism was especially bad on the res back then. One night when I arrived at her place, I walked in on a man beating her. He was drunk out of his mind. A blind rage took over my being. All I wanted to do was pound the life out of that man. Grandfather stopped me. Made me quit before I killed him."

Logan laid a log on the fire. "Did the woman live?"

"No. She died moments later, in my arms."

"And after all these years, you wish you would've killed the bastard?"

Walker continued working a moment before answering. "Yes, I do." Walker looked up from his work, stared hard at Logan. "But Grandfather was right. It would've made me no better than the drunk who killed Haiwi."

Logan lay back, his feet toward the fire, his hands behind his head, watching the flames twist and twirl in the darkness. He looked over at the sleeping form of Walker, his hand on his knife.

If he actually does sleep.

The man was hard to read, and his story about a lost love had surprised Logan, but gave him comfort that he wasn't alone in his pain.

Does he guess at my true relationship with Nicole?

One thing was for sure. Walker had once again made his point about why Logan shouldn't kill the man who murdered Nicole.

Intellectually he knew Walker was right, but that didn't change what in his heart he longed to do. What he still planned to do.

Besides, he knew something Walker didn't understand. It didn't matter if Selden had evidence of what Logan knew or didn't know. Selden would never let him live. The risk was too great.

CHAPTER THIRTY-EIGHT

Seattle, Washington

D ean McClure stepped outside and strolled down the sidewalk, heading toward the wharf. The Seattle skies were clear and blue, the slight breeze pleasant, something residents knew to take advantage of. Besides, he needed some time and space to think.

Nataya had called him that morning, and although the information she passed along was helpful, it left him with more questions than answers. The fact that Walker trusted Logan did give him some comfort that his own instincts were valid. But since Walker had played the GPS card, McClure felt the pressure increase. Time would run out for Logan eventually. He needed to find answers to this if he still hoped to help clear Logan's name.

The most interesting bit of data, though, came from the fact that Nicole had been the one to contact Logan the day she died, said she had been threatened by a man named John Selden. That she was frightened.

That's saying a lot for a woman who spent years as an FBI agent.

After Nataya's phone call, McClure had looked up the guy. Looked like Selden was a big-time player in Colorado. Made his money in real estate. Used it to hold some clout in the political world, enough to attract politicians hoping for donations and notoriety in their careers. So why had Selden taken an interest in Nicole's husband's career? Maybe he looked at Conrad as a politician to keep in his pocket in the future.

McClure needed to talk to Jeff Conrad in person, find out how Selden recently became buddy-buddy with him. Which sounded easier than it would be. He wasn't sure how he could pull this one off, when he had no jurisdiction in the case.

McClure walked across the street to the Pike Place Market and meandered his way past the shops, barely noticing them as he contemplated the facts. The one point he kept coming back to, over and over, that the house had been tossed, like a robbery, even though Nicole hadn't been killed there.

The prosecutor had convinced the jury that Logan had confronted Nicole, forced her to leave with him. Then when things didn't go his way, he killed her in a fit of rage and dumped her in the park. Then he went back to the house to make it look like a robbery, as if Nicole walked in on it and was kidnapped as a hostage for a getaway, then disposed of. Sounded elaborate, but the jury had bought it.

Knowing about Nicole's investigation, he re-thought the scene. The man who threatened Nicole needed to silence her without causing suspicion as to why. So he made it look like a robbery gone wrong, even stealing a couple of laptops, some jewelry and a piece of art, all to throw the law off his trail. It had been pure luck for the guy that Logan's DNA showed up on Nicole's body and sent suspicions Logan's way.

McClure stepped off the sidewalk to the nearest wooden pier jutting into Elliott Bay and followed it to the end. There he gazed out over the waves, the wind riffling through his gray hair, the fresh air invigorating.

Wait a minute. The laptops.

McClure gripped the pier railing.

This is important.

Of course. The staged robbery. Whoever did it could have been covering the fact they were searching for something.

Nicole's notes.

McClure paced back and forth on the pier, not caring who watched. He needed to sort this out. Before Nicole was killed, she had already been threatened. She would've been paranoid that this guy might try to find her notes. She wouldn't have left anything on her computer. She would have physically hidden whatever she had on this guy, somewhere, and not any place easily found. The sheriff's department didn't find anything, but they would've been looking for a murder weapon, not documents.

It could be possible that her notes were still there, waiting to be discovered.

More than ever he had reason to meet Conrad, talk to him face to face. He needed to somehow convince Conrad that Nicole might have hidden something of importance, somewhere in the home.

But how do I involve Conrad in this without making him a target as well?

CHAPTER THIRTY-NINE

San Juan National Forest, Colorado

The morning sun danced across the ripples of water as the shallow creek meandered its way across the valley floor. If it possessed memory it would recall the robust current and powerful eddies from high above, as the ice-cold snowmelt cascaded its way down the mountainside, calming, finally, to this serene pace through the trees.

It paid no attention to the foreign object that bobbed contentedly along on the surface, a servant to the whims of the ebb and flow as it coursed over and around the rocks, exposed tree roots, and water-loving plants. Until, at last, a fallen tree limb lay across the shallow depth and trapped the package against the water-soaked bark. And there it stayed, resting finally from its journey down the mountainside.

The GPS signal would continue though, steadily sending out its location.

CHAPTER FORTY

Boulder, Colorado

Dean McClure walked along the sidewalk enjoying the warmth of the sun on his back. He could never get over the intensity of the sunshine in Colorado, but then, comparing it to the Seattle weather didn't seem fair. He found the house number he needed and entered the lot.

He knocked on the front door of the house, not looking forward to the conversation about to take place. He looked around the neighborhood while he waited. Nice, upscale, with kids playing outside. The yards were all neatly manicured. The door cracked open and McClure had to look down to see the curly blonde head of a little girl looking up at him with wide blue eyes.

"Are you the man who is coming to talk to my daddy?"

"Yes, I am. And what is your name?"

"I'm not supposed to tell strangers. And I don't know you."

McClure smiled. "That's okay. We can let your daddy tell me your name. Would that be better?"

Curls bounced around the girl's head in agreement. Then a man walked up behind her.

"Here's my daddy now. Daddy, can you tell the man my name?"

The man leaned down and picked up the little girl. His neatly trimmed dark hair showed a sprinkling of gray at the temples, his face clean-shaven. *Typical politician.* The man looked hard at Dean before speaking.

"I presume you are Dean McClure?"

"That's right," McClure said, holding out his hand. The man hesitated, then disengaged one hand from holding the girl and tentatively shook McClure's.

"Jeff ... Jeff Conrad."

"Daddy, tell him my name," the girl said.

The man looked at McClure again. "This is Charlene."

"Nice to meet you, Charlene. You are a very pretty young lady."

The little girl smiled, then wiggled from her father's arms. He let her down to run off with an older boy who came running through the house. Her brother, McClure figured, since they both had that curly blonde hair.

"I still don't want to talk with you, Mr. McClure. But I had you checked out and my ... friend gave you a thumbs-up. Said I should hear what you have to say. And since you've gone to the trouble to travel all the way here, I'll give you the time you've requested, but I'm not thrilled about it."

"I understand, Mr. Conrad, and I do appreciate your cooperation."

The man led McClure through the living room and into the dining room. The house was neat, clean, and tastefully decorated. A house used for formal entertaining, but still a home.

Conrad offered him a seat at the table, showing him this was not a social call. It was business. Then he disappeared into the kitchen and brought them each a cup of coffee. McClure thanked him. The simple act told McClure a lot about this man. That even though Conrad didn't want to do this, he was also too well mannered to be rude.

Conrad sat down on the opposite side of the table, wrapping his hands around the coffee cup as if for warmth and comfort. McClure studied the man. The lines of fatigue and worry were etched into an otherwise handsome face. McClure could read the anguish that lay beneath the surface. This was what McClure had needed to see in person, the real-life emotion that could not be covered up with words or actions. He needed to *see* that this man had deeply loved his wife.

Seeing the home, the children, the man's face, told Dean that Nicole did have a nice life, something precious and worth saving, worth fighting for.

"Go ahead and ask your questions, Mr. McClure. I doubt you have anything that hasn't already been asked. My life has already been drawn and quartered before the public and laid open for all to see."

McClure leaned forward on his elbows, clasping his hands. "Tell me, Mr. Conrad, how soon after Nicole's death did the FBI approach you about her murder?"

The man looked up with a start. "Perhaps I have underestimated you, Mr. McClure. How did you know that the FBI spoke to me? It wasn't part of the investigation or trial."

McClure worked hard to show no emotion, but his mind shouted in jubilation. He had gambled with the question, and it worked. "You know I'm retired from the FBI. I understand how they operate."

"Yeah, I suppose you do. I still don't see what this has to do with me."

"It's important for me to know what questions they asked you."

"Why? And why should I give you that information?"

McClure took a deep breath and exhaled, steadying himself, then looked straight at Conrad. "Because I need to make sure the courts have convicted the right man for the crime."

Conrad's face went through a range of emotions from surprise and confusion to anger. He shoved back his chair and stood, his body trembling. He struggled to contain the rage in his voice.

"You bastard! You are not going to come in here and even suggest this has all been for nothing, being put through that trial, believing justice has been done. Why should I even talk to you and bring back all the pain again? Hasn't my family gone through enough as it is? There was a trial and the man was convicted, for god's sake!"

Conrad's children came running into the dining room. "Daddy. What's wrong?"

He knelt and hugged them both. "Nothing's wrong. Daddy needs you to go upstairs and play in your rooms for a while, okay?" Both children bounded off, leaving Conrad standing by the table.

McClure softened his tone, made sure it didn't sound patronizing. "I'm truly sorry to put you through this. But let me ask you, what if the man convicted of the crime didn't do this? And I have enough doubts to qualify that question. What if the real killer is still out there, free to harm you, or your children? I have to make sure, that's all."

There was a heavy sigh from Conrad then, and McClure took advantage of the moment.

"If you can just tell me what kind of questions the Bureau asked when they talked to you, it will be a huge help. No one else needs to know we even met. And then I'll leave you alone."

Conrad stood a moment longer, but McClure could see the resolve give way as the tension eased from his body. He moved over to the chair and slid in, his anger spent. "It's all mostly a blur to me. I was still trying to comprehend that my wife was gone, had been murdered. I was still in shock. Later, it dawned on me that they weren't even a part of the investigation, so why were they asking me questions? But then the trial started, and I was too overwrought to think about it anymore."

"Just relax and think back to the first question ... let it flow back into your memory ..."

"The first thing they asked me was if we had any backups to the laptops that got stolen."

"Did you?"

"No. Never thought about it. I do all my work on the computer in my office. Whatever was on the laptops is gone now. I learned that lesson too late."

"What did they ask next?"

"It was a strange question, now that I think about it. They wanted to know if Nicole had talked to me about any type of investigation she had been doing?"

"And?"

"Well, no. Of course not. She gave that up years ago, before we even married." Conrad grew silent, staring into his coffee cup.

"Anything else that you can remember?"

"No, except they wanted to know who my close friends were. Guess they wanted to talk to them."

"Can you give me a list of the names you gave them?"

"Only if you promise not to contact them, or bother them in any way."

"Promise."

McClure pulled a tablet and pen from his jacket pocket and slid them across the table. Conrad wrote out the names, shoved the tablet toward McClure and stood. "Is that all?"

McClure stared at the names on the tablet, saw the name, John Selden, listed. "There is something else."

Conrad sat back down reluctantly, waiting, the lines of exhaustion showing on his face.

McClure struggled with the guilt that swamped him, for what he had already put this man through, for what he still had to ask of him. McClure had lain awake most of the night wrestling with it. "I've got to ask you a question that won't make sense to you, but it's extremely important."

"Okay …" Conrad said hesitantly.

"For just a moment, I need you to think like Nicole would. If she had some papers, or documents she wanted to keep safe, where no one would look, where do you think she'd put them?"

Conrad's eyes widened in surprise, then narrowed. "What kind of question is that? What are you implying?"

"I'm not implying anything. I just need you to think about it." This time McClure stood and walked over to where Conrad still sat in stunned silence. Seeing Selden listed on that piece of paper had changed his strategy. He couldn't directly ask Conrad about Selden. What if Nicole's notes were never found? The line of questioning would be a for-sure tip-off to Conrad—giving him knowledge that he'd never be able to hide from someone like Selden. It would be like handing Conrad a for-certain death card. McClure couldn't bring himself to go that route. This ploy pushed the limits beyond what McClure wanted to do as it was.

McClure laid his business card next to Conrad's hand. "I've written where I'm staying on the back. Please, it's important. A man's life hangs in the balance." When Conrad remained silent, McClure turned to leave. "I'll show myself out."

CHAPTER FORTY-ONE

San Juan National Forest, Colorado

Firelight flickered against the growing darkness as the sun dropped behind the mountains, crickets just beginning their evening songs. Matt Logan and Fox Walker sat at the campfire, each absorbed in their own form of relaxation. Walker whittled at a piece of wood with his knife. Logan cleaned his pistol. He picked up the barrel and sighted through it, inspecting the interior. Then looked over at Walker.

"What are you working on? A spear?"

Walker nodded. "This one is V-shaped … more efficient at holding a fish once it's caught." He continued to work without looking up.

"You don't much care for guns, do you," Logan stated.

"No, I don't."

"Can I ask why?"

Walker didn't say anything for a moment. Logan waited patiently. He had learned to give the man lots of space in a conversation. Walker didn't look up, but spoke as he worked.

"Guns make killing too easy."

Logan put the gun barrel down to give Walker his full attention. "Explain."

"When I hunt with bow and arrow, my knife, or set traps, I have to know my quarry intimately. I have to understand how the animal or bird thinks, its daily habits, how it survives. As I stalk my prey, we become as one. When I release the animal's spirit to the Creator, the animal leaves its body to me as a gift. We are joined in death this way. In return, it's my responsibility to waste nothing."

Logan studied Walker for a long moment. "I do understand what you are saying. And I appreciate your beliefs and why you live as you do. I even admire that about you. But there's something that you are forgetting."

Walker looked up from his work and waited for Logan to continue.

"I too had to stalk my prey. I had to know everything I could learn about him … his strength and weakness, his fears, and how he would react to set circumstances. I too felt a deep connection. The difference is, I couldn't get all romantic about it. If I didn't kill him first—he would kill me. Plain and simple."

Walker nodded. "Agreed. You were a warrior. Your responsibilities were different."

Logan picked up the barrel and started sliding the Glock back together. "Damn right I'm a warrior, Walker. Always will be. And you know, you Indians had your share of famous warriors as well. If we could talk to some of the pioneers, they'd tell us some gruesome tales. You say that guns make killing easier, and I suppose in a sense you're right. But humans have been finding ways to maim and kill other humans for thousands of years. Some of them downright horrific. Me—I'd far rather die from a bullet than from having my gullet flayed open by a knife." Logan stopped when he saw Walker slowly smile.

"You misunderstand. I'm not saying you were wrong, Logan. You did what you were trained to do. I'm saying you no longer need to be a warrior. You can leave that behind now. I can teach you, if you want."

Logan stared at Walker for a long moment. "I don't know. I'm not sure I can do that."

CHAPTER FORTY-TWO

Denver, Colorado

Dean McClure checked out the window of his hotel room. The sun had set hours ago, leaving the parking lot lights the only brightness in the dark sky, drowning out the stars. He left the room, rode the elevator to the lobby and took a seat, watching the entrance.

A few minutes later, Jeff Conrad walked through the doors and stood a moment in the entry, surveying the room. McClure caught his eye and motioned him over.

McClure studied the man's face as he drew closer. He looked haggard and tired, but there was something else there, too. Resolve? When they met, his handshake was firm.

"Thanks for seeing me, McClure. I know it's late."

"No problem. I appreciate it that you are willing to talk to me. We can take the table in the corner over there. Is that private enough?"

Conrad nodded and they both walked over and sat down.

McClure leaned forward, resting his forearms on the small table between them. "You said you found something."

"I thought a lot about what you said. I had to face the fact that until now my life has been all about my political career. Nicole played a big part of that, supported me, was proud of me. Now with Nicole gone, my two children are all I have left. It's not the career that's so important anymore, and I want to make sure they are safe. I want the man who destroyed our lives behind bars. So I started looking through the house. All the places the sheriff's department didn't already check."

Conrad pulled a bulky envelope from his jacket pocket and opened it. He began to pull out copies of newspaper clippings, laying them on the table for McClure to examine. "First, I found these. Nicole had hidden them in the pages of a cookbook in the kitchen. Once I found these, I started searching all of her cookbooks and found more papers."

McClure picked up the articles and flipped through them. "These are from twenty years ago."

Conrad nodded. "Yes. Each article is a story about a missing young lady who disappeared from her college dorm. They never found her, or a body." He reached over and handed McClure a different batch of clippings. "These are another case, another coed, but five years later, when Nicole was in the Bureau. She has written notes in the margins. Reads like her memories of a case, like she worked on this during that time frame."

McClure scanned the copy. "Both cases had the exact same circumstances. Both missing women had admitted to close friends that they were pregnant before they disappeared."

"Exactly." Conrad handed more papers to McClure.

He leafed through them, skimmed over the hand-written notes, then looked up at Conrad. "Nicole believed these women were both killed by the same man."

"Yes, and she believed the killer was never caught. I've spent the last four hours reading every word of her notes, studying them. It all started at one of our parties. Someone mentioned a rumor about John Selden, and it set off some memories, reminded her of this case. I found all kinds of research on the guy in her papers. My conclusion is that evidently she was on the right track, and that's why she's dead. I think she discovered Selden's secret past." Conrad pointed to a particular section of papers on the table.

McClure picked up the papers and read through them. "I can see how she has tied this guy into all this, and I believe she's on the right trail, but there's nothing here that could be used for hard evidence." McClure watched Conrad's shoulders sag. "You know as well as anybody that Selden is not some little nobody, your average Joe. From what I've read, the man is a powerful and influential man. That's why you let him become a close acquaintance."

Conrad sat back in the chair and sighed. "Yes. He began to approach me about a year ago, at parties and political gatherings. Made it clear he was interested in getting to know me. I considered it quite an honor to get his attention. A backing from John Selden meant a great deal. He tends to pick winners. Or they became winners because of his backing. Not sure which. Nicole was elated as well, in the beginning. But in recent months I noticed a change in her attitude about me spending so much time with Selden. She even seemed nervous, jumpy. But when I tried to talk to her about it, she'd brush it off and evade the question."

"Could be this Selden guy picked up on Nicole's nervousness as well. Especially if all of you were together often. If this man is her killer, and murdered those college girls years ago, he isn't going to get rattled easily. Besides, a man who has gained this kind of power through wealth knows how to handle people who get in his way, and he has no problem doing it."

Conrad leaned over the table, sorting through the papers. "Isn't there something here in these notes that we can use to at least get him arrested?"

"If we are going to have him arrested, we want to have enough evidence to keep him there, and take him to court. If this is all true, he's an extremely dangerous man. We don't want to arrest him, or alert him to our suspicions, only to have him get released again, knowing who we are."

"Of course, you're right. I can't even think clearly right now."

"Don't be so hard on yourself. I'd be in the same boat at this point."

Conrad rested his elbows on his knees. "What I don't understand is why Nicole didn't come to me about this. I thought we had a great relationship. We could talk about anything."

McClure laid the papers down and gave Conrad his full attention. "Because she was smart. And because she loved you."

Conrad looked at him, puzzled.

"She knew she didn't have enough evidence yet to put Selden away. And if she told you about it, your attitude toward the man would change. She knew Selden would notice it and realize you knew of his past deeds as well. She was keeping you in the dark to keep you safe."

Conrad's eyes widened, then filled with tears. He lowered his head, and McClure could see the man struggle to compose himself. McClure waited. When Conrad finally looked up he had a determination to his jaw that had been missing before.

"Let's finish this for Nicole. Let's find what we need to take this bastard down."

McClure studied the man a moment. "There can be no 'we' to this, Conrad. You can't do anything to tip Selden off that you know anything about his past. You've got to carry on as normally as possible. One slip and—well, you know. Your life is on the line here.

That's why I hesitated to involve you, but ultimately it was the only way I knew to go, to find Nicole's true murderer."

"But, you'll do whatever it takes, right? Selden *can't* have my wife's life in return for his. She was worth more than that."

McClure could see the pain in Conrad's eyes and knew the man suffered. He hoped that when Conrad played his part as a politician he was not as easy to read. Someone like Selden would see right through him.

I've got to move fast on this—get Selden behind bars before he can do more harm.

McClure gathered up the papers scattered across the tabletop. "You can bet I'll be doing everything in my power to put this man away. In the meantime, I want you to use your current situation as an excuse to pull back out of the public spotlight a while longer. It's a valid reason to want to be alone with your family. Even Selden should not question that. Stay away from the man as much as possible without causing any suspicion, okay?"

"Sure. I can do that. But you've got to let me know if there is anything else. And you'll keep me informed, right?"

"Right. You can count on it. And Conrad, thanks again for doing this. I know it wasn't easy."

"It's the least I can do, for Nicole, and the children." Conrad handed McClure the envelope for the papers. "I want you to keep these. For safe keeping. So, will you be contacting the sheriff now?"

McClure folded the papers, slid them into the envelope and tucked them safely away in his jacket. "No. I think it's time to confront the FBI and find out what they know. I have something they'll want, and it gives me some leverage."

CHAPTER FORTY-THREE

Denver, Colorado

Sean Logan paced the hardwood floor of the living room, stopped and stared at the photos of himself and Matt, then paced again. He didn't know which was worse, being worried that the FBI would confront him again, or waiting around worrying about his brother.

He walked over to the dining room table and riffled through the papers scattered across the top, newspaper clippings of Matt's trial, scribbled notes. He had tried to keep himself occupied while waiting to hear back from McClure that Matt was safe, and had hoped to find something, anything that might help. Even being at work didn't help. His mind constantly wandered back to Matt and what might be happening. Each day had stretched into the other, until five long days passed. Then came the relief. Knowing that McClure had made it happen. Nataya had found Walker, and they connected with Logan.

But another two days had passed while he waited to hear any more news. This level of frustration ate at him. The sense of helplessness had started to take over his every waking moment.

Matt needs me *this time. Lord knows he was there for me when I need-ed help.*

He jumped when the disposable cell phone vibrated on the cof-fee table, then snatched it up and answered.

"Hi, Sean. Dean McClure here."

"Yeah? Everything okay?"

"Going well. I made contact with Nicole's husband and con-vinced him to search the house. Got some good luck there. He found some papers that Nicole had hidden. Articles and notes which give us a solid lead to the real killer. The name matches with what Nataya got from Logan."

"Which is?"

"Don't worry about that yet, Sean. We don't have enough to get an arrest, but we will. And in the meantime, I'm going to the Bureau with what I've got. It should be enough to convince them to let Walker bring Matt in safely while we sort all of this out."

"I don't think Matt will do that. Come in, I mean. He has plans."

"What do you mean, Logan 'has plans'?

"That's why I asked about the name. All I know is Matt men-tioned 'handing out his own form of justice.' Figured that meant he had plans for Nicole's killer."

"Shit. That's not good. The man's name is Selden. Ring a bell?"

"No, sorry."

"Look, if your brother means to go after Selden, we need to get to him before he does. We're trying to prove Matt's not a murderer. We don't need him to prove that he is."

Sean stared out the window after the call ended. He couldn't stand waiting by the phone anymore. And McClure was right. They needed to prove this Selden's guilt quickly and get him out of Matt's path.

But how could he help Matt? He had never trained as a fighter.

He stood and walked over to the photos sitting on the fire-place mantel. Picked up a photo from his college graduation. Matt beside him, his arm slung around Sean's shoulders. He could see the pride in his brother's eyes, could hear him say, "You're the brains of the family."

A slow smile came to Sean's face. He grabbed his jacket and car keys, and rushed out the door.

CHAPTER FORTY-FOUR

San Juan National Forest, Colorado

F ox Walker opened his eyes with a start, seeing only darkness at first, then the sliver of moon hanging in the star-filled sky overhead. He guessed it to be around midnight. He didn't know what woke him, so he stayed still, listening. He heard Logan's breath— not the slow rhythm of sleep. Could tell he was also awake.

There. A low eerie humming, growing in volume. Walker couldn't place the sound. Heard Logan roll up to his knees and begin to throw dirt over the hot coals left from their fire, at the same time whispering a command, his voice hoarse with urgency.

"Walker. Quick. Under the trees."

Both men scrambled to the shelter of the dense foliage and waited. Logan spoke first.

"Chopper. Blackhawk."

They crouched among the trees as the noise grew louder. Even with the echoes resonating off the nearby mountains, the chopper sounded as if it passed directly above them. Walker sensed Logan's tenseness. Could tell he slid his gun from the shoulder holster, and felt his own body preparing for fight-or-flight mode, his hand automatically resting on his knife.

The seconds seemed to stretch into forever until Walker heard the machine move beyond them, then up over the top of the mountain, the noise fading as it reached the other side. He heard Logan breathe a sigh of relief and did the same before he spoke.

"It's heading down into the valley. It's been three days since we released the GPS into the water. It should be in that region by now."

"Yeah. Must have snagged on something and stopped. They're probably dropping in some guys to check it out. It won't take them long to find it."

Both men listened as the helicopter noise shifted from a faraway hovering sound, then rapidly faded away completely, out of earshot.

Walker sat up, relieved that the machine had taken a different route out. He brushed leaves and debris from his shirt. "And when they find the GPS, and no sign of me, you know what they're going to assume."

Logan returned his gun to the holster. "Yeah. That I killed you and sent the GPS as a decoy."

"They'll be forced to follow the stream back up to the source, though, up the mountainside, to find you. Should keep them busy for a while. And we're on the opposite side, miles into the deepest part of this wilderness."

Logan was silent for a moment. "Let's hope that's the case, but I have to wonder ..."

"What?"

Logan shook his head. "No way. They wouldn't bring in the HRT for someone like me."

"HRT. Who or what is that?'

"The Hostage Rescue Team is the FBI's version of an enhanced SWAT and counter-terror team, based out of Quantico. But they can be brought in for searches or manhunts when the regional field office isn't equipped for the situation."

"How do you know that?"

"The HRT conducts joint training exercises with US military units, and they participate in exchange programs. I've worked with these guys. They're top-notch."

"If that's the case, why the hell did they bring me into this? Why didn't they just bring in the HRT from the start?"

"Like I said, I can't imagine them bringing in the big guns for the likes of me. Besides, it was all about timing, I'm guessing. They could get you inserted into the forest the quickest. And you know it better than most."

Walker looked back up to the sky, reassured when he saw only stars scattered about in the darkness. "There's something else. The FBI knew I wouldn't come in here carrying a gun."

"So?"

"Maybe they want to make sure you come out of here alive. Too many weapons out here and it's easy for an 'accidental' shooting to take place in the wilderness. With no witnesses."

Logan looked at Walker thoughtfully. "Good point. But why? Why am I so damn important to them in the first place?"

CHAPTER FORTY-FIVE

San Juan National Forest, Colorado

The sweet melody of morning bird song floated between the rustling leaves. Fingertips of a breeze traced over his cheek. He felt Nataya's lips brush his ear ... her whispers ... slowly opened his eyes.

Fox Walker lay on his back, blinking against the glare of the low-slung, early morning sun, wondering how late he had slept. Then realized that the sunbeams radiated out from the dark silhouette of a man. He blinked again and recognized Logan, standing over him. His gun pointing directly at Walker's head. His heart thumped and his still-sleepy mind jerked fully awake.

Stay calm.

Thoughts tumbled and tripped over themselves as he tried to make sense of what he saw.

The helicopter. Does Logan believe I betrayed him?

Walker opened his mouth to speak, but no words came. He saw Logan bring his index finger to his lips, motioning him to silence.

What the hell?

Then Logan whispered, "Don't move."

Walker's mind and senses went into a hyper-alert state. Every sound near him focused and amplified. Logan shifted ever so slightly, his body blocking more of the light behind him. Walker could see Logan's eyes. Followed the line of their stare and the angle of the gun barrel. They were aimed at a point just above and to the left of Walker's head.

Not me. Something close.

Again Logan whispered. "Rattlesnake."

In the instant that followed Walker realized what was about to take place. Spit out the word "No!" causing Logan to bring his gun up away from his target, a startled expression on his face. But he held his fire.

"No need to give away our position to the FBI. The snake won't strike. Trust me."

Logan didn't move. His expression said he wasn't convinced.

Walker moved in slow motion, gradually rolling away from the snake until out of striking distance. Then in one swift move he went to his knees, his knife already in his hand. A second later it sliced through the air, striking the rattler just inches behind its head, the body convulsing.

Logan still stood in the same position, staring at Walker. "I don't get it. When I came back with firewood that snake was sidling up, getting ready to get cozy with you. I was convinced that one move and he'd strike."

"The snake wanted the warmth of the fire, not to attack me. Rattlers only strike if provoked."

"That's what I've heard, but I wasn't about to take a chance."

"Thanks." The act revealed more about Logan than the man probably realized. He was willing to shoot, thinking he had to—to save Walker's life—even if it meant letting the FBI know their location. And Walker had to admit that right at that moment he felt pretty damn relieved Logan had been aiming at the snake, and not his head. He watched Logan holster his gun.

"But I'm confused, Walker. You didn't have to kill the snake to escape it. Doesn't that go against one of those 'codes of life' of yours?"

Walker knelt by the snake a moment and said something in Shoshone, then completed severing the head from the body. He stood up, holding the three-foot length of snake and handed it to Logan. "We need protein."

Logan smiled. "Glad you see it my way this time," he said as he laid the coiling body of the snake over a couple of low branches, waiting for the muscle spasms to ease up.

Walker returned to the snakehead lying on the ground. Using the tip of his knife, he dug out a hole from the soft dirt and shoved the severed head in, then covered it.

Logan watched him. "I know the poison is still dangerous even after the snake is dead, but why bury the head?"

"Just a precaution, so another person or animal doesn't accidentally get hurt."

"Good idea. I didn't learn that in my training."

"Grandfather taught me to do that."

"Your grandfather sounds like an interesting fellow."

"He was. But he wasn't my paternal grandfather. It's a term of respect for elders who share their knowledge with others. You would think of him as a teacher, a mentor."

"Ah. That makes sense. I thought you called people like that a medicine man."

"Not in this case. He trained as a scout in his youth, and never stopped learning about nature." Walker picked up the snake, made an incision in the skin where the head had been, and began to work the skin down a few inches until he could get a solid grip. Then, holding the meat with one hand, and with a steady pull, he peeled the skin down, the action turning the skin inside out.

Logan took the skin from Walker and began the process of turning it right-side out again, while Walker cleaned the snake. "So what about your father?" Logan asked.

"He was a hard worker, Walker replied. "Always busy trying to keep food on the table for the family, Mom, my younger sister, and me. He didn't have the time or energy to take notice of me. Grandfather saw that I was always running off from school to the remote parts of the reservation. He took me in as a pupil. Started teaching me when I was eight years old."

"Were your parents okay with that?"

"Mom was happy that Grandfather made me stay in school, because he would only teach me after my classes. Father never said much, but seemed pleased when I learned to bring game home for the table."

Walker pulled out the snake's entrails in one swift jerk, cut the snake meat into large sections and handed half to Logan. They both skewered the meat on sticks and laid them over the hot coals at the edge of the fire.

"Sounds like Grandfather took the place of a father for you."

"Yeah, in many ways. He taught me more than just survival skills. He taught me about life and death, and the spiritual world, and my place in it."

Logan was silent for a moment as he watched the meat cooking. "My father was the center of my life. I admired him, wanted to be like him. But I had such a rebellious attitude, and it often got me into trouble. I've always regretted that I caused my father so much grief. As a kid you just never realize that your parents might not be there someday. He was a policeman. He died saving his partner's life."

"I am sorry to hear that."

"It was an honorable way to die, and he was doing what he wanted. What he believed in. But it helped change my mind-set. I had my younger brother, Sean, and my mom to worry about after that. It was up to me to protect them. It's what kept me trying to be a better person."

Logan turned the skewers of meat so they would cook evenly. "The military took the place of my father, I guess. A strict, no-nonsense, nose-to-the-grindstone, sink-or-swim, trial-by-fire kind of parental love. They didn't teach me how to live as one with nature, like you were taught. I learned how to exploit it for my needs."

Walker picked up a small piece of firewood and laid it over the flames in the center of the campfire. "The military may have trained you differently than Grandfather trained me, but your training served a different purpose. Like I said before, they helped make you a warrior to keep you alive."

"Yeah. I guess you're right." Logan watched Walker pick up a piece of wood and begin working it with the smaller knife he took from his ankle sheath. "You wouldn't choose to be a warrior, would you." It was a statement, not a question.

"My path is not your path. It doesn't mean that either one is wrong. Just different."

Logan nodded in agreement. "You seem wise to me, about life. I think I could learn a lot from you. I wish I had wisdom like that to share with people."

Walker didn't look up, continued carving at the wood. "When I became a young adult, because of all my training and living in the wilderness, I was a misfit in society. I didn't understand how I belonged in the world. Grandfather suggested that I simply start helping people. So I assisted with search and rescues. Soon I received calls from the law enforcement, wanting my help. Then individuals started asking me to teach them about survival. Soon my Wilderness Survival School was born. I found a way to make a living doing something I love. But it started by just helping others."

"That's a great idea, but I don't see how my skills could help people."

"You were trained to protect others, and to survive. As young men, we both struggled to find our place in the world. There are young boys and teenagers today who could use some guidance. Maybe you can begin by teaching people self-defense, help them gain their confidence. It's a place to start. But first we've got to get you out of this mess."

Logan remained quiet for a long time, staring into the fire. When he spoke, his voice cracked a moment with emotion. "I've never thought of myself that way, except with Sean. And even then, it wasn't to teach him or inspire him. Just to protect him. I like your idea." He looked up at Walker. "You know, up until now all I had was the desire to bring justice to Nicole's killer. Uphold her honor. But you just gave me something else worth living for."

As soon as I take care of that one bit of business with Selden.

CHAPTER FORTY-SIX

FBI Headquarters, Denver, Colorado

D ean McClure looked around at the furnishings in the Denver regional FBI offices as he made his way through the building. Couldn't help but compare the newness of them to the older Seattle offices he had frequented. The glass-and-girder structure sat on what used to be the tarmac for the Stapleton Airport. The offices even boasted a view of the Rocky Mountains.

But he couldn't lambaste them for the apparent costly expenditure. He clearly remembered visiting the cramped, old building of twenty-plus years ago, when they were still located downtown. Back then agents joked that you could find a cockroach or rat easier than you could find a parking place. And he had agreed that they weren't far from the truth.

McClure reached his destination and the receptionist ushered him into the room where Special Agent Susan Mueller sat behind a polished walnut desk. She motioned him over to a chair in front as she wrapped up a phone call—sounded like problems with their phone service.

McClure sat down and tried not to look too obvious about checking her out, and her office. He had done his research before requesting the meeting with the special agent in charge of the Logan manhunt. Having worked in this system his whole career, he knew to find out how she worked, how best to approach her. He expected a less than warm reception. What he hadn't expected was how young she looked, slender with shoulder-length, brunette hair. It made him feel old. No, more like ancient.

Agent Mueller placed the phone in its cradle, stood and walked around the desk toward McClure, her hand extended.

"So nice to finally have the opportunity to meet you in person, Mr. McClure."

He stood and took her offered hand. "I appreciate you taking the time to speak with me."

She gave him a firm handshake and smiled. "I wasn't about to miss the chance to meet the infamous profiler, Dean McClure."

He hadn't anticipated the friendly greeting, and the momentary surprise must have shown on his face because she gave a short laugh. "I'm not so young that I don't remember you. You're a legend in the Bureau." She turned toward some cabinets on the sidewall and said over her shoulder, "Coffee?" He nodded.

She handed him a cup of the hot brew and kept up the light conversation as she poured a cup for herself. "I studied every case you worked. Your insight into the criminal mind inspired me. There was a time when I even considered going into profiling."

To his surprise she settled into one of the chairs next to his, instead of behind her desk. This wasn't what he expected at all, but he figured it worked to his benefit, and he planned on taking full advantage of it. "So what changed your mind?"

She gave him a long, knowing look, one that told him she knew more about him than maybe he would have liked. "I saw what that particular vocation could do to a person. The extreme emotional toll it takes on a truly talented person, such as yourself."

McClure mentally squirmed under that stare. It raked up memories of anguish, flashes of tortured insight. He struggled to suppress them, relegating them to that part of his mind where he usually managed to keep them tucked away.

In the next instant he realized what she had just done. She had let him know she respected his work, but had done *her* homework and knew his weaknesses. She had deliberately made sure he understood she knew how to do her job, and that they were on an equal playing field. McClure looked at her with new respect, but he had played this game far longer than she had. "Yes, that's true. Profiling does take a toll on your life. That's why it takes courage to even attempt it, knowing the price one must pay."

She smiled, and he could see in her eyes she knew he had beaten her hand, but she seemed to be enjoying the game. He did not. The political games within the Bureau were one of the things he didn't miss from his career. She must have sensed it and changed the subject.

"You mentioned you have some information we might be interested in, concerning Matthew Logan and Nicole Conrad. I'm, of course, curious."

McClure noticed she laid out the statement in an open, vague fashion. No specific questions, such as "how did you obtain your information," or "why do you think I would be interested?" He knew she hoped he would jump in, fill in all the blanks on his own. But he had intel he wanted as well. So, he took the offensive stance.

"I don't know for a fact that you will be interested. But, since the FBI has used Logan's escape into a national forest as an excuse to insert themselves into Nicole Conrad's murder case, there is a distinct possibility."

She contemplated the statement a moment before answering. "I could ask you for your source. How you came to that conclusion."

"And I would tell you that I deduced it from the public information available to everyone."

"Okay." She stood and leaned against her desk, looking down at him. "Let's say the Bureau is interested in what you know. I presume you are not here to simply offer it up out of the goodness of your heart. You want something in exchange for it."

"I do. And I know your time is valuable. I suggest we skip the hours of bartering, each of us trying to position ourselves to get what we want without giving up more than we want." He saw a flicker of humor in her eyes. "We both know how the game goes. You're good at this, but I've got years of experience on you. And I'm retired. I've got all the time in the world."

McClure watched her study him in silence for a moment. Then she surprised him with a full out laugh.

"You're right, of course. But oh what fun the two of us could have had."

McClure smiled. He had no illusion that she would still withhold as much from him as possible, and he would do the same, but at least they both knew the score.

Agent Mueller returned to her chair and maneuvered it to face McClure, then sat down. "You first, since you requested this meeting."

"Fair enough." He pulled the envelope from his jacket pocket and began to extract the copies of clippings and various notes, while Mueller made room on the edge of her desk for him to lay out the papers. "Nicole had these hidden in her house." He looked up to see her staring at him.

"You found them?" She emphasized you.

He shook his head. "No, her husband did."

"And he just happened to stumble upon them?"

McClure shrugged and continued to distribute the papers across the desktop.

"But why do you have—" She stopped herself, bit her lip, and instead picked up a pair of reading glasses from her desk and began to scan the articles and notes. The more she read, the faster she picked up the next piece of paper. She soon ignored McClure altogether, pouring over the notes.

At last she leaned back in her chair again and took off the glasses, looking at McClure. "After Nicole's murder, we began to suspect this might be the circumstance. She worked a serial murder case with us years ago, one we are currently still working. With Selden recently getting close to her husband, we feared she had picked up on the same clues we were following. And that Selden figured it out."

"But you had no proof. And the laptops are missing."

"Right. We had to presume Selden got them, that he used the ruse of a robbery to steal them and throw everyone off the scent."

"How long have you been watching him?"

"For years. And I'm disappointed to say that even with all the information Nicole has here, it's pretty much what we already have. Selden has learned a lot since his college years. And now he has the monetary resources to better hide his tracks, and gain political influence. Makes him a powerful man to bring down."

"But Nicole's notes here give him motive for the kill."

"True. If we can prove he knew about them. But we'll need more than that to make an arrest stick."

McClure nodded. "So, you never believed that Logan killed Nicole, did you?"

"No."

"You couldn't help him?"

Muller pressed her fingertips together and brought them to her lips thoughtfully, then sighed. "That was a tough one. Bad luck on his part, with the DNA and his past records."

"Bad luck? We're talking about a man's life here."

"I know it sounds calloused, but it would've compromised our case. We can't let Selden know we even suspect him of anything at this point. There's a bigger picture here, beyond the murders. Don't misunderstand me here—we do hope to help Logan clear his name, just as soon as we get the evidence we need to convict Selden for his past *and* present crimes … and now, hopefully, for Nicole's death as well."

"But in the meantime, you've got a manhunt going on for Logan."

"That's all a part of the plan to keep him safe."

"Excuse me?"

"Okay, so you're correct. We used the excuse of Logan being on federal lands to take over the manhunt. We didn't expect him to escape. We had to act quickly, otherwise the sheriff's department would have sent in an armed search team, and who knows what else. We want him brought in alive. With his DNA being found on Nicole, we believe he possibly talked with her the day she was killed. If we could get a statement from him that in any way confirms our suspicions, that Selden figured out what Nicole was doing, we'd be getting somewhere with this case. But we didn't have enough during his trial to do it—we still need more evidence to go after Selden publicly."

McClure nodded, considering everything he had learned. Then he pieced it together. "That's why you elected to send in Walker. You knew he wouldn't carry in firearms or any communication devices. You're counting on Walker to keep track of Logan, but you're not worried about him confronting Logan, or backing him into a corner where he has no choice but to come out firing."

"Exactly." Muller hesitated a moment before she continued. "But we've had a bit of a setback on that end."

McClure raised his eyebrows. "Yes?"

She sighed. "The GPS tracking device we gave Walker stopped moving for twenty-four hours, so we dropped in a couple of agents last night to find it, make sure Walker was okay."

"And?"

"They found the device alright. But it had clearly been rigged to act as a decoy, to divert us from Logan's real location. The only conclusion we can come up with is that Logan has … disabled … Walker in some way and has taken off in another direction. We have no idea where he is now, or Walker."

McClure rested his forearms on his thighs and stared at the floor a moment. "What if I could reassure you that Walker is okay?"

"You know that for a fact?"

"Yes."

"How—"

"Let's just say that Walker agrees with all of us, that Logan is not a murderer."

Mueller didn't even try to hide her relief at the news. "Thanks. I mean that. It helps us make decisions moving forward."

"Like leaving Logan out there in the wilderness for now?"

"Yes."

"Good."

She gave him a questioning glance, waited for him to explain.

"I came here hoping I could convince you to call off the search for Logan, let Walker bring him in. But, now I believe he's safer out there for now."

Mueller stared at him for a moment, then sat up straight in her chair. "You know that Nicole did talk to Logan before she was killed. And Logan knows about Selden."

McClure remained mute, watched the revelation in her eyes.

Geez, but she's good. She definitely missed her calling. Should have been a profiler.

CHAPTER FORTY-SEVEN

FBI Headquarters, Denver, Colorado

Special Agent Susan Mueller sat at her desk, alone in her thoughts, her hands wrapped around the coffee cup. She stared into the dark liquid, willing it to give her some kind of relief from the feelings of self-reproach.

She liked Dean McClure, wished she could have worked with him when he was at the Bureau. That's why guilt weighed heavy on her. Not because he had managed to pull more insight from her about the case than she had planned to reveal, more because of the intel she still withheld from him. But security on this case had to be her top priority. Too many people's lives depended on secrecy.

Mueller sighed, set the coffee cup aside and shuffled through Nicole's papers. She knew, of course, that McClure had made copies before bringing these in, but she appreciated that he left them behind. She planned to give them to her team to scrutinize further, hoping they could find a detail she had missed in her quick perusal, something they could use on Selden.

The level of frustration she had endured while watching Selden stay free, out in society, hiding behind his wealth and power, behind his bodyguards, had threatened to eat her alive in the beginning. But she was a survivor and came to realize that to beat Selden she had to learn how to control her anger and turn it into hardcore, dogged determination.

It had taken her months to win the confidence and loyalty of her team, but once she did, real progress began to happen. She inserted undercover agents, patiently waiting as they infiltrated Selden's personal circle. The Bureau began to take notice of her and the team's work. She noticed a newfound respect from fellow agents in her interactions.

Mueller looked at the plaque on her desk, a reminder to keep her ego in check.

Pride goeth before the fall.

Dealing with despicable people like Selden had taught her to anticipate the unexpected—to never underestimate how low a person would go to achieve their goal, or to remain free.

Mueller had experienced failure, and knew she had to … to learn and become better at her job. She knew, too, to be the most alert to disaster when everything seemed to finally be falling into place a little too easily. Maybe it sounded cynical to others, but it worked for her.

Good thing. too, because once she had established a steady stream of data coming from Selden's personal and political world, she discovered something far more sinister. Someone feeding Selden info from the Bureau.

They had a mole.

CHAPTER FORTY-EIGHT

San Juan National Forest, Colorado

Walker and Logan climbed the steep bank, moving away from the quick-running stream they had been following all morning, then stood amid the trees to survey the woodland scene before them. Aspen, maples, ash, and oak trees mingled with the spruce, firs, and junipers, creating a lush canopy above them, blocking out most of the bright sunshine.

The coolness felt refreshing to Walker after hours of hiking upstream in the sun, using the waterway to guide them to their designated meeting place with Nataya. Logan turned to him.

"So this is where Nataya is to meet us?"

Walker nodded. "Yeah. We made good time. Earlier than I anticipated. She probably won't be driving up this way until the day after tomorrow. Once she reaches the forest, she'll hike for two days to reach this spot."

Logan looked around thoughtfully. "That still leaves us hanging out here all day today, tomorrow, and the next day. I don't like the thought of us being in one place that long."

"I agree. We're too close to civilization here. And I'm still thinking about the possibility that the helicopter we heard dropped in agents to find the GPS device."

"I know. Me, too. Wouldn't put it past them to follow the stream up the mountainside, hoping to pick up my trail," Logan added. "Feels too risky to stay here, waiting. Unless we can find a place to hide out."

Walker took his bearings from the surrounding mountains towering above the trees. "There should be a deep ravine to the left of this area. Follow me, I have an idea."

Logan gave a nod. "I think I know what you're thinking. Lead on."

⋙⋘

Walker watched as Logan inched his way down the steep rock wall, placing the toe of his boots carefully, making sure the rock would hold before putting all his weight onto it. He used protruding stones and indentations in the wall for handholds.

"This is it," Logan shouted up to Walker. "Just as you thought."

"Good." Walker knew how to spot the indications of an opening in the rock wall; otherwise it would be almost impossible to spot from above, on top of the ravine.

Logan worked his way over to the cave-like indention, partially covered by some scrawny shrubs clinging to existence. He made sure not to disturb them, as they created a natural camouflage for the entrance. He swung his feet in and lowered his body into the compact stone chamber, crouching to keep from banging his head on the rock overhead.

Walker followed from above, swinging in and looking around. "This could work."

Logan agreed and peered out of the cave opening to the bottom of the ravine. "Perfect. If anyone comes in from below, I doubt they would notice this opening in such a steep rock wall. And even if they did, they'd be crazy to try to climb it."

Walker nodded. "Should be a safe place to retreat to, if need be."

"I say we stay here during the nights. They brought that helicopter in after dark. I don't want to try to climb down this wall at night with someone hot on my tail."

"Good idea."

Logan leaned out the opening. "I'll retrieve the backpack from topside."

"Okay."

Logan climbed out of the cave, heading up the ravine wall while Walker brushed away pebbles and dirt clods to make the surface smooth for sleeping.

Being here reminded him of Nataya and their times together in a similar cave. He remembered the night he had dug out a shallow hole in the cave floor and transferred hot rocks from the campfire to it, the warmth radiating into the space, their bodies huddled together for warmth throughout the night.

He shook his head to clear the vision from his mind. Thoughts of her had surfaced often as he and Logan hiked through the forest. In fact, since her departure, he noticed he struggled at times to stay focused on the work at hand, something he'd never experienced before. He'd even begun to wonder if perhaps it was a detriment to not have her here with him.

Logan returned with the backpack as Walker finished clearing the floor of rubble. They both sat crossed-legged on the floor and emptied out the contents of the pack. Logan gathered all the remaining food packages.

"We have some dried fruit left, and one package of beef jerky."

"I'll hunt today. And we can fish. Since we'll be staying close by the cave for a few days, I can keep a small fire going and dry some meat. Replenish our supplies."

"Sounds good. I'll help in whatever way I can." Logan picked up the metal water bottles and set them against the cave wall. They had filled them at the cabin before leaving. He turned to Walker.

"Guess we should discuss what our game plan might be going forward. I realize we have to see what news Nataya brings, but what are your thoughts at this point?"

"You had a plan when you escaped. What was it?"

Logan stuffed the food packages into the backpack. "I knew how much time I had to reach the cabin and rendezvous with Victor. He and some of my other team members were—and still are, as far as I know—gathering info on Selden. They're watching his habits, figuring out ways to get past those bodyguards he has with him all the time. Since we couldn't count on the conventional method to prove his guilt, we planned to take up where the justice system failed. The cabin would have served as a safe place for Vic and me to meet. That's where we were going to review what info he had gathered and figure out how to implement our plan."

"And now?"

Logan didn't look up at Walker. Instead he rummaged through the remaining items on the ground and, one by one, added them to the backpack. "The circumstances have changed, but my mission remains the same."

Walker didn't reply. He sat and watched Logan. Quiet filled the cave until Logan looked up at Walker.

"I know what you're thinking. You've made it clear you believe I'm wrong for planning to seek revenge for Nicole's murder. But that's where you and I are different, Walker. I always repay my debts, and I owe this to Nicole."

"Why?"

Logan hesitated, then answered, his voice tight with anger. "It's my damn fault she's dead. That's why."

Walker studied Logan for a moment, then spoke. "Nataya told me about why you feel this way. About how Nicole came to you, afraid and asking for help."

"That right."

"But the truth is, Logan, that Nicole was investigating Selden because she wanted to protect her husband's reputation and career. It had nothing to do with you."

"It has everything to do with me."

CHAPTER FORTY-NINE

Denver, Colorado

Sean Logan stood facing the bathroom's full-length mirror, scrutinizing his appearance. He picked up a handheld mirror and turned his head to catch a glimpse from the side. He had to admit, the clerk had been right, the Bluetooth earpiece was completely hidden. In fact, he would have to use a strong magnet that came with the kit to even remove it from his ear canal—which made him a bit nervous. But the sales clerk told him the secret service guys used this unit, boasted that it is the smallest headset in the world.

Sean turned left and right, noting in the mirror that his button-down shirt collar covered the wire loop around his neck. The thin microphone wire ran invisibly down the long sleeve of his shirt, letting the tiny mic lie just under the cuff at his wrist.

Sean flexed his pant leg. Good, it showed no evidence of the wire running down to his shoe. Under his toes lay a signal pad that allowed him to press it and send a silent signal to another cell phone, like Morse code.

On one hand, scenes of James Bond came to mind, but flip-flops in his stomach dashed them away. He took a deep breath. All he had to do was find this John Selden and figure out a way to get a face-to-face with the guy. He'd been working on a plan, rolling it over and over in his head.

Sean read the rest of the instruction booklet that came with his spy set. For the earpiece to function, he needed to have his cell phone within fifteen meters. He did the math. If one meter equaled roughly three feet, then he needed to keep his phone within forty-five feet. That should be easy enough.

He gave a sigh. Well, with all this gear on, he might as well give it a try. He pulled his cell phone from his pocket and punched in Victor's phone number. In three rings Vic answered.

"What's up, kid?"

Sean smiled when he heard Vic's voice in his ear, clear and strong. He dropped the phone into his pocket to see if Vic could hear him speak via the hidden mic.

"Just doing a quick test of my new Bluetooth earpiece. I can hear you loud and clear. How 'bout you? Can you hear me okay?"

"Sure. Sounds a little different, but I can hear you fine."

Sean smiled. Super. The microphone worked as well. Next he tested the footpad. "Hey, Vic, I got this phone app that lets me send a signal, like Morse code," Sean lied. "Want to hear it?" Sean heard a sigh on the other end, but Vic answered patiently.

"Sure, kid, give it a try."

"I'll give you one beep for 'yes' and two beeps for 'no,' okay?"

"I said go ahead."

Sean tapped his toe one time on the pad in his shoe.

"Hey, that's pretty cool, I have to say," Vic said.

As Victor spoke, Sean heard the neighbors' dog go into an all-out rage of barking. It sounded as if he wanted to eat someone alive.

"Hey, Vic, while I have you on the phone, let me check and see why my landlord's dog is so upset. He never barks like this, unless someone's messing around our yards."

"Sure. But stay inside."

Sean usually ignored the barking dog, but wearing all this espionage gear made him doubly paranoid and jumpy. He walked into the dark living room, and, without turning any lights on, peeked around the edge of the drapes. At first he couldn't see anything, but he kept staring and noticed a dark shadow not far from his house. The shape of a van.

Crap!

He heard Vic's voice in his ear and jumped. He'd forgotten the earpiece.

"Sean. What's going on?"

"There's a black van parked out front. Never seen it before. It doesn't belong to the neighbors."

"Okay, don't get all nervous."

"The dog stopped barking, real sudden-like."

"Okay, look. Make sure all your doors and windows are locked."

Sean raced to the front door, glad he had his hands free to check everything as quickly as possible. Vic continued giving instructions.

"Leave off any lights that you can without someone noticing."

"Just the bedroom and bathroom lights are on."

"Good. Leave it that way."

"Vic?"

"Yeah, kid?"

"Should I be worried?"

"Probably nothing. But, I'm getting into my car now and heading your way. Look, most likely it's just a couple of agents watching ya."

Sean felt an immediate release of tension with the thought. Of course. Victor had to be right. It was probably just the FBI keeping an eye on him, or trying to intimidate him. He headed for the back door in the kitchen to make sure it was locked. He resisted the urge to flip on the light, instead walking across the floor in the darkness.

Arms grabbed his torso from behind, trapping his arms. He managed a yell of astonishment just as a cloth hood went over his head. He couldn't see a thing, but instincts took over as he thrashed against his attacker, kicking, twisting, and trying to throw the person off balance. He could feel his body banging into objects, hear thuds of furniture hitting the walls. More hands grabbed him.

Only when his captors had subdued him did he hear Vic's voice in his ear—shouting—wanting to know what was going on. When Sean didn't answer, he heard Vic ask the same question over and over until Sean remembered the pad in his shoe. He managed to tap it once to say "Yes," he could hear Vic.

Then Vic asked another question and Sean tapped twice. "No" he wasn't okay. He wasn't okay at all.

Victor went into battle mode. Before leaving his house, he grabbed body armor and an armload of equipment, then threw it into the trunk of his car. He sped down Denver's side streets at breakneck speeds, swerving around slower traffic, staying away from stoplights, barely hesitating for stop signs. All the while he listened to what he could hear on Sean's end, trying to figure out what was happening, listening for clues. All he could tell so far was that Sean had been taken by surprise, and wouldn't—or couldn't—talk. He'd been abducted. But by whom?

He could understand why Sean could hear him on the Bluetooth earpiece and others wouldn't know. But he didn't know why he could hear what was happening with Sean. The phone could be in his pocket and still on.

Unless Sean wired himself?

Geeez! What a bonehead thing to do. Victor had no idea who the kidnappers might be, but finding a wire on Sean wouldn't be a good scenario, no matter what.

Vic took a tight curve, squealing his tires. He had to take advantage of being able to communicate with Sean before someone figured it out. Meanwhile he kept up a steady stream of reassuring words to Sean, letting him know help was on the way. But in the back of his mind, Vic wondered how the hell he was going to get the kid out of this.

⭿⭿ ⭿⭿

Sean focused on Vic's voice in his ear to keep panic from taking over. He could feel his body trembling, struggled to calm it. He had to be able to think. And to be able to think he had to calm down. And stay calm.

Is that even possible?

Hands led him across the grassy lawn, his hands bound in front of his body, and with what felt like a gun barrel against the cloth hood covering his head. He didn't want to test the theory as to whether it was real or not. Even though he was disoriented without his sight, he was certain they took him in the direction of the van he had seen outside. When his feet stumbled down a step and he felt pavement under his shoes, they stopped him. Strong hands lifted him into an already running vehicle and tossed him onto the floor. He could feel rough carpet underneath, hear men's voices muttering. One man volunteered to guard him, and the others must have moved away because their voices faded. The vehicle bounced with the weight of someone climbing inside. He sensed a man settle in next to him. Heard the other doors opening and the quick staccato of slamming closed again.

The van began moving and Sean thought of all those movies he'd watched where the kidnapped person memorized which directions their captors were taking them. Then he remembered the microphone in his sleeve. He was lying on his side, ankles and wrists bound. All he had to do was curl up in a fetal position to get the mic closer to his face. He could act like he was frightened, and he didn't even have to pretend. Not being able to see anything made him paranoid to move, though. He had no idea if the guard watched him, or looked out the window. He decided to try moving in super-slow motion. No reaction from the guard. Okay, so far. He continued moving until he could position his arms up close to his chest, bringing the microphone right up to his chin.

He concentrated on the vibration of the tires on the pavement. They had moved forward and made two stops so far, so they were still in his neighborhood. He tried his first whisper into the mic, hoping and praying that the road noise of the van would drown it out. His guard remained silent.

He gave directions into the mic for Victor. "Two stops … forward … third stop … right."

Victor encouraged him on. "Look, kid, as soon as I get to your place, I'll start following this trail of breadcrumbs and get to you ASAP."

Sean continued to feed the info to Vic, trying to keep his directions straight, a difficult task without any visual references, on top of being scared out of his wits. He tried to think of it as simply a challenge. Not as a life-or-death situation. If he had his directions correct, they were headed for downtown Denver, which surprised him. Wouldn't kidnappers head out of town to some remote location? But his thoughts were interrupted when the van began to slow. One of the guys up front shouted back to the man guarding him.

"Hey, Tony, make sure you frisk the guy before we take him in to Selden."

Selden.

That was the name of the man he wanted to talk to. Sean heard the man called Tony grunt a response, felt hands begin to pat him down. He tensed. What would happen if the guy found the wires?

The hands found the phone in his pocket and removed it. Sean reassured himself that it was still okay. The screen would be dark. No one would think about him being on a live call. And as long as this guy stayed within forty-five feet, he wouldn't lose his signal. Then the hands continued doing the pat down, lightly touched the wires and hesitated.

Sean realized he had been holding his breath. No way the guy didn't feel those wires. What was going on?

He sensed the guard leaning over him, froze and waited. His body gave an involuntarily spasm when he heard the man speak into his ear through the cloth hood.

"Shit. You're wired? Listen, I'm FBI. Undercover. Tell whoever is listening not to follow. You got that? This guy who kidnapped you is extremely dangerous. We've got this under control. Let the FBI handle this."

Sean was too stunned to speak. He heard Vic reply in his ear. "Yeah, I heard that. Act like I agree."

Sean nodded his head for the guard's sake.

"Good," the man whispered. "I've got to get this off of you before they find it. We'll be stopping soon."

While the guard frantically cut and pulled the wires free, Sean heard Vic's voice on his still-hidden earpiece. "I've lost the mic, Sean. If you can still hear me and can signal me, do it."

Sean managed to press the pad in his shoe for the "yes" before the guard stripped out the wire. He heard Vic's voice, reassuring him.

"I'm telling you, kid, there is no way in hell I'm not coming for you now—you got that?"

But Sean couldn't do anything to respond to Vic. He closed his eyes and concentrated on trying to breathe without hyperventilating.

CHAPTER FIFTY

Denver, Colorado

Victor skidded the car into a parking spot in front of Sean's house, exited, and raced to the back yard. He remembered Sean saying the front door was locked, so he felt sure that the kidnappers had gotten in at the back. He rounded the corner of the house, with no dog barking frantically. He didn't want to think about what might have happened to it. He guessed no one had discovered it yet, or the cops would already be there.

The back door into the kitchen stood slightly ajar. He slipped in and flipped on the light, immediately noticing the scattered chairs, the breakfast table pushed against the wall. As he passed through the small room, Vic noted the knocked over blender and drinking glass on the counter. At least Sean put up a good fight.

Vic located the landline phone on a desk in the living room. His cell phone still showed that he had a live connection with Sean's cell. Whether Sean still had the earpiece in he didn't know, but he didn't want to break the connection. He dialed up

McClure's number on Sean's desk phone, heard him pick up after just two rings. The grogginess in McClure's voice made Vic check his watch. Midnight.

"McClure, Vic here. Sean's been kidnapped from his home." He could almost hear the man snap to full awareness in that next second.

"How do you know that?"

"No time to explain now. But I've got Sean's general location. They're headed downtown. I need your help. I heard the name 'Selden' mentioned by the kidnappers. I think it's John Selden."

"Could be."

"Yeah, well, the FBI has an undercover agent in there with the kidnappers."

"That's him, then. Bureau's doing an investigation on him."

"Good. John Selden built his wealth through commercial real estate. What do you want to bet he owns a building somewhere in the location where they're taking Sean?"

"Good point."

"I need you to get me the name of any buildings he owns around the Lower Downtown—LoDo District in Denver. Can you do that?"

"I can't. But I have someone who can. It's going to take a bit of time, though. I'll have to call you back with the info."

"No, don't call. I'm keeping my cell free. I'll pick up a burner phone and call when I get closer to LoDo."

"What's your game plan, Vic?"

"I'm kinda winging it. My gut tells me the only reason someone would kidnap Sean is to use him as bait, to lure Logan out of hiding. Beyond that I'm not sure. But I feel certain I need to get to Sean before these people have time to put their plan into action."

"I think your instincts are right on target. But with an agent in place within this organization, maybe the FBI already has a plan in action?"

"Are you willing to stake Sean's life on that assumption?"

"I see what you mean."

"Gotta go. I'll call you for the building info when I get as far as I can go without it."

⇒⇐ ⇐⇒

Dean McClure disconnected the call, then immediately dialed a new number. No need to look up Clay Evans's number. He had it memorized. He counted on Clay for anything that had to do with computers or online info. The guy hadn't let him down yet. McClure heard the ringing stop and Clay answer.

"Hey, Clay, Dean here."

"Yeah, where you calling from? I didn't recognize the prefix."

"I'm in Denver."

"You can't sleep?"

"Sorry to wake you, Clay."

"You didn't."

"Good. You sitting at your computer?"

"Where else would I be?"

"Got a hot request. Life or death, you could say."

"The hotter, the better. Give it over, man."

CHAPTER FIFTY-ONE

LoDo District, Downtown Denver, Colorado

S ean Logan, his head still covered with the hood, was lifted to
the ground, then the bindings on his ankles cut loose so he
could walk. Hands pushed him forward across pavement—maybe
a parking lot—and into a building. He tried to get his bearings
by the sounds around him. The airflow and echoes of voices gave
him the impression that they were in a high-ceilinged room. He
noticed a distinct scent to the air, not unpleasant, tried to place
it. Maybe sawdust? The smooth floor under his shoes felt like con-
crete. Could be a warehouse.

Someone guided him into a chair. Strong hands held both of
his arms while someone clipped the plastic tie binding his wrists,
then forced his arms back until his hands were behind the chair
and the binding replaced. The position immediately put a strain
on his shoulders and neck. He found himself leaning his head forward to ease the tension. Using one hand to grab the wrist of the
other relieved some of the pressure on the binding and made the
pain a little less.

To avoid thinking about his discomfort, Sean switched his concentration to his surroundings. With his sight out of commission, he could focus on the conversation going on around him and pick up words here and there. He wondered at the fact that the kidnappers weren't being secretive about their conversation. Didn't they care that he was within earshot? After a few minutes he could distinguish between some of the kidnappers' voices, the ones doing most of the talking, anyway.

One man spoke slowly, perhaps considering each word before he said it out loud. His words came across clear, easy to understand. Sean tuned in.

"Anybody got the whole story on this yet? All I've heard is that our hostage here is for some sort of exchange."

A gravelly voice laughed. "Too bad you aren't further up the food chain there, Danny Boy. The rest of us know the score. Guess this is a 'need to know basis' and you don't need to know."

Sean heard chuckles from various men.

Slow Talker waited for the laughter to end. "Oh yeah? You all think you're so much smarter, eh? Well, how 'bout if I tell you that I know there ain't gonna be no exchange."

Quiet in the room. Sean could hear his own heartbeat.

A nasal voice broke the silence. "And just how would you know something like that?"

Slow Talker seemed to take a moment to savor the fact that he had everyone's attention. "Because I know Nick here is one of the top snipers there is. Why would he be here, unless they plan to lure this Logan guy out in the open, using Peachfuzz here for bait? And then BAM. He gets blown away before he knows what hit him." He laughed at his own story.

Sean had involuntarily jumped when Slow Talker did his gunshot imitation. All he could think of was that he had to get word to Matt. Warn him. Then it struck him. If they didn't plan to exchange him for his brother, they'd have no need for him either, once the sniper took out his target.

Nasal Voice spoke after a few seconds. "That's really good there, Danny Boy. I'm going to have to put in a good word for you with the chief. Maybe get you a promotion from expendable grunt to hired hand."

More chuckles, subdued this time. Gravel Voice added his comment. "Yeah, the chief might even let you carry a gun."

Sean tried to tune out the conversation. A tingle of dread ran through his body, and he found it difficult to breathe as his heart pounded against his rib cage. He had to stave off the wave of panic that threatened so he could formulate some sort of plan.

How could he warn Matt? He thought of the missing microphone. He could still hear Vic on his earpiece, but Vic had no way to hear what was going on. Sean couldn't communicate to the outside world.

He then understood why Vic seemed so dead set on getting to him before the kidnappers put their plan into action. Vic instinctively knew it wouldn't go well.

They still had the hood over his head so he couldn't see his captors. He tried to cling to that tiny thread of hope. Vic had told him he'd be there soon, but the fact remained that Sean's wire had been disabled before Vic got the final destination. How would Vic figure out which building held him and the kidnappers?

What about the undercover guy? Maybe he could figure out a way to talk to him again—at least get a warning to Matt. This brought his thoughts back to his situation and his discomfort. All this stress was taking a toll on his body, and he needed to pee badly. He could use that. And it would be the truth, too.

He found it ironic that fear gave him the courage to speak. "Hey," he said. It came out muffled through the cloth hood. So he shouted the next time.

"Hey. Somebody. I need a break to go to the john."

The room went silent. He tried again. "I'm sure no one wants to have to clean up the floor."

Then he heard the voice of the undercover agent speak up. "I'll take him."

Gravel Voice shouted, "Hey, Tony. What're you, his nanny?" Others laughed and so did Tony, as he helped Sean to his feet.

"No way. Hey, Danny, toss me another one of those plastic ties. I ain't gonna be handling the merchandise."

Sean heard Nasal Voice shout over the laughter. "Hey, check out his hardware. Maybe we can get a good price for him on the black market. He's young and pretty. Just like they like 'em." This brought another chorus of laughter.

Tony grabbed Sean's shoulders and turned him around, then pushed him forward as he continued the banter with the guys. He stayed behind Sean, shoving him by the shoulders, and guided him around a turn, where the sound of the men's voices faded.

The airspace and echoing of their footsteps made Sean believe they walked through a narrow hallway. Tony whispered behind him. "That was good thinking, asking to go to the john."

Sean didn't want to admit that it wasn't as much about strategy as a real need. So he only nodded.

The agent tugged him to a stop. "Look, I'm going to pull up this hood just enough for you to see to do your work here. Now, let me cut loose the bindings. I'll be holding a gun on you, in case one of the guys decides to wander down this way."

Sean took care of business, surprised at how much his hands shook. He guessed his gut had grown so used to being scared at this point, that it seemed like a normal state to experience.

He turned around to see the agent watching the hall. His movement caught the agent's attention, and his head turned back to Sean.

"Look, I know this all sounds scary. Just try to stay calm and remember my face. I'm the one on your side, okay?"

Sean nodded but spoke as he turned around and the agent pulled down the hood. "You've got to get word to Matt. Warn him."

Sean positioned his arms behind his back again. But as Sean waited, Tony leaned up close to Sean's ear. "*Geesuz*, kid. Be careful what you say here."

Sean reprimanded himself for not being more cautious. After all, this guy's life was at stake, too. He thought about his brother and how much he had had to know to do his job as SEAL team leader. But when Tony spoke again, his tone was less harsh.

"Now, listen carefully. I'm going to put the binding back on this one wrist, but not the other one. The end of the tie is going to be loose. Keep holding your position like you have been ... that's right. Here's the loose end. Hide it in your free hand. Perfect."

Sean whispered. "Thanks."

"No problem. Just be alert for what's happening around you. As for your brother, let's take care of your situation first. They're coming in for a rescue before the kidnappers can set up their 'exchange' plan."

Sean opened his mouth to speak, then snapped it shut. He decided not to voice his thoughts, about how on TV this is when the hostage usually gets killed.

⊷⊹ ⊹⊶

Victor pulled into the gas station, parked and walked into the attached convenience store. He found and paid cash for a disposable phone, then hurried back to his car. He dialed up McClure's number the moment he slid into the driver's seat.

McClure picked up on the first ring.

"McClure here."

"You got what I need?"

"Yep. Selden owns a furniture store called Wooden Galley in the LoDo District. It's on the corner of First and Walnut. There's an alley behind the store, where you can gain access to the delivery entrance."

"Perfect. Thanks."

"Something to keep in mind, Vic."

"Yeah?"

"Like I said earlier, the Bureau has been investigating Selden for years and the fact they have that undercover agent in there probably means that they know what's going down as well. Be careful you don't end up getting caught in any cross fire."

"Good point. I'll keep my head down."

CHAPTER FIFTY-TWO

LoDo District, Downtown Denver, Colorado

Victor turned off the car's headlights and pulled into the alleyway behind a row of stores that included the Wooden Galley, let the vehicle creep forward. One faint light on the backside of the buildings shone into the dark shadows, allowing him to see a black van parked behind the furniture warehouse. He pulled his own car into a space behind a restaurant, one building away. A dumpster sitting against the brick building partially hid his car.

He hated the fact he had to park so close, but his plan called for a quick escape. Running down a long alley with the bad guys firing guns at him and Sean didn't sound like his idea of fun. He did a quick inspection of the body armor he had hurriedly donned before leaving Sean's place. Everything was in place.

He switched off the car's dome light before opening the door, eased out and closed it quietly. Made a check of his weapons. Although he hoped to make a silent entry, extradite Sean and make the escape without anyone taking notice, he knew how Murphy's

Law loved to come along for the ride on missions. He knew from experience how quickly a situation could go from SNAFU to the worst-case scenario of FUBAR. So he came prepared, with everything from a stun gun to real guns, from a lock pick to flash-bang grenades, ready for anything Murphy's Law might throw at him.

Victor began to make his way down the alley, his backside sliding along the building walls, skimming in and out of doorways, staying in the shadows. Any object he encountered along the way became a momentary shield. He sidled up to the cold brick of the furniture warehouse and took a quick peek around the corner. No surprise that the kidnappers had left a guy out back to keep watch. While Vic waited, the man walked down to the other end of the building, turned his back to the light breeze, and Vic. The guard began the process of lighting up a cigarette.

Thanks for the open invitation, dickhead.

Vic and the stun gun took quick advantage of it. He left behind the unconscious, bound-and-gagged guard and tried the side door positioned next to the large, overhead delivery doors. Found it locked. A quick pick of the lock and Vic slid inside to a dark room, an office, by the looks of the equipment. An open door on the opposite side of the office led to a narrow hallway that ran parallel with the delivery room. He walked silently along the tiled floor, noted a staircase to his right, but continued along the hall toward the light, streaming in from an opening on the right side of the hallway. He figured it must open to the delivery room. Soon he heard the muffled sound of voices coming from the opening at the end of the hallway. He hesitated

The stairs.

⊶ ⊷

The men around Sean abruptly quit talking, and he could hear the footsteps of someone entering the room. A cell phone rang and the footsteps stopped. A voice he hadn't heard before answered, "Selden." Sean's chest tightened. The man McClure mentioned, the man who threatened Nicole, who'd probably killed her. He forced himself to try to breathe normally, which only aggravated it. He could still hear the man talking on the phone. Everyone around him had gone dead silent, listening.

Sean nearly jumped when he sensed something next to his head, but just as quickly recognized the undercover agent's voice, his words hissing into Sean's ear.

"Something's wrong. You've got to remember this. Tell Mueller it's Samson. Don't forget!"

Sean knew he couldn't acknowledge, but instantly repeated the info to himself, memorizing it, even though he had no idea what it meant. He could tell it meant something important to the man he had come to know as Tony.

The man talking on the phone ended the conversation, and footsteps told Sean the man had joined the group of men surrounding him. Still, silence prevailed, and Sean felt an immediate shift in the tension. Then the man spoke.

"Take the hood off. I want to see his face."

Sean felt the cloth pulled from his head but squeezed his eyes shut. He didn't want to see his captors. He knew from movies what that meant. Certain death.

Sean heard men chuckling, then a command. "Open your eyes. Or I'll kill you right now."

Sean reluctantly obeyed, blinking in the sudden brightness until his eyes adjusted to the light. It wasn't difficult to see who the leader was in the group. The perfectly groomed man in the suit held everyone's attention as he addressed Sean. *Selden.* Whatever had made him think he would've been able to talk to this guy—let alone get a confession on tape?

Sean realized then what a dire mistake he'd made. He'd wanted to help Matt so badly that he'd lost his good sense of judgment. He could very well end up being the cause of Matt's death. There was no way Matt wouldn't try to come to his rescue and do whatever the kidnappers demanded. Sean felt his insides roil and worked hard to gain control of his body. He didn't want to be embarrassed by throwing up.

Selden studied Sean, then spoke.

"Ah, there is a family resemblance. And as I understand it, your brother would do anything to save your life. I have to say that I had looked forward to dealing with Matt in my own way, but there's been a change of plans," he said as he addressed not only Sean, but the other men as well. "There's not going to be any exchange."

Sean felt a second of relief for Matt, then the thud of fear hit his chest wall as he understood the full impact of the statement. They no longer needed him.

Selden had everyone's attention. He pointed to one man. "I've got a special assignment for you, Nick. Instead of playing sniper during the exchange for Logan, I want you to head out right now to the forest, where you'll hunt him down and make it look like a hunting accident. I've got coordinates and will feed you updated location info as I get it, so keep in touch."

Nick nodded and headed for the door. The other three men looked on, waiting for instructions.

"Tony, go get the van ready. We need to take a little trip here with the other piece of the equation," he said, indicating Sean.

Tony also nodded and turned to leave. Sean sensed the split-second of hesitation that told him Tony did not want to leave him unprotected, but had no choice. The next moment happened in slow motion for Sean.

Tony turned to walk away. Selden made a quick hand signal to his two bodyguards, and, before Sean could even comprehend it, or the other kidnappers could react, the bodyguards had pulled their guns. Shots rang out. Sean cringed at the blasts echoing in the open room, then watched as Tony fell face forward and lay still.

It couldn't be real. Just a movie stunt. He stared at the red stains appearing on the back of Tony's jacket.

The other two men, a look of bewilderment on their faces, stared at the barrels of the two bodyguards' weapons. One of the men didn't have a gun. The other man had his hand on his gun, but didn't move. Selden waved his hand nonchalantly. "Don't worry. You're not next. Seems we had an uninvited guest in our midst."

Selden held his hand out to one of the bodyguards, took the man's gun, calmly walked over to the agent's body and shot the man in the head. Execution style. "Nobody double-crosses me."

⊶⊷

Vic had retraced his steps to the staircase, took his time climbing the metal rungs, placing each foot carefully to avoid making any noise. Once he reached the top of the staircase, he peered over the edge. A wooden floor stretched out in front of him, stacked with various shapes and sizes of furniture, but he could see where the balcony ended. He pulled himself over the staircase edge, staying on his belly as he slithered his way toward the edge, where he could look between plastic-wrapped chairs to the room below, just as the gunshots rang out.

Damn!

Vic peered over the edge to see boxes and furniture piled all around the sides of the space, but the middle of the room sat open. On the ground lay a man bleeding out.

It's not Sean!

Vic recognized the well-dressed Selden standing over the body, along with his two ever-present body guards. A couple of other men stood to the side, fear on their faces. Then he spotted Sean. He had hoped to find Sean being held in a room elsewhere, with maybe only one guard.

Shit.

Looked like Murphy's Law had joined the party. Status had just changed from SNAFU to FUBAR.

⊨⊧ ⊨⊧

Sean fought against the nausea of unrelenting fear. He tried to calm his racing heart and almost jumped again when he heard his Bluetooth earpiece static to life with Vic's voice. It took a second to remember no one could hear it except him.

"Stay alert, kid. I'm here. If you can hear me, move your left foot forward."

Sean slowly shifted his left foot.

"Good. Listen, when the action starts, tip your chair to the right side and go to the floor as fast as you can. See ya soon, kid."

When the action starts?

What the hell did Vic think had been happening? But he tried to focus and keep his mind clear to think and react. He forced himself to look away from Tony and the blood, watched Selden hand the gun back to the bodyguard, turn and look at Sean.

Sean stared at the two bodyguards as they both moved their raised weapons until the guns pointed at him. It didn't feel real. It had to be a bad dream and he'd wake up any time at any second. Time slowed. Everything appeared in detailed relief against the background. Sean noticed every minute feature, his heartbeat, the airflow in the large, open room. The smell of gunpowder.

Selden studied Sean. "I'm sorry the exchange didn't work out. I don't have anything against you, only your brother. This one," he said, indicating Tony, "had to be dealt with on a more 'personal' level. But I can't go around shooting everyone, so what are we going to do with you?" Selden smiled.

An explosive burst of light and thunderous boom stunned Sean. He dove sideways from the chair and sprawled to the floor, thankful Tony had freed his wrists.

Smoke blurred the scene, but he could see shadows running away from him and diving for cover as gunshots rang out. He scrambled behind some cartons of furniture closest to him. Another fiery eruption and reverberating assault of sound. He covered his ears, crouching low to the ground. What the hell was that, anyway? Strong hands grabbed him and he lashed out with adrenaline-fired strength. Until he recognized Vic yelling at him through the buzzing in his ears.

"It's me, kid. Come on!"

Vic pulled him to his feet, and, shielding Sean with his own body, began to push him toward the opening to the hallway. Sean made it through the doorway with Vic right behind him. But before they rounded the corner to the safety of the hall, Sean heard returning gunfire and Vic let out a grunt of pain. Sean tried to turn but was shoved forward by Vic, who yelled, "Move it!"

They half ran, half stumbled down the long hallway, rounds hitting the walls beside them, Vic returning fire back at their pursuers. Sean couldn't think, he just ran and listened to Vic shouting directions. They reached a small office room, rushed through it and spilled out into the dark night. Vic slammed the door, snapped the lock closed and fell to his knees. Blood streamed down his side from under his armpit, the one spot of body exposed in his armor. He pushed keys into Sean's hand and pointed him toward the car just peeking out from behind a dumpster, one building over.

"No way. I'm not leaving you behind." Sean tugged at Vic, pulling him to his feet. He let Vic lean on him as he struggled to haul them both across the space.

Halfway to the waiting car, Sean heard shouts and the sound of gunfire from behind, the ricochet of bullets hitting the metal of the dumpster ahead of them and the ground around them.

Vic pushed him to the ground and fell next to him. That's when, over the noise, Sean heard men shouting and the sudden halt of gunshots. He peered back over his shoulder and saw armed men, dressed in black, converge upon the two gunmen who had just moments ago been firing at him and Vic.

The FBI.

Sean dragged at Vic, shouting, "I'm not leaving without you, so get the hell up!" With Sean tugging at him, Vic managed to stagger to his feet. Sean began dragging Vic toward the car when he heard the agents behind him shouting to wait. He kept moving. Somehow he got Vic into the passenger seat, slammed the door shut, propelled his body up and slid over the hood of the car. He yanked open the door and jumped into the driver's seat. If he hadn't been so scared he would've been proud of his maneuver. A quick glance in the rearview mirror showed FBI agents running toward him. The engine roared to life and Sean skidded the car out of the alley.

Once on the streets, and thankful for the early predawn hour, he blew through the intersections and ran lights on the nearly deserted streets. He glanced at Vic's pale face, the blood soaking through his clothing. Damn. There was so much of it. He kept talking to Vic, making him answer questions. When Vic's weak voice finally faded and stopped, Sean bit his lip in nervousness.

To combat his terror, Sean pushed the pedal to the floor and screamed at Vic, "Don't you dare die on me. I need you to live. You hear me?"

CHAPTER FIFTY-THREE

San Juan National Forest, Colorado

Fox Walker made his way up the slight rise and into a small clearing where he and Logan had set up a day camp after sleeping in the cave. It gave them a place to dry meat in the full sun, along with the smoke of a fire, yet they remained close enough to the thick cover of nearby trees for safety. If needed, they could make a run for the cave, only seconds away.

Walker carried a rabbit, retrieved from a snare he had set the night before. He knelt, prepared everything for a fire and had it blazing within a few minutes.

He had just finished skinning the cottontail when a movement at the tree line caught his attention. He looked up to see Logan returning from his early morning fishing trip. He carried a large trout and wore an even bigger smile on his face. Walker stood and helped Logan lower the heavy fish to the ground for cleaning.

"Good catch, Logan. There's enough here for breakfast and still leave plenty of meat to dry, along with the rabbit."

"Yeah. And I'm looking forward to the breakfast part," Logan said as he knelt and prepared to clean his catch. "He put up one helluva fight. I've worked up an appetite."

Both men worked at their tasks next to the campfire. Walker added another piece of wood to the flames, using fire as well as the sun to dry the strips of meat.

After a few moments Logan spoke while he labored over the fish.

"I've been thinking a lot about what you said to me the other night, about Nicole. I don't think you understand. It's true that we knew each other, intimately, for many years. But beyond that we had some crazy adventures together over the years. The kind of things that formed a special bond between us, the kind of bond that even being apart for years couldn't break."

Walker cut the rabbit meat into strips and began to lay them across the small wooden rack he had built. The smoke from the fire flowed over the meat. "You cast the die many moons ago, when you couldn't make a commitment to her. She had no choice but to move on with her life. She was married to Conrad, and he's the one who made the commitment to her, not you. She got into this mess by trying to protect her husband and his career, not you."

"But she came to me asking for help. And I failed her," Logan argued.

"She came to you too late. There was no way for you to succeed. But the guilt you feel is not because you failed to protect her."

Logan raised his eyebrows in question. "Oh yeah? You think you know what I'm feeling? So tell me, since you're so much wiser."

"It has nothing to do with wisdom. Sometimes we can't see clearly, until we are on the outside looking in, set apart from our emotions."

"You're talking in circles again. I hate it when you do that. Just spit it out."

Walker sighed. "After Nicole left for another life, you realized your mistake. That you still loved her. The guilt you feel now is because you came back into her life again, knowing full well that she couldn't resist being with you, even though she loved her husband."

A quick moment of surprise showed in Logan's eyes before they narrowed. "You're guessing now."

Walker shrugged. "So tell me I'm wrong."

Logan glared at Walker but said nothing.

CHAPTER FIFTY-FOUR

Denver Health Trauma Center, Colorado

S ean Logan sat alone in the corner of the emergency trauma
waiting room, staring at the large clock on the wall, watching
as the minutes marched by. A couple of FBI agents had followed
him there, interviewed him and insisted he needed them to keep
a watch, for his safety. And they made it clear they weren't finished
with him yet.

He leaned forward, elbows on his knees, head lowered into his
hands.

How did we end up here, Vic?

He knew Vic had saved his life. And the only way he knew how
to pay that debt back was pray that he had gotten Vic there in
time—time enough for the doctors to save Vic's life.

He looked up when a nurse pushed opened the large doors
leading to the trauma rooms and motioned for him to come to
her. He made his way toward her on shaky legs, and they both
stepped behind the doors. Sean tried not to notice the blood on

her scrubs, or think about where it came from. He stood there, his heart pounding, and tried to get a read on the nurse's face. She must have read his expression without any problem because she spoke before he could get the words to come out.

"Yes. He's still with us. He's stabilized enough for surgery. That's where he's going right now. One of our best surgeons is on this. Your friend is in good hands."

"But he's going to be okay, right?"

"He's going into surgery. We can't speculate beyond that."

"But you know his condition. He's got a chance, doesn't he?"

"We know the bullet pierced his lung, but can't tell what other damage it has done until we get in there. That's all I can say."

Sean couldn't look at her anymore, for fear he'd lose it. He felt her place a hand on his shoulder. She spoke quietly, so only he could hear. "Look, his chances are better because you rushed him here so fast. He wouldn't have made it if you had waited for a rescue unit." She turned to leave.

Small consolation.

Sean mentally kicked himself for the negative thought. Of course Vic was going to be okay. He had to be. Victor had been there for Matt when he needed him, *and now he's been there for me.* Thinking about Matt brought back memories of the conversation he overheard from the kidnappers. He spun around and scrambled after the nurse, grabbing her arm to get her attention.

"Is there a phone somewhere that I can use? I don't have my cell, or a wallet. And it's really important that I reach someone right now."

"Sure," the nurse said. She led him over to the registration desk and relayed his request to the lady there. "Follow Anita. She'll help you."

Anita led Sean to a small business room where he could use a phone in privacy.

He sat at the table and tried to calm his mind so he could re-member what hotel McClure had said he was staying in, finally recalled the name. He called information, made the connection and asked to be put through to Dean's room. Sean heard him pick up on the first ring.

"McClure here."

"It's me, Sean."

"Sean. You're okay! Thank the heavens. Where's Vic?"

Sean could hear the concern in McClure's voice, figured he had been expecting a call from Victor. Heck, he'd probably been up all night waiting for it.

"Vic's in the hospital. I'm not going to sugarcoat it, McClure. They won't tell me if he's going to make it or not. He's stabilized enough to go into surgery right now."

"What happened? Gunshot?"

"Yeah, he took a bullet under the armpit. He had body armor on, but had his arm up, pushing me forward, with that small area unprotected. He lost a lot of blood."

"Don't worry, Sean. He'll make it. He's tough. How are you holding up?"

"I'm not sure yet. Still trying to comprehend it all."

"You'll be fine. You come from strong stock, Sean."

Sean had never remotely thought to compare himself to his father, or Matt. The compliment felt good. But it reminded him of Matt's situation.

"There's more. You've got to help Matt. I heard that man, Selden, give orders to a sniper. Sent him out to the forest with instructions to hunt Matt down and make it look like a hunting accident. You've got to find a way to warn Matt."

"Good job, Sean. I'll make sure he gets the warning. Matt will be proud of you. It's not easy to stay calm and remember facts while you're under fire. Look. Don't worry about your brother. You just worry about yourself and Vic right now."

"Thanks. That reminds me, there was an undercover FBI agent there. They called him Tony. Guess his cover got blown, because Selden shot him. But before Tony was killed he made me promise to memorize this message. He said, 'Tell Mueller … it's Samson.' That's it. I didn't tell the FBI agents here about this, since Tony was obviously ratted out. Thought you could make sure that this Mueller person gets it as a private message?"

"Good thinking. I know who Mueller is. I'll make sure she gets the message."

"She?"

"Yeah, she's the special agent in charge of Logan's manhunt."

"McClure?"

"Yeah?"

"Can you make sure she knows Tony tried to help me?" Sean felt his voice crack. All the emotions of the day finally floated to the surface. The terror of not knowing what would happen to him. The hope against hope that he would be rescued in time. The reality of watching Tony die in front of him. Not knowing if Vic would make it, or not. It all hit at once.

He heard McClure answer, "Sure, Sean. I can do that." But all Sean could do was hang up the phone.

CHAPTER FIFTY-FIVE

Elk Meadow, Colorado

Nataya set the enamel coffee pot on top of the wood stove to heat water for tea. The cabin still felt chilly from the night before, and she needed something to help her relax. Even though she had all day to prepare for her departure the next morning, an anxiety had set in when she first arose, before dawn. She picked up her bow and quiver of arrows, carried them to the countertop next to the front door, and added them to the articles already lying there, a sheath knife and flint. In the kitchen she picked up two small packages containing dried fruit and meat. These were also added to the awaiting items.

She didn't know if her anxiety stemmed from being excited that she would soon see Walker again, or if there were other reasons that lay hidden from her at this time. But Walker had taught her to stay tuned to and conscious of her instinctual feelings. More than a few times, they had proved to be valuable insights, giving her an edge, or a chance to react quicker to a threat or emergency.

A peek out of the kitchen window revealed long shadows on the valley as the sun rose up from behind the nearby trees. Nataya decided to walk down to the large outbuilding that Walker used for survival classes. She knew that he kept it unlocked throughout the winter, in case a lost hiker needed shelter from the weather. But spring had settled in, and with her plans to leave in the morning, and no one there to keep an eye on the property, she would feel better knowing it would be securely locked in her absence.

The early morning air felt brisk when she opened the cabin door and stepped out. Tiny watery jewels sparkled off each blade of grass as she walked toward the lake and outbuilding, the ducks and geese splashing about in the water as they awoke. She sat down on the bench by the lake.

Nataya looked out over the lake to the surrounding woods, trees in the fullness of spring leaves mingled with rigid evergreens and the mountains in the distance. As much as she missed Walker, being surrounded by nature like this gave her a sense of peace and tranquility that helped take the edge off the anxiety that itched at her, and the worry, always there at the back of her mind.

When she finally stood up, a sense of peace surrounded her. She made her way to the large wooden door of the outbuilding and tugged it open. Nataya scanned the cavernous room, empty except for wooden bleachers sitting beneath the high, open rafters of the ceiling. At the head of the room sat a desk and whiteboard for instruction. She inhaled the cut-wood smell of the space and exhaled with a sigh. She looked forward to the spring survival class arriving, working with Walker … together again.

She pulled shut and locked the heavy door.

I've stalled off going back into the empty cabin long enough.

She turned and began her walk.

Before she stepped onto the porch, she picked up an armload of firewood to bring inside. The phone was ringing as she opened the door. She dropped the wood by the stove and rushed to the phone, wondering who would be calling. It was far too early in the day for the agent. *Unless—*

"Hello," she said, breathless.

"Nataya. Thank the heavens you're there."

McClure's voice!

She could breathe again. "Dean. I'm so glad it's you."

"I thought I'd missed you. I've been calling over and over."

"So sorry. I was outside and didn't hear the phone."

"I'm just glad you haven't left."

"Not yet. Planning on tomorrow morning. Why? Is everything okay?"

"Walker and Logan are fine, for the moment. Any chance you can leave sooner?"

"Sure. I could leave right now. But why? What's happened?"

"No time for the whole story. But I'll give you the skinny, and I need you to pass it along to Logan and Walker."

"Okay."

"Remember the man named Selden? Logan told you about him. The man who threatened Nicole?"

"Yes."

"Selden has sent a sniper into the forest to hunt down Logan. The sniper's instructions are to make it look like a hunting accident."

Nataya felt her stomach lurch upon hearing the message. Anyone sent in to kill Logan would also mean danger for Walker.

Dean continued. "So the sniper will probably be dressed in hunter camouflage, and most likely using a semiautomatic assault rifle. Logan will know which brands pass as licensed hunting equipment."

As Nataya listened, the reality of the situation set in. "McClure, even if I leave right now and drive to the entry point of the forest today, I'll need two full days of hiking before I can reach the meeting location."

"Shit. I didn't know that. Okay. Let me think this through. So, if we take the worst-case scenario … say even if Selden has a contact at the Bureau he can squeeze for intel … the FBI has recovered the GPS, but they can only guess at Logan's general location based on where they found the device and what direction they think he may have gone. You're the only one who knows the exact location for the meet."

"Yes, that should give me the extra time I need to get to Logan first, before the sniper can pick up his trail and track him down."

"Exactly. But wait, couldn't you give me the map coordinates of where you and the guys agreed to meet?"

"Sure, but what good will that do?"

"I've been in contact with an agent at the Bureau, the one handling Logan's case. She might be able to pull some strings, get someone dropped in there by helicopter and pass the info along to Logan faster than you can. If anyone can get that done, it would be her. But I don't have a guarantee the Bureau will work with us."

"Won't hurt to try, Dean. But there's no way I won't be going out there at this point. I'm not taking any chances."

"Agreed. So, give me the longitude and latitude for the location where you'll be heading. I'll do what I can on my end."

⊷⊰⊱⊶

Nataya took one last look around the cabin. The wood stove was damped down so the remaining hot coals would soon grow cold, and the few supplies she needed sat on the truck seat.

Anxiety to get on the road tugged at her, but she took a breath and blew it out to stay calm.

Better to take a moment now than be sorry later.

She glanced at the phone. One last loose end. The agent would call that night and not get an answer. But since she had been absent before, and had given him the excuse of being called away for a search and rescue, she figured he'd automatically guess that as the case again.

She left the cabin, locked the door and hurried to the truck. The urgency of getting to Walker and Logan pulled at her constantly, but letting panic rule would leave her open to making mistakes. And right then, even though every minute counted, so did doing everything correctly.

CHAPTER FIFTY-SIX

Denver, Colorado

Dean McClure pushed the button to disconnect his call with Nataya and immediately dialed the direct number to Special Agent Mueller. He heard the message come on saying she was away from her desk.

No. Not now.

He glanced at the clock. Damnit.

He tried three more times, every fifteen minutes. Time was passing by far too quickly. While he listened once again to the recorded message, he made up his mind. It went against his better judgment, but he had to at least get the coordinates to her so she could act on it the instant she got his message. The rest of his information could wait. He heard the beep for voice mail.

"Agent Mueller, it's Dean McClure. I have urgent intel for you regarding Logan's situation. Selden has sent a sniper into the forest to hunt him down and make it look like a hunting accident. I have map coordinates for where Logan and Walker are located.

Don't ask. I'm hoping you can drop in someone from a helicopter ASAP to warn them or extradite them. I have additional info I need to pass along to you, but it can wait until after we deal with the urgency of this one. Please return my call as soon as you can."

He gave her the coordinates, then added his phone number to the message and hung up.

Crap.

He hated feeling so helpless. He could only pass along information and hope all the players made the right moves.

CHAPTER FIFTY-SEVEN

FBI Headquarters, Denver, Colorado

Special Agent Susan Mueller rapped her fingers on the desk in frustration. She had done nothing but field calls all morning since sending in the rescue team for Sean Logan. And although the mission could be counted as a success—Sean was safe—she'd lost her chief undercover agent, a man she highly regarded. But she couldn't dwell on the sting of that loss. More work awaited her, including this call from Dean. She picked up the phone and dialed his number. He answered immediately.

"McClure, Agent Mueller here."

"Thanks for calling. You got my message?"

"Yes. And thanks for the coordinates. I've just relayed them to the helicopter pilot. I'm sending in a team to that location with the orders to bring in Logan and Walker, safe and sound. I've got them scrambling now, to drop in before dusk. I don't want Logan thinking it's a covert operation. It's going to be tricky as it is, contacting him."

"Yeah, I understand. Appreciate your help with this Mueller."

"No problem. Thanks for sharing."

"Speaking of which, I have a message for you from Sean Logan."

"Yes?"

"He wanted me to relay to you how much that undercover agent helped him. The kidnappers called the guy 'Tony.' According to Sean, Tony helped protect him from Selden's men."

"Good to hear. Thanks for passing that along. He was an exceptional agent and will be missed."

"That's not all of it. Sean said that the agent evidently sensed something was going wrong. Before he was killed, Tony gave Sean a message to pass along. The message is this, 'Tell Mueller ... it's Samson.' Hope that means something to you."

Agent Mueller sat up straight in her desk chair.

Samson is Seldon's mole.

She rummaged rapidly through her brain for a connection. Samson. The name sounded so familiar. She ran through the names of the agents she knew, people working the desks, in the lab. Nothing. She heard the growing silence on the phone.

The phone.

A face came to her then, that of the technician who handled their communication equipment, a young guy, pleasant and rather good-looking. The voice-mail system on her desk phone had recently developed some strange glitches, and she had called the tech department for service, and Samson had been more than a little helpful about fixing it for her.

Shit.

He had probably created the so-called 'problems' on her voice mail in the first place, to gain access to her phone system and hack into her messages. Not a difficult task for a techie.

And McClure's message had been sitting there just long enough that morning for it to happen, too. Which meant the sniper most likely had those same coordinates as her helicopter pilot.

Damnit.

McClure's voice finally broke the quiet. "You still there?"

"Yes. Sorry. Just trying to place the name. Guess I'll have to see if others can figure it out. But thanks. I appreciate you passing along the message."

"No problem. Seemed important, a dying man's last request, so to say …"

She noticed he left the thought hanging, probably hoping she would pick it up and say more. She waited instead for McClure to speak again.

"So, can I presume Selden is now in your custody?"

Mueller gave him another long moment of silence. He waited her out this time. "No. No you can't presume that." She sighed. "When agents arrived for Sean, they heard gunfire and explosions. They secured two men who were chasing and exchanging fire with Sean and his friend, but in the confusion Selden slipped out with one of his bodyguards. They found the other bodyguard shot dead."

"So Selden is still out there somewhere?"

"Afraid so."

"That's bad news."

"Don't worry. We have agents watching Sean, but I don't expect Selden to risk coming after him. He knows that right now it's just Sean's word against his about the kidnapping. He's probably out recruiting alibis as we speak."

"Seriously? The man believes he is that untouchable?"

"Well, so far he has been."

"Guess you have a point. Hope we can change that soon. But right now I'm concerned for Conrad's safety. He has no idea any of this has gone down. Selden might decide to cut his losses and take out anyone he feels can point a finger at him."

"A valid point. I'll put you in touch with the sheriff department, and ask them to get someone over there to keep an eye on Conrad's house until we can reel in Selden."

Susan Mueller hung up the phone and put her head in her hands. It felt wrong not to let McClure know about the sniper situation, but it was what she had to do to maintain the integrity of the mission. Besides, what could McClure do about it anyway?

But it did change things on her end, and not in a good way. She picked the phone up and contacted the helicopter pilot.

"Zack. Mueller here. Disregard my previous order to use an overhead broadcast system to announce your arrival and intentions to Logan from the air. We have a complication. We can't risk having Logan come out into the open for you. There may soon be a sniper out there. You'll have to send the team in covertly, find Logan, and convince him you're there to help. Sorry. I know it sucks."

CHAPTER FIFTY-EIGHT

San Juan National Forest, Colorado

The shadows of nearby trees were beginning their march across the large meadow, and a serene quiet filled the late afternoon air. Evening wouldn't be far behind. Fox Walker and Matt Logan began to break camp and prepare to retire to their cave hideout for the night. The process took some time and they wanted to be done well before dusk.

Walker gathered up the strips of meat that had dried in the sunlight and smoke of the fire. They would eat the jerky and smoked trout when they didn't have time to hunt, but their bellies were full from their earlier feast, thanks to Logan's catch that morning.

Logan covered the fire with dirt and shouldered the backpack. By then Walker had joined him and began brushing away their tracks as they made their way toward the ravine.

Although they planned to hide their trail to the cave every night as a precaution, they had decided on a strategy of always leaving behind prints from their daytime treks into the woods, where they would be hunting or fishing. That way, if indeed agents were nearby and found their trail, hopefully they would follow the prints leading into the woods, far away from where Walker and Logan hid in the cave.

Logan led the way with Walker behind him, disguising the trail. Walker mused on Logan's more patient passage across the scrubby, brush-filled land that ran along the edge of the ravine. The man continued to learn how to relax into nature's slower rhythm. It hadn't been an easy transition for him. Logan loved action. He enjoyed hunting with Walker. But sitting quietly, being one with nature, remained a foreign concept to him. Although, he had been unusually quiet, after their earlier conversation about Nicole.

They were within a few yards of the ridgeline when Walker halted. He looked skyward a second before Logan, but this time even *he* knew the sound.

Chopper.

They simultaneously dove for cover. Walker saw Logan roll under some bushes, his camo clothing blending perfectly. Walker's jeans weren't so easy to hide. He crawled under a young evergreen's dense foliage and took a quick sideways glance at Logan. The man had scraped out some moist soil from under the bush and was smearing it on his face. Walker did the same, realizing that they needed to watch the helicopter, but didn't want anyone picking out their shining faces from the landscape. It was the same trick Walker used to hide from his prey. The two of them weren't so different. Logan had learned to hide from the enemy while executing a mission, Walker had learned to hide from his prey as he hunted.

The whomp-whomp sound of the rotary blades came closer. Walker peered through the branches to see the helicopter hovering over the meadow, where they had just left. Coincidence? It might be the largest opening in the forest for a few miles, but what made them pick this area, out of the entire wilderness? The chopper moved just out of his range of vision. Hopefully Logan could still see it from where he hid. Walker could only hear it hovering.

Within what seemed like mere seconds to Walker, the chopper's engine revved to a higher pitch and a moment later sped out of range over the treetops. Before Walker could move, Logan was beside him, snapping out orders.

"FBI. They dropped in four men. Move it! Get to the cave. Now!"

Walker tried to comprehend what he heard Logan saying. It could only have been a minute. How did they drop in four men? He suddenly got a vision of what Logan might be capable of, beyond the wilderness survival. He found himself scrambling to his feet and following Logan's commands.

Logan crouched low and rushed forward through the shrubs, Walker following, quickly brushing away their tracks behind them until they came to the edge of the ravine, above the cave. Logan signaled Walker to go down first, while he knelt and took point. Walker caught a brief glimpse of Logan, his gun drawn and ready, before he slipped over the side. All of his attention had to be directed to the climb down. One missed step and none of this would matter.

Walker swung his legs into the cave and let go of the ledge, landing on his feet, crouching to keep from hitting his head. A moment later Logan dropped in and knelt next to Walker, motioning him toward the back of the enclosure, as far from the entrance as possible. Only then did he speak in a harsh whisper.

"What the hell. Sending in agents during the evening? A covert operation would come in using the cover of full darkness." Logan's eyes narrowed. "It's like they wanted to announce their arrival. Make sure we saw them."

"What do you think? Is there a chance they are trying to contact us as friendlies?"

"Do you want to take a chance on that?"

Walker shook his head.

"Yeah, me neither."

"But out of the whole wilderness, how did they know to come to this location? Just luck?"

"Good point." Logan considered this for a moment. "Maybe the Bureau has been secretly watching Nataya. Maybe followed her while she drove up here, then picked the closest open area they could find to drop in the agents."

Walker felt his skin go cold. "You could be right. And I don't think she would be watching for something like that while driving. It's a possibility. But once Nataya enters the forest, she would know if she is being followed."

"Good to know. Let's hope that if they had anyone on the ground trying to track her, she's lost them by now."

"Yeah. Except that she'll be heading straight for this location, not knowing agents are out here, right where she's supposed to meet us."

CHAPTER FIFTY-NINE

San Juan National Forest, Colorado

Nataya leaned forward, her hands on her knees, trying to gulp in air. The dusky shadows surrounding her set off conflicting messages running through her mind. One part of her brain shouted for her to keep running at full speed toward Walker, before darkness took over. The other warned her to stop and prepare for the night, and the cold it would bring.

She replayed her actions of the past hour. She had practically jumped from the truck as she brought it to a halt and rushed into the forest, sprinting faster and faster, until the trees were a blur in her vision. She had run until she could no longer draw breath and her body forced her to stop.

Only then did she realize that she had let panic set in. Panic to get to Walker and warn Logan of the sniper.

Walker had taught her better than that.

She let her body slowly recover, then stood up straight and took stock of her position in relationship to the mountain peaks rearing up over the treetops ahead of her. The sun would soon set and she needed to have shelter to keep warm for the night.

She thought back to all the lessons Walker had taught her about survival, shelter being the most important when low temperatures could threaten maintaining her body heat. She wouldn't do him any good if she died of hypothermia during the night.

She had no choice. She had to stop and build a shelter.

CHAPTER SIXTY

San Juan National Forest, Colorado

A heavy mist had settled into the ravine during the night and lingered as Matt Logan climbed out of the cave at daybreak. Walker watched from the cave opening as Logan peered over the rocky ledge and studied the surroundings. He then motioned Walker up as he pulled himself to the top.

Walker joined Logan, both of them lying prone in the dirt, the shrubs serving as the only camouflage. He watched the trees in the distance, listened to the noises of nature close by, then spoke quietly.

"No one is near here."

"How can you be sure?"

"The bird songs and insects tell me."

Logan stared at him for a moment. "You've got to teach me that trick someday."

Walker nodded, then followed Logan as he stood and began to move forward, cautious and attentive to their environment.

This time they *knew* there were others in their territory—and how many. It put them on hyper-alert. Walker could tell from Logan's body language that the man had gone into battle mode. Walker used his stalking techniques as he moved through the terrain.

As they made their way closer to the meadow and their camp of the previous day, Walker thought about Nataya, hiking through the forest as well. He had found sleep difficult during the night, so he took the opportunity to think about the lay of the land between them, visualizing what path she would most likely take to reach him. It gave him some sort of comfort. Not that he had any illusions of control in the situation, but it gave him a connection to her in his mind that brought a degree of peace with it.

He also knew he couldn't let worry for her override his thoughts and actions in this moment. He had to believe in her skills, and trust that she would be able to stay safe and hidden from the agents. He brought his focus back to the here and now.

Logan stopped and waited for Walker, then pointed to the ground. Walker squatted next to the boot print, studied it, felt the ground for moisture.

"From last night."

They both began searching the ground for more prints, circling the meadow where they had made camp, Walker frequently dropping to his knees to study the sign he found. After many minutes he stood and looked toward the nearby trees.

"You were right. Four men. They searched the perimeter of our camp last night, before dark came. These tracks are fresher. This morning they started following our trail into the woods. Just as we hoped."

"Good." Logan glanced at the sun just rising above the treetops. "Been light for an hour, so they are probably not too far ahead of us. My trail from yesterday will take them down to the stream where I fished, but I entered the water and walked downstream for an hour before coming out on the other side."

Walker nodded. "Once they reach the stream, they may take the time to try and find your trail on the other side of the water before they give up and think it's a dead end. They might double back then."

"Gives us about an hour to get as far from this camp as possible. Which direction?"

Walker studied the trees and mountains around him. "Nataya planned on entering the forest northeast of this location. We can take that angle through the woods. It runs parallel to the trail the agents are following, so we can avoid them. My hope is to move forward quick enough to meet Nataya at the halfway point from here, before agents can track us, or accidently find her."

Logan pulled out his compass and took a reading. "Sounds good to me." He began to head out, but abruptly halted, turning to look back at Walker. "Look. The FBI has no beef with you or Nataya. As far as they know I took that GPS from you and used it as a decoy. I'm the one they want. You should go find Nataya and get out of here. I could take off in the opposite direction, purposefully lead these guys away from the two of you."

"And then what?"

"I'll figure it out. I can hide out here for a while, then find a way to contact Vic."

Walker studied him, remembered Logan's ultimate plan for revenge. "Thanks for the offer, but our path has become one now. Besides, you need any updates Nataya is bringing to us. We don't know what's going on outside this wilderness."

Logan nodded. "That's true. Appreciate it, Walker."

Both men entered the trees, silent and thoughtful. Walker didn't voice his other concern.

As long as I have Logan in sight, I can make sure he doesn't do something he'll regret.

CHAPTER SIXTY-ONE

San Juan National Forest, Colorado

One good thing about studying the topo map for so many hours, Nataya knew exactly where the fastest route lay to get to where Walker and Logan were to meet her. She wasn't tracking anyone, so she could move quickly through the woods, just not in the uncontrolled fashion of the day before.

She pulled out a package from her pocket, selected a strip of beef jerky and used her teeth to rip off a piece. She walked as she chewed, letting her mind settle into a world she knew intimately. She thought back to all the lessons Walker had taught her about listening and being aware of the animals and birds around her, watching where the plants flourish, knowing where she could find water.

Soon she moved smoothly, efficiently through the terrain, insightful thoughts flowing in her mind, instinctively selecting the easiest passages through the trees and boulders. She fell into a rhythm that allowed her to maintain a strong, steady pace. One that gave her a sense of peace, of being at one with her surroundings.

Hours flowed by, the land changing subtly as she entered valleys that led to fast moving streams, then hiked uphill into dense stands of evergreen trees, sometimes skirting open meadows where the elk roamed amid the spring flowers.

Nataya reached the top of the ridge she had been steadily climbing for the last thirty minutes and stopped to gaze at the land in front of her. She was almost to the halfway point. If she pushed harder and hiked until dark, she could make the meeting point by early morning instead of the afternoon.

Excitement at seeing Walker drove her forward, as well as the warning that she needed to pass along to Logan. Which made her think about the sniper. As she drew closer to where Logan and Walker might already be waiting, she should be more careful about her movement through the woods. Who knew what direction the sniper took through the forest?

Nataya stopped.

What if the sniper didn't hike in?

She hadn't considered that before. He could have been dropped in by helicopter or airplane. She had heard a few helicopters and small planes the day before, always far enough away that she couldn't see them through the forest canopy.

What if the sniper discovered her while he searched for Logan? If he had been hired to take out Logan, whom else might he be willing to kill to get to his target?

CHAPTER SIXTY-TWO

San Juan National Forest, Colorado

Matt Logan cautiously lifted his head from the damp earth to get a look at Fox Walker. They both lay on their stomachs, flat against the ground, knowing the slightest movement could alert the men below to their presence. They had been hiking along a ridge high above the valley next to them, moving at a good clip when Walker picked up the sound of voices. Both men had dropped, but Walker must have first gotten a look at the men. He mouthed the words 'FBI' and held up two fingers.

Logan could hear a discussion, but the sound of water in the background drowned out individual words. The agents were following the stream where he had fished. Two of them must have decided to try to pick up his trail by following the stream and looking for prints. *Damn.* How did these guys end up this close to them? Logan knew he had only followed the stream for a mile. The only explanation had to be that the agents missed seeing his prints on the opposite side of the water. It was the only way they could get this close to the parallel path he and Walker were on. *Geez.* He hadn't counted on them *not* being able to follow a trail.

While Logan waited, he watched Walker. The man looked relaxed, his head tilted as if he listened to something beyond Logan's earshot. Logan recognized how tense his body felt and tried to relax, began to listen ... really listen. Little noises came to him, beyond the sound of water, including insects and birds calling in the forest canopy. That's when he heard the men's voices change. Why did they sound differently? He strained to pick up every minuscule bit of sound.

They've turned away from us.

Walker made eye contact and smiled. Logan grinned back. The agents were returning the way they had come. Within a few minutes Logan and Walker felt safe to stand up and continue their trek. At least they knew where two of the agents were. But that left two other men. Hopefully the two pairs were staying in close contact and not getting too far afield of each other. The last thing Logan and Walker needed was to run into the other pair unexpectedly.

Logan let Walker lead the way. He seemed to be confident about which direction Nataya would be coming from. Even though Logan found the pace too slow for his taste, Walker always managed to find the easiest routes through the woods, making their passage go quickly and noiselessly. Steady and sure, that's how Logan would describe Walker. And at the same time, driven. Logan wondered how much of Walker's determination was due to the fact Nataya was on the other side of the woods, coming toward them. He couldn't blame the man. He knew what it felt like to love someone that much.

Walker glanced up toward the sun as if getting his bearings, or maybe the time? Then he halted. Logan froze, not knowing if Walker heard or saw something ahead, but Walker simply cupped his hands to his mouth and did what sounded like a perfect owl imitation. If Logan hadn't seen him do it, he wouldn't have believed it. Walker repeated the series of calls before moving forward again.

Logan took a couple of long strides to join Walker. He spoke in a whisper. "What was that all about?"

Walker kept up his pace. "Nataya will know that is my call if she is within hearing."

"But it sounds so real. How can she tell it's you?"

"Because a Great Horned Owl would not be making that call this time of day and in the springtime."

Logan shook his head. If he had met Walker under different circumstances, he'd swear the man was a genuine medicine man, or a sorcerer. No wonder people still believed some of these people had special powers. They did. The power of observation.

They continued to move forward, Walker still in front of him, weaving in and out through the trees and brush, in a slow dance with the terrain. Logan had to admire the way the man's movements seemed to flow with energy, yet stay under Walker's complete control.

The trees around them became less dense and sunlight entered the foliage once in a while, like small spotlights, highlighting a plant here, a flower there, the bark on that tree. Walker continued to stop and do his owl call every so often, listening, perhaps for a return call? This time, when his call went unanswered and Walker started walking again, he changed his pace to a slower moving, long, drawn-out, exaggerated movement. The stalking-like motion allowed Walker to glide through the trees and plants noiselessly.

Logan had always prided himself on his stealth, but this made his technique seem noisy and cumbersome in comparison. He studied Walker's action, trying to imitate his style and quickly realizing that it would take much practice to achieve the same results.

Up ahead, Walker had stopped at the edge of a small meadow, a dense cover of trees surrounding the open grasses.

Logan made his way to the tracker's side, thinking it was time for another owl imitation. But Walker stood still, watching the trees around them intently before putting his fingers to his lips to signal silence.

He must sense someone near us.

Nataya?

Logan felt his body being shoved to the ground. A bullet whizzed overhead where he had stood just a second before, followed by the distinctive sound of a rifle shot.

Logan rolled behind a fallen log and pulled his gun. The shot had come from directly in front of them. He had recognized the sound. While in the military he knew it as an M16 semiautomatic rifle, but Colt had begun marketing it as the AR-15. He knew the Bureau used it. He expected the FBI to try to capture him. But shoot first and ask questions later?

He checked over his shoulder at the nearby weeds, but couldn't see Walker. He must have dove for cover in the opposite direction and used his shove against Logan as momentum to push his body away. For a non-military man, Walker had good instincts, giving the gunman two targets to worry about.

Logan ran through the battle options in his head as he crawled along the log barrier, trying to get an angle on the shooter. He had to assume that there were two gunmen out there. The Bureau's special forces men trained with the SEALS and had the same two-man-team system.

Logan peeked through the weeds growing up next to the rotten tree trunk. It took him a moment to spot Walker, and even then he could only see the blue of jeans through the plants. It looked as though Walker had positioned himself behind some low boulders.

Seconds ticked away before Logan saw any kind of movement from the trees, and then only shadows moving amongst them. Whoever navigated the terrain out there had circled around, coming up behind Walker.

Shit.

Did Walker know? Logan watched Walker's legs for any indication of movement. Saw that Walker tried to maneuver his body into a different angle, so he must see the danger. But Logan could also see that Walker didn't dare leave the protection of the boulders, and there wasn't anything else close enough to use for cover. Logan swore under his breath. He knew Walker's skills with his knife, but doubted Walker could pull off an accurate throw from his position on the ground. And where the hell was the target anyway?

He'd need to find a way to circle around behind the shooter if he was to offer any assistance to Walker. A movement caught his attention. He held his breath as the figure of a man slipped into an opening between the trees. The lone man wore typical hunter's camouflage, his assault rifle shouldered and ready to fire. Not the FBI.

A hunter?

Logan's mind raced, considering the unexpected scenario. AR rifles were legal for hunting there, and it wouldn't be the first time a hunter had mistaken a person for an animal.

Logan studied the man's movements, the rifle and scope. Remembered hunting season was months away.

A sniper!

So why hadn't the sniper taken him out from a distance? Why take the chance of being seen or heard before shooting?

Then Logan knew.

It's supposed to look like a hunting accident.

A cold fury settled over him. Someone had sent in a lone sniper to take him out.

Selden?

Well, he'd see about that. And he sure as hell wasn't going to let the guy get Walker.

But Logan still needed to move to a different location to get a clean shot at the guy. He saw the sniper moving into position.

Damnit. No time to circle around.

Logan had one choice. He'd have to expose his position and draw the fire of the shooter to give Walker a chance to escape, or throw his knife. At least the sniper would have as much trouble trying to make his shot as Logan would. He just had to hope that luck was on his side.

He saw the gunman drawing a bead on Walker. Logan brought his pistol up, gathered his body to make the lunge. To run and fire.

But before Logan could make his move, he heard a curious whisper of a noise—and watched in stunned silence—as an arrow sliced through the air, piercing the sniper's throat. The man dropped the rifle, grabbed at his neck and stood still for a heartbeat, before crumpling to the ground.

Logan found himself standing. He didn't remember getting to his feet. He stared in disbelief.

A movement in the trees to his left. He swiveled, swinging his pistol to the new target.

Nataya.

She stepped from the shadows, still holding her bow in shooting position, another arrow nocked and ready, aimed toward the fallen man.

She walked up to the dying sniper and pushed the rifle away with her foot. Only then did she let up her guard. Logan saw Walker hurrying toward her. Logan holstered his pistol and sprinted toward them.

Nataya turned, and Logan saw the expression on her face as she looked at the man in his last death throes, strangling on his own blood.

She's never had to kill someone.

Logan knew that look. The impact of having to take the life of another human being. She'd done what had been necessary. But reality had set in, and the finality of that split-second decision.

He did the first thing that came to mind. He stood before her, went to attention and saluted her. She stared at him, not understanding.

He relaxed his stance and took her hands in his. "Nataya, you are truly a warrior. You protected the lives of your teammates without regard for your own safety. I'm proud to be in your company." Then he surprised even himself by wrapping his arms around her slender frame and giving her a bear hug.

When he released her, she had tears in her eyes, but smiled at him.

Walker held her while all three looked back to the fallen sniper. Logan leaned down and checked for a pulse. None. He straightened up and looked to Nataya.

"How did you know?"

"McClure sent me to warn you about the sniper. I heard Walker's owl calls and followed the sound. Evidently, so did he," she said, nodding toward the dead man. "I've been trailing him for a while, afraid to let him out of my sight."

Logan leaned down, picked up the AR-15 and straightened. He saw Nataya's gaze shift from the rifle to over his shoulder. Something behind him made her eyes grow wide. He spun around, bringing the weapon up at the same time. Couldn't believe the scene in front of him.

From out of the shadows of nearby trees stepped four fully armed FBI agents, their guns drawn and aimed at him. The men began to advance and circle Logan. The tallest of the agents shouted. "Logan. Drop the gun. We need you to come with us. Walker and Nataya, too."

Logan took the offensive stance, legs wide, blocking the agents from clearly seeing Walker or Nataya. He shouted to them. "Leave these two out of this. I took them prisoner. They had nothing to do with my actions."

The agents didn't flinch, kept advancing. The same man replied. "We have no intentions of harming your friends, or you. Put down your weapon, Logan. We need to talk."

Logan opened his mouth, ready to tell them to go to hell, felt Nataya touch his arm. Heard the urgency in her voice. "It's okay, Logan. I think McClure got the Bureau to drop in these guys to warn you about the sniper. In case I couldn't make it in time."

Logan didn't move. "It's a trick. They're here to take me back." He shouted at the agents. "I'm not going with you."

The delegated speaker slowly lowered his gun. "We're here to help you, Logan." He took one step toward the trio. "Your brother, Sean, can clear your name, but your friend Victor was critically wounded when he helped Sean escape his kidnappers."

An avalanche of emotion slid through Logan's mind.

Sean did what? Victor hurt? In critical condition? Kidnappers?

What the hell happened out there while he was in the mountains and out of touch?

The agent took two more steps, talking as he moved. "We've got a chopper coming in. We're here to take you directly to the hospital."

Logan felt the presence of Walker and Nataya beside him and tried to comprehend everything the agent was telling him. He heard the helicopter coming in overhead, felt the chop of wind, but everything seemed surreal as he moved through it as if in a haze, expecting to awake from the dream any moment.

CHAPTER SIXTY-THREE

Denver, Colorado

D ean McClure sat on the edge of the hotel bed, next to the phone, his mind still on the previous call. Mueller had let him know that Logan, Walker, and Nataya were safely aboard a helicopter, heading to the hospital where Victor lay unconscious and Sean anxiously waited. The sniper, dead.

He flinched when the hotel room phone rang, interrupting his thoughts. He picked up the handset, wondering who else would be calling his room instead of his cell phone.

Maybe Conrad?

Heard the sheriff.

"McClure?"

"Hi, Sheriff. Any news on Conrad?"

"That's why I'm calling. We went to his house. No one home. Checked with his parents. They have the kids. Conrad told them he needed to work late at the office tonight and wanted the kids to spend the night with them."

"I take it you've already checked his office?"

"Yep, sent deputies to the office building where he works. Nothing. Security guard checked the videos. Conrad never entered the building tonight."

"What about Selden?"

"He's not at his house. Expected that. Probably gathering his cronies to make sure they all have his alibi story. Right now it's Sean's word against Selden's that he was even there at the warehouse. FBI didn't see him. The agent that did see him is dead. Sean thinks Victor saw him, but who knows if ..."

McClure tried not to think about how the story with Victor might go. He focused on Selden. "Any chance Selden might go to his office? Maybe do a little cleanup, just in case?"

"Thought crossed my mind. We're heading there now. You want to ride along?"

"Thought you'd never ask."

"We're pulling up out front of the hotel now. I kinda figured you'd want to join us."

McClure smiled.

CHAPTER SIXTY-FOUR

Suburbs of Denver, Colorado

Conrad worked to calm his heartbeat as he stood outside Selden's office door. Could just make out a dim light inside. He remembered Selden mentioning he liked to work at his desk late at night, when phones had stopped ringing, people were gone, and his bodyguards weren't hovering around.

Conrad double-checked the small recorder in his pocket. Yes, switched to "on." He gently tried the doorknob, found it locked, gulped in a deep breath and knocked. A moment of quiet was followed by small-office sounds inside, before he heard Selden's voice.

"Who's there?"

"It's John—John Conrad."

Footsteps then, and soon Selden unlocked the door and cracked it open enough to see out. When he saw that Conrad stood there alone, he pulled the door back and motioned him in.

"What brings you out this late at night? Where are your kids?"

"I dropped them off at my parents' house earlier. Knew it'd be a late night at the office. Trying to catch up from … everything."

Selden nodded soberly, then indicated a chair to Conrad and turned his back to walk over to his desk. Conrad watched the man's body language, wondering how the guy could act so nonchalant, so calm and collected. How could he lie the way he did and never have his conscience bother him? Maybe men like Selden didn't have one.

Conrad undid the button that closed his suit jacket and slid his hand around the pistol handle tucked into his waistband as Selden walked across the room. He slid the gun free and pointed it at Selden, who turned to face him, now standing behind the desk.

Selden took in the scene for a moment, then surprised Conrad with a laugh. He didn't act one bit intimidated by the gun pointed at him, merely slid down into his desk chair, his hands in his lap, and stared at Conrad.

"Well, my friend, what have we here?"

Conrad didn't know which made him angrier, the fact that Selden seemed so unfazed about the scenario, or that he had simply dismissed Conrad as a threat.

"I know all about your past, Selden. How you got those college girls pregnant and then killed them. Made them disappear. What were they to you, an inconvenience? A mere gnat that irritated you. So you swatted it away?"

Selden continued to smile his charming, you-can-never-defeat-me smile. "Conrad, you're distraught over Nicole's death. You have no idea what you're saying. Put that gun away and come sit down so we can talk this through. I can help you."

Conrad hated the patronizing tone of Selden's voice. Hated the fact the man had no fear of him. Hated the man's confidence, that no one could touch him.

"I know you murdered Nicole. You knew she was on to you, didn't you? Knew she could ruin you."

"Poor Nicole. The misguided wife and mom who couldn't give up playing secret agent. I don't know what she told you, but she was mistaken, Conrad. You and I can straighten this all out now, work together to make it right."

"I have Nicole's notes."

Selden's smile faded. Conrad felt a wave of triumph splash over him.

Finally.

He had cracked that pompous shell of confidence, felt a lift of some confidence himself. He didn't wait for Selden's response. He took a step forward, the gun still pointing at Selden. Plunged on ahead into unknown waters.

"Yeah, you know, the notes you killed Nicole for. The ones you searched for in our home. The ones you thought were on our computers. Must have been so disappointing to find nothing."

Selden's eyes narrowed. "You're bluffing, Conrad. And you're not good at it. You're in over your head on this."

"Bluffing? How else would I know about your despicable past if I didn't have Nicole's notes? How else would I know what a liar and coward you are? The truth you hide from the world."

Selden made the slightest move and Conrad found himself staring at a gun pointed directly at him. His heart thumped so loud he swore Selden could hear it and would know his fear.

Selden smiled and tsk-tsked him. "You really are inexperienced at this, aren't you? Didn't you even once think about the fact I'd have a weapon handy, especially with someone knocking on my door this late at night?"

Both men aimed their guns at each other, neither speaking. Conrad's hand trembled ever so slightly. Selden's did not.

Conrad desperately tried to remember everything he had planned to say, but it all fell short with the gun targeting his chest.

Selden began to speak again, the voice of reason. "You don't need to die like this, Conrad. There's no reason to sacrifice your life for Nicole. She was following a false lead and became obsessed with this whole misunderstanding. She wouldn't listen to reason. You know the saying, you can take the agent out of the Bureau, but you can't take the 'agent' out of the agent. This was her mistake, not yours. You and I can put this behind us. Put the gun down. Think about your children … without a father."

Conrad did think about his children and felt his heart breaking. He also knew the moment he lowered the gun, Selden wouldn't hesitate to shoot him.

The thoughts ran through his mind like the tide coming in, knowing he had no choice but to pull the trigger, and would die as a consequence. He hated the idea of being remembered as merely a murderer, but knew of no way to change the obvious outcome.

Conrad sensed his life as a mere fleeting moment before Selden would end it, just as the bastard had done with Nicole. He had wanted so badly to avenge Nicole's life, set the falsely convicted man free, do the right thing.

Then he remembered the recorder. What did he have to lose? He gathered his courage for one last desperate gamble. Spoke with as much authority as he could muster.

"So, you knew she had you, didn't you?"

Selden cocked his head slightly. "Had me?" He chuckled. "You're not going to give up on this are you?"

Conrad held his breath and his words. Waited.

Selden looked disappointed. "This saddens me. But if you insist …" He shrugged. "Yes, she was good, I will grant you that, after all those years connecting the past to me. That took some talent and tenacity. But, in the end, she let fear get a hold of her. Not for herself, mind you, but for you, and those little brats of yours. She would do anything to save you from me. It was her downfall. I couldn't risk letting her live."

Conrad felt the sharp pain of truth. Accepted it and held it close to his heart. She had loved him that much. And he had accomplished what he set out to do for Nicole. He'd recorded the truth, for others to find and know.

Now I go for the gold ring ... for myself.

He let all the anger and pain rise to the surface, but held it in tight restraint, translating it into cold and contemptuous words aimed at his opponent.

"You smug son-of-a-bitch. You think you're so untouchable? Not this time. Nicole outsmarted you, Selden. She hid the evidence from you. Knew you would come looking for it. So she hid it where only I would find it. And I did."

Conrad felt the seconds ticking away. Knew his time was coming to a quick close. He grasped at anything he could think of to throw pain at the bastard. "And guess what? Nicole's research gives the authorities everything they need to put you away forever. She not only tied you to your past crimes, she made sure that if anything happened to her, you would be linked to her murder as well. It's all coming to light now. And of course all of this 'attention' will warrant an investigation into all your business dealings, past and present. All those healthy political donations will come under scrutiny. You won't be able to buy your way out this time, Selden. You can kill me now, but you won't win."

Conrad heard a helicopter, low and overhead, decided to weave it into his story.

"You see, I gave all of Nicole's evidence to the FBI." He nodded his head toward the noise overhead. "It's just a matter of time now before they are the ones knocking on your door."

Selden's cold stare wavered for a heartbeat, and Conrad thought he had him, but then it took on new conviction. Conrad knew the cold dread of death staring him down. He held his gun steady, finger on the trigger, his blood pounding in his ears.

So, this is what it feels like to be a hero.

CHAPTER SIXTY-FIVE

Suburb of Denver, Colorado

Dean McClure peered out the windshield of the cruiser from the backseat. The deputy driving the cruiser had it at full speed, no siren but lights flashing, the colors sliding along the buildings they passed. When they made the next turn, the sheriff motioned for him to go dark. McClure watched as they neared a business complex on the right-hand side of the street and pulled in. A half dozen other officers' cars followed, lights out, in stealth mode. A helicopter had already made a pass over, giving them the heads-up.

The sheriff pointed out Conrad's car, parked a few spaces down from Selden's office. McClure felt his stomach lurch.

Shit. I was worried about Logan taking matters into his own hands. Never thought Conrad capable of it.

He said a silent prayer that they had made it in time.

Officers eased out of the cruisers and began to creep forward. McClure did the same, staying behind the sheriff, hoping no one noticed him tagging along.

There was a faint light in the office window. A desk lamp? Maybe Conrad had merely broken into Selden's office and was in there alone, searching through papers? McClure glanced around the parking lot and at first didn't see any other vehicles. Then spotted the back end of a Mercedes peeking out from the end of the building complex.

Selden's car?

That's when the single gunshot exploded the quiet. Everything went from slow motion to fast-forward in one beat of his heart. McClure followed the group of officers as they stormed the office, splintering the door from its hinges. The group halted abruptly and the sheriff pushed through the men to the front. McClure followed in his wake, vaguely conscious of his heart pumping furiously.

In the center of the dimly lit office stood Conrad, his back to the door, arms hanging limply at his side. His right hand held a semiautomatic pistol, barrel pointed to the floor. He didn't respond to the group behind him, just continued to stare ahead. Dean followed his gaze.

Behind the desk slumped Selden. Or what was left of him. Blood and brains spattered the wall behind him.

The sheriff gently removed the gun from Conrad's hand. The man offered no resistance. The sheriff dropped the magazine and saw that it was full, then he racked the slide and ejected the still chambered bullet, took a whiff of the barrel. "It hasn't been fired." He held it out to an officer. "Bag it."

McClure felt a weight lift from his heart.

Thank the heavens.

He heard the sheriff talking with Conrad, explaining that they needed to go downtown to get a statement. Routine stuff.

Conrad turned to leave with the sheriff, spotted McClure and stopped in front of him. "Thank you. Now I know the right man has paid for what happened to Nicole." He patted his suit jacket pocket. "Got it all right here."

Conrad turned to leave, hesitated, then faced McClure again. "Funny. I thought I was a goner, standing there, each of us pointing a gun at the other. So I just kept talking, trying to record everything I could against the guy before we blew each other away. Just when I think he's going to shoot, he suddenly sticks the gun into his mouth and fires. What a chicken shit."

⇒+ +⇐

Dean McClure sat in his rental car in the dark outside the sheriff's department. Both hands gripped the steering wheel, even though he hadn't cranked the engine over. He couldn't get that scene out of his head. Conrad standing there with the gun in his hand.

It's my fault he was even there.

He'd been the one to push Conrad. Make him accept that Logan might not be the real killer. He'd been the one who urged him to look for Nicole's notes. It was his doing that Conrad found out Selden was Nicole's murderer.

All to help me meet my own agenda.

All the years of playing mind games with mental cases had taken their toll on him a long time ago. But he had recovered from that and had found a way to keep his hand in the mix, by working as a consultant. Thought he had to do it, to keep himself from growing old and senile. To keep his mind sharp.

But this … this time he took it too far. He had made the conscious decision to involve this decent man, just to make his case, when he knew it would endanger Conrad's life. He had done something out of desperation, took the easier route, and put someone's life at risk.

McClure stared out the windshield into the night sky. He didn't see the snow-capped Rocky Mountains rising high above the city lights. Instead he saw a vision of himself standing in the rushing, cold-water streams of the mountains in Washington state, waders on, breathing in the clean, fresh air, casting out his line ... searching for that next steelhead to hit.

Maybe it's finally time to truly retire.

Then he grinned and started the car.

Time to go home, to Seattle.

CHAPTER SIXTY-SIX

Denver Health Trauma Center, Colorado

The helicopter settled onto the hospital's rooftop landing pad.
The rotors still slowing, Walker watched Logan jump out,
then he and Nataya followed after him. They were ushered into
the hospital and led to the ICU waiting room, where they drew curious stares. Logan was still in full camouflage, Walker and Nataya
in buckskin shirts and moccasin boots.

Walker watched the wide-eyed people shift in their seats and
look at each other. How ironic. He felt the same way about them.
He hated hospitals and being around all these strangers.

He and Nataya went directly to a corner of the room where no
one else sat. Logan joined them after he finished talking to the
lady at the front desk. He sat down next to Walker, and looked at
him and Nataya.

"Sean is in there with Vic right now. They're changing Vic's
dressing and will send Sean to come get me when they're done."

Walker nodded, then noticed one of the FBI agents walking toward them and nudged Logan. It was the same agent who had briefed them while on the helicopter, telling them about the kidnapping, Victor's rescue of Sean and Selden's escape from the FBI. He had reassured them that Sean and Vic were under FBI protection at the hospital.

The agent approached the three of them, then lowered his body to one knee, encouraging them to lean forward as a small, tight group. He spoke discreetly, keeping it a private conversation. "Dean McClure asked that I update you on the situation with Selden."

Walker glanced sideways at Logan's expression while the agent explained the recent event and about Selden taking his own life, noticing the look of relief mixed with disappointment. After the agent left, Walker waited for Logan's reaction. It didn't take long.

"It's not right. I should've been the one who confronted Selden and got revenge for Nicole. She came to me for help."

Walker fixed him with a hard stare. "Nicole was never yours to save."

Logan turned his gaze toward the hallway, staring into emptiness before speaking. "You're right of course. I've been feeling guilty for being selfish, for putting my own wants and needs before hers. She never felt right about it, really. I knew that, but I ignored it, tried to rationalize it, to make myself feel better about it."

Nataya spoke softly. "But she did love you, in the only way you let her. What you did at the trial was courageous. And you did honor her, by not letting her husband know about the two of you. After all, you knew she loved him. You've repaid the debt."

Logan looked down for a long moment, then up to Walker and Nataya. "Thank you for that. It helps."

Someone shouted Matt's name. Walker looked over to see a young man standing in the doorway, his face wearing a haggard but weak grin. Logan made the distance in four long strides, grabbed the guy in a bear of a hug, then held him at arms' length.

"You okay, little brother?"

Sean nodded. "Yeah, I'm okay. Been a tough day, though."

"What's the word on Vic?"

"He made it through surgery and is stable. Still hasn't come to, though. The doc says they've done everything they can. It's up to him now, and how bad he wants to live."

"We'll see about that. Take me to him."

═╬ ╬═

Logan dreaded this part, that first moment of walking into an ICU and seeing one of his buddies lying there, looking so vulnerable and feeling so helpless. It was never easy. And this was even harder. Victor was his brother, in a way that Sean never could be.

Logan walked up to Victor's bed, looked past all the tubes and wires attached to him and studied his face. He thought about what the doctors had said. That it was up to Victor.

Logan took a deep breath and blew it out slowly. Tensed his body. He knew he was taking a helluva gamble on this, but he knew Victor better than anyone. Knew what made him tick.

Logan snapped to attention and began his performance.

"Atten-*hut*, Soldier! This is your commanding officer. Why is your sorry ass in that bed? What the hell do you think you're doing. Sleeping on the job?"

A nurse ran over and tried to stop Logan, but he gently picked her up and set her down away from Vic, and gave her a look that backed her off. She tried the FBI agent watching the room, but he merely nodded at Logan. She took off, running for reinforcements. Logan continued his rant, the volume going up with each word.

"Now get your good-for-nothing, shit-for-brains ass up out of that bed before I come over there and kick some sense into that pea-sized brain of yours."

The nurse and a security guard arrived, heading straight for Logan. Without turning, Logan put out his hand, signaling them to stop, and pointed to Victor, who had opened one eye and was squinting up at Logan. Then the other eye opened. He gave Logan the slightest hint of a grin and croaked out, "Good to see you, too ... asshole."

EPILOGUE

Fox Walker and Nataya followed Matt and Sean Logan out onto the front porch of their cabin. Walker offered Matt a firm handshake. "Are you sure you and Sean don't want to spend a few days with us?"

"Thanks for the offer, but I know you two are looking forward to some quiet time as much as we are. But we appreciate your kindness in letting us stop off here as we head out."

"We're glad you could. It has been good to see you both, away from the city."

"Agreed. To tell you the truth, I'm anxious to get back to Dad's cabin, as a free man this time. It's been years since Sean's seen it, and Dad would be happy to know his sons are enjoying it."

Sean stuck out his hand to Walker. "You might say a little prayer for me. Matt says he's going to use me as a guinea pig, so he can figure out how to train guys like me in the art of self-defense." But he laughed and looked up at his big brother. Walker felt sure Sean could see the mirror of admiration in Matt's eyes.

Matt gave Walker a sidelong look. "I haven't forgotten our conversation out there in the woods, Walker. Maybe I can help a few troubled youths find a better path in life." Then he laughed and gave Sean's head a brotherly thump. "If this guy can go through what he did and come out okay, I should be able to work miracles with the others. But, seriously, I'm putting together some plans, and Victor has agreed to help me out when he's fully recovered."

"That's great news, Logan."

Walker watched Nataya hug each man in farewell, then moved to stand next to her as they watched the men drive away. He shifted his gaze out across the valley and leaned forward on the porch railing. They watched the sunlight dancing on the lake water, how it partnered with the shadows of the surrounding woods, green leaves and evergreens, the mountains rearing up in the background, still wearing their winter crowns of snow.

Nataya straightened and took a deep breath. "It's warm enough now to open up the cabin and freshen the air inside." She paused and looked at Walker. "Feels good to be home again."

Walker smiled, and they turned to enter the cabin together. He heard Nataya gently close the door behind him and walk into the kitchen. Vaguely heard her open windows, feeling the warm spring breeze float through the room as he thought about the past few days, and his time out in the wilderness, without Nataya.

He found himself standing next to the bow-and-arrow collection on the wall, reaching out to finger the bow that Nataya had used in the forest. So much had happened since that day, a blur of activity. No time to think, or talk to her the way he had wanted to.

Somewhere in his mind he heard Nataya say something about taking out the canoe, maybe camping along the river. He turned to find her standing next to him. She gave him a questioning look but remained silent … waiting for his full attention, he guessed.

He picked up the bow and looked her. "I haven't forgotten how you saved my life with this." She reached out and touched the bow, a melancholy look on her face. He wrapped his arm around her waist, pulled her close. "I also know what it cost you to save me. Having to take another's life. It's not an easy thing to live with."

Nataya looked up, and he could see the depth of love in her eyes. And when she spoke, he could hear it in her voice. "You did that for me once as well. But only now do I understand how steep the price was for you." She touched his cheek, then leaned in to kiss him.

Walker felt her lips on his, the warmth of her love filling his heart and wished he knew a way to keep a moment like this frozen in time forever. But perhaps the spirits were wiser than he, for if these moments weren't so rare and so hard fought, they wouldn't be so treasured, so cherished.

Life had been difficult, disappointing and at times excruciatingly painful. But he had continued living and working and trying. That's why having Nataya in his life was so precious.

This time when the tug of fear twisted at his gut, when his mind tried to make him see what his life would be like without her love, he didn't flinch. He acknowledged his fear of losing her.

Instead of denying it—or running away from it—he embraced it. He faced it and made it a part of his devotion to her.

He whispered in her ear. "I'll never make you do that again. I promise."

She pulled back to look at him, confused. "Never make me do what?"

"Stay behind."

ACKNOWLEDGEMENT

I am fortunate to be surrounded by supportive family members, my mother, brother, my two sons and daughter-in-law, aunts and uncles, nieces and nephews, and lots of cousins. For some odd reason, they believe in me and my writing. I don't take that for granted. I thank you all for your continued love and support.

Readers are the life blood of writers. My stories would go unread without your support. My sincere thanks and heartfelt gratitude to every one of you.

My profound appreciation and thanks to Mark Clements and Larry Edwards, my editors for PURSUIT and accomplished authors in their own rights.

To my writer friends, you cheer me on even as you strive to find your own way. I fear I would forget someone if I try to list you all, but know that I am thankful for your friendship.

I am grateful also for the organizations in San Diego that help writers find each other. Kudos to San Diego Writers Ink, Sisters in Crime (Partners in Crime San Diego Chapter), and Romance Writers of America San Diego Chapter. A special thank you to the Mysterious Galaxy Bookstore and Jonathan Maberry for hosting the Writers Coffeehouse.

I would like to thank the following authors who continue to offer me encouragement, instruction and ongoing support: Dale

Amidei, Mark Clements, Larry Edwards, Jill G. Hall, Lois Joy Hoffman, Lynne Kennedy, Jonathan Maberry, John Mullen, Leslie Nack, Matt Pallamary, Judy Reeves, Mike Sirota, John Kevin Smith, Lynne Spreen, Laura Taylor and Jennifer Silva Redmond.

Through it all, one person is always there for me, encourages me and believes in me without fail, Michael, my husband. To you I say, "To the moon and back, Babe."

AUTHOR BIO

Indy Quillen has always loved to write but took many side adventures along the path to publication, including raising a family while organic gardening and learning self-reliance skills, owning and running a natural food store, training and competing in martial arts, creating and selling nature-themed watercolors, as well as designing gemstone jewelry. She grew up in Indiana, lived in Colorado and the San Diego area, and now resides with her husband in the Pacific Northwest. When she's not writing (or camping and practicing her survival skills) she enjoys reading, gardening, traveling, hiking, bike riding and swimming.

Made in the USA
Middletown, DE
22 December 2019